More praise for
BREWSTER

"Intense and elegiac. . . . [W]e keep burning through the pages. . . . [W]e're gripping the book for dear life. . . . Slouka's storytelling is sure and patient, deceptively steady and devastatingly agile."
—*New York Times Book Review*

"[A] terrific novel . . . [from] an author of particular sensitivity and significance."
—*Boston Globe*

"Slouka's laconic dialogue resonates with regional authenticity, his late-1960s pop culture references ring true, and the stripped-down prose style in his masterful coming-of-age novel recalls the likes of Tobias Wolff and Raymond Carver."
—*Publishers Weekly,*
starred review

"The subtle tragedy Slouka points to is how we can remember false things so precisely that they come to replace the truth—and the heartbreak that what once mattered so much will never matter again except in our struggle to keep its meaning alive. . . . *Brewster* is subtly wrought and wholly moving, capturing with beautiful desperation the sense of personal insecurity overshadowed by an era of unwieldy international concerns."
—*The Rumpus*

"Slouka brings a Richard Russo–like compassion and his own powerfully stripped-down prose to this poignant coming-of-age story. . . . What Slouka captures so well here is the burning desire of the four teens to leave their hardscrabble town behind and the restricted circumstances that seem to make tragedy an inevitable outcome.

What Slouka also draws, with unerring accuracy, is the primacy of friendship and loyalty among teens who feel they are powerless."

—*Booklist*, starred review

"From J.D. Salinger's *The Catcher in the Rye* to S.E. Hinton's *The Outsiders*, classic male coming-of-age stories attract generations of readers by delivering plainspoken narratives that seem to bleed from the page, yet are neither maudlin nor precious. Such is the case with author Mark Slouka's evocative new novel. . . . [A]chingly realistic. . . . [A]s often comic and delightful as it is brutal and devastating."

—*Bookpage*

"Taut, honest. . . . [I]n *Brewster*, Slouka has created something wholly original and more deeply impressive than an entire bookshelf of conventional coming-of-age novels."

—20somethingreads.com

"A masterful story about teenage boys and friendship surrounded by violence."

—Best Books 4 Teens

"This is an intense, brutally honest story that you won't easily forget. It's both a story of the meaning of friendship and a microcosm of the generational clash of the 1960s. . . . For a true life coming-of-age story, *Brewster* is the book to read this year."—Chicksdigbooks.com

"Moves at a rapid and accelerating pace, and with ruthless precision, toward a surprising conclusion. . . . [U]nmistakably the work of an accomplished writer."

—*Kirkus Reviews*

"The dark undertow of Slouka's prose makes *Brewster* instantly mesmerizing, a novel that whirls the reader into small-town, late 1960s America with mastery, originality, and heart."

—Jennifer Egan, Pulitzer Prize–winning author of *A Visit from the Goon Squad*

also by **Mark Slouka**

Essays from the Nick of Time

The Visible World

God's Fool

Lost Lake: Stories

War of the Worlds: Cyberspace and the Assault on Reality

BREWSTER
A Novel

Mark Slouka

W. W. NORTON & COMPANY

NEW YORK | LONDON

For information about permission to reproduce selections from this book,
write to Permissions, W. W. Norton & Company, Inc.,
500 Fifth Avenue, New York, NY 10110

For information about special discounts for bulk purchases, please contact
W. W. Norton Special Sales at specialsales@wwnorton.com or 800-233-4830

Manufacturing by Courier Westford
Book design by Fearn Cutler de Vicq
Production manager: Devon Zahn

Library of Congress Cataloging-in-Publication Data

Slouka, Mark.
Brewster : a novel / Mark Slouka. — First Edition.
pages cm
ISBN 978-0-393-23975-1 (hardcover)
1. Teenage boys—Fiction. 2. Life change events—Fiction. 3. Vietnam War, 1961–
1975—Fiction. I. Title.
PS3569.L697B74 2013
813'.54—dc23

2013009415

ISBN 978-0-393-34883-5 pbk.

W. W. Norton & Company, Inc.
500 Fifth Avenue, New York, N.Y. 10110
www.wwnorton.com

W. W. Norton & Company Ltd.
Castle House, 75/76 Wells Street, London W1T 3QT

1 2 3 4 5 6 7 8 9 0

Awake, arise or be for ever fall'n.

Milton

To my father, Zdenek Slouka, who was a runner once,
and who finished his race the day after I finished this book.
I didn't believe a heart so big could ever stop.

The baton has passed, Dad.
May I run my time half as well.

BREWSTER

THE FIRST TIME I saw him fight was right in front of the school, winter. It was before I knew him. I noticed him walking across the parking lot—that long coat, his hair tossing around in the wind—with some guy I'd never seen before following twenty feet behind and two others fanned back like wings on a jet. It was the way the three of them were walking—tight, fast, closing quickly. That and the fact that instead of speeding up he seemed to be deliberately slowing down, one hand in his pocket, the other still bringing the cigarette to his mouth. His head at that "too late" angle I didn't know yet. And then he turned around as if to tie his shoe, the hair blowing over his face, tossed the butt and tackled the guy with such fury—low, head down—that the two of them were actually airborne before they crashed into the icy slush. And then one of the others was being pulled off his back and he'd shaken free and was walking away, ignoring the yelling, the threats, the small crowd gathered around the figure still lying on the ground. I watched him cut between the cars, walking easy, running a lazy finger along a fin, tapping a sideview mirror. At the edge of the parking lot he stopped, though there wasn't any traffic. Like nothing had happened, like there was nothing behind him. And I saw his shoulders hunch and his head bend forward and realized he was lighting up.

BREWSTER. It's where I knew them all, Ray and Frank and Karen Dorsey and the rest. I can talk about it now. I can see the big brown hills, the reservoirs, the tracks. For some reason it's always winter. When I try I can remember summer evenings with kids running through the tunnels of smoke from the barbeques and the parents yelling "If I catch you doin' that one more time" like it's a joke, but what I really see is winter: weeks-old crusts of ice covering the sidewalks and the yards, a gray, windy sky, smoke torn sideways from the brick chimneys. The houses were small and smelled like upholstered furniture and fingernail polish, and if there were old people in the house, upholstered furniture and garlic, and if there were babies, upholstered furniture and garlic and shit.

I think I always hated the place. It's one of the things Ray and I had in common—one of the biggest, maybe—and we played it over and over like a favorite record. Hate is a big deal when you're sixteen. Of course it wasn't really about Brewster. Brewster just made it easy to pretend it was.

I didn't know that then. I thought it was the place. On bad afternoons when the track was iced over or the sleet was sweeping down in sheets, Falvo would have us run intervals in the upstairs hallway of the high school, twenty-three of us in three groups of six and one of five pounding down the linoleum in waves, slowing into the curve by the science classrooms, stretching it out, then slowing again by the guidance office, then finishing up, three sets of ten with a slow jog back for recovery, and flying past the darkened classrooms I'd see the gray squares flashing by—rain, rain, rain—like empty slides in a projector, and think: Everything out there is Brewster, and turn up the pain as if I could run it all down, all of it—the town, the ice, the December dark. As if there was something to beat.

For three years I carried around a picture I'd cut out of the paper of Tommie Smith and John Carlos on the medal stand in Mexico City after the Olympic 200-meter final, heads bent, shoeless, gloved hands raised in protest. I used to take it out and look at it. I knew they were fucked. It didn't matter. If anything, it made it better. They'd done it, they said, for all the people nobody said a prayer for.

"Yeah?" Ray said when I showed him the picture. "So what? Somebody's gonna say a prayer now?"

I shrugged.

"Somebody's gonna give a shit because a couple of soul brothers took off their shoes in fuckin' Mexico?"

I put the picture away.

"Lemme see it again," he said, and I took it out and he looked at it for a while, then handed it back to me and I put it away. I knew what he meant. We could change the world, rearrange the world, but that's not how it felt, ever. Not in Brewster. How it felt was like somebody twice as strong as you had their hand around your throat. You could choke or fight.

WE DIDN'T HAVE A CAR. We walked. We walked like convicts testing an invisible fence. How far did we get those three years? If you could untie that knot, straighten it out, all the times we walked to school with the rain coming down the streets in ridges like a shell or out to Dykeman's in the dark, slipping around on the ice pond where they actually used to get ice, grabbing on to the trunks of trees—how far would we have made it? St. Louis? Denver? Ray would just show up at my door, sometimes after school, sometimes at dusk, wearing that coat and I'd say "It's rainin'," and he'd say "I know it's fuckin' rainin'," and I'd throw on a sweater and a sweatshirt and a jacket and close the door behind me.

It was the winter after the summer of love, and it went on for a long time. It's hard to describe. Things were changing, but we couldn't feel it. The children of God came through in their sandals and ponchos—we'd see them hitching backward up Route 22 with the wind whipping their hair into their faces, adjusting their packs or their guitars—but they kept going. Woodstock may have been just across the river, but Brewster was a different world. It wasn't interested in getting back to the garden. It had to resurface the driveway, it had to mow the fuckin' lawn, it had to right one of the angels in front of Our Lady of the Immaculate Conception Church whose 20-pound test had snapped, leaving it dangling from its heel, one arm out, one knee forward as if sprinting madly for the earth. No, we felt like a cog in something turning all right—the dead, unmoving cog at the center of things, the pivot point, the pin in the tie-dye pinwheel. Watching the colors blur just made it worse.

We'd talk, or drink beer if we had some. Sometimes we'd just throw stuff into the East Branch, which always seemed to be running high with snow melt, or go up into the woods around the reservoir. The ice shelves along the river were thin as china. By the last year, things weren't good, but that didn't keep us from walking—the wind marbling the empty frozen streets, the red-brick buildings shuttered on Main. It was all we had. He'd still knock on the door, then look away almost like he was embarrassed, and sometimes my mother would walk by and he'd say "Hiya doin', Mrs. Mosher?" and she'd say "Hello, Raymond, how is your family? and he'd say, "OK if me and Jon go out?" and her mouth would tighten and she'd say "He can do what he wants," and go up the stairs.

He met Karen, or first saw her, anyway, the fall of our sophomore year, but I can't tell you when it was we were walking down Doanesburg Road the night Rizzolo and his partner pulled up behind us—it was later, that's all I know. Maybe a year. More.

We were walking to Putnam Lake. He couldn't knock on her door, Ray said; he just wanted to look at her house. I had nowhere else to go. It was dark, freezing, and we'd just passed over the little bridge down from Green Chimneys where they brought city kids to straighten them out when we heard the bleep of the siren. I'd never had a problem with the cops. With our hands in our pockets, hunched in our coats, I guess we must have looked like something. We weren't.

"Police," said a voice over the loudspeaker, like there was any doubt about it, and then the cruiser pulled up next to us and a flashlight beam hit us in the face.

"Where you think *you're* goin'?" said the cop behind the flashlight. "Nothin'—Cappicciano's kid," he said into the car. He turned back to Ray and whistled softly. "Will you look at you. What's a matter with you, you been leadin' with your face again? Joe, take a look at this." He played the flashlight under Ray's hood. "Jesus, you look like one of them dogs with the black eyes."

"Buster Brown," said the other cop.

"What?"

"The dog that sells the shoes."

The cop with the light turned to look at him. "You have to believe me when I tell you I don't know what the fuck you're talkin' about." He turned back to Ray. "So you ever think, like, to duck might be a good idea?"

"Yeah, OK," Ray said.

"Yeah, OK. So where'd you get the shiner?"

"Danbury."

"Danbury. What is there, like a store?"

"Yeah."

"Let me tell you somethin', smartass—you're gonna get yourself killed. You got a thick head for a punk, but these little spics can fight, an' one of these days one of 'em's gonna cut himself a window in your chest the size of Puerto Rico." He turned the light on me. "Who the hell's this?"

I told him.

"What're you doin' with this moron?"

The driver said something I couldn't make out.

"Yeah? Track star, huh? You gonna try out for football?"

"No."

"Why not, you can run, right?"

"I don't know."

"He doesn't know," said the driver.

"Another genius."

He switched back to Ray. "Your father know about Danbury? How's your father?"

Ray didn't say anything.

"Well, you tell him I said hello. *We* said hello. It's a goddamn crime what they did to him. OK." He tapped twice on the hood. "Stay outta trouble, track star." And the car pulled away.

LATE AT NIGHT a place can look older. Walking down the hill into Putnam Lake with everything frozen and just the three streetlights, the flag hanging quiet in front of the firehouse, the war memorial on its pedestal where the road split, it felt like we'd walked back in time. Like it was the 1940s or something. Maybe that's why I remember that night. Or maybe it's because six miles each way was crazy even for us. Ray didn't talk much after the cops left. I didn't mind—I didn't need to talk all the time.

By the time we found the house a short way up from the lake, it was just after midnight. It was a big, light-colored house with a wide porch with quiet blue Christmas lights around it like a frame. The windows were dark. We just stood across the street and looked at it.

"I always liked that house," Ray said.

"Yeah," I said. I did a little dance to keep my feet from going numb.

"She's probably asleep."

"Probably," I said.

He reached into his coat pocket and pulled out half a Snickers bar and unwrapped the end.

"Sure?"

"Go ahead, track star."

"Fuck you, I'm gonna try out for football."

He was still looking at the house, hugging himself in his coat. I could see his lip, like he'd stuffed a big grape under it, lifting his mouth into a comic book sneer. "Weird how things can change," he said.

"Yeah," I said. I wiped my nose but it didn't do much.

"I don't know why she's with me, you know?"

"Me, either," I said.

"I guess we should go. Fuck, it's cold."

"I think we should stay here. Stare at the house some more."

And we started the long walk back, along Putnam Lake like a flat white field in the dark, past the war memorial and the fire-house, then Lost Lake, curved and still behind the trees, and it was almost two when I let myself in the back door. I'd go in late to school—nobody would care.

THE STORY IS that my parents moved to Brewster in 1956, when I was three, because my father wanted to open a shoe store and the rent was cheaper than in White Plains. It made sense. Brewster wasn't much: small wooden houses with dark yards, a train station, a river—no more or less than most places—but it was cheap. It had some things. A bank. Basic services. Folks from the city stopped in Brewster on the way to nicer places in the Berkshires. There were big reservoirs in the woods that the city had put in for its water supply, and out on Route 22, past the Elk's Club, there was an A&P with a conveyer belt that took your groceries in a metal cart with your number out to the curb. When I was a kid I'd spin the metal rollers with my hand.

Sam's Shoes was on Main across from Bob's Diner. Everybody knew Sam. He and Vera had come from Germany where it seemed they'd had a hard time of it during the war. Sam was Jewish but he knew shoes.

They were there for sixteen years. They'd meant to move on—to a bigger town with a park and a library, maybe even to the city— but when I was four my brother Aaron, who had blond hair after my mother's father, plugged in a lamp he'd found on the street and died. It happens. I was playing in the living room when I heard my father screaming and a few seconds later, my mother. I'd passed

Aaron on the stairs a few minutes before, carrying something up. "Shhh," he said. I never saw him again.

I could have said something. I didn't. And anything I said after that didn't really matter much. The things you don't say you can't take back.

And that was that. We didn't talk about him. I remember walking by his room and seeing his bed, his shelf, the punching-bag dinosaur in the corner, the toys on his desk—all quiet like in an aquarium—and thinking he'd be coming home from school.

I think now they just broke. People break, just like anything else. They'd lost everything once, now they'd lost it again. And they broke. No more to it.

I'm not making any claim to anything. You read worse stories in the paper every day.

NOTHING CHANGED—and everything did. My father went back to work because the store was there—because somebody had to go. We ate at the same table, I watched the same shows. Every morning for fourteen years my mother went into my brother's room and pulled the curtains, then closed them at night. Once a week she dusted and vacuumed. She didn't talk to me much. It was like something inside her had frozen. When I was little and couldn't sleep I'd come downstairs to find my father in the leather chair looking over the top of some book by Stifter or Büchner or Musil as if he was confused by something he'd read. My mother would be sitting at the kitchen table in front of a closed magazine, and she'd push herself up with her arms and make me some warm milk.

I was four when he died, so I don't remember much. I remember going into his room and taking a toy and my mother grabbing the hair on the back of my head and slapping my face three times, not back and forth but the same side, then bursting into tears. And

I remember standing in our yard watching Mr. Perillo reaching down into the gutters and throwing big flapping handfuls of wet leaves off our roof and my father pleading in that accent like Colonel Klink's in *Hogan's Heroes*, "Really, Tony, you do not haff to do zat," and Mr. Perillo not even looking at him, saying, "Forget about it, Sam, almost done."

When I was five or six the neighbors had a block party on the Fourth like every year. The cops blocked off the street and there were hanging paper lanterns and kids running everywhere and people laughing from the porches or standing around in groups in the shadows so all you could see was their light-colored shirts or pants. It was hot and sticky and if you looked into the backyards you could see the fireflies sparking up in the weeds. The air smelled like smoke and grass and burning meat. I found my father sitting on the top step of the Montourris' porch in his dress shirt and slacks and I sat down next to him between the paper plates and the half-filled Dixie cups and even though it was dark, I remember watching yellow jackets moving in the beer like something trying to wake up.

"The wood is still warm," he said, putting his hand on the boards next to him, and then he didn't say anything more until I heard a kind of hissing sound and realized he was crying. He'd taken his glasses off and he was holding his nose with his right hand like he wanted to hide it and his shoulders were jerking up and down. I didn't know what to do. His left hand was just lying next to him on the porch, palm up, so I put my hand in it but nothing happened—it was like it had fallen asleep—and after a while I took my hand back.

Sometimes it felt like there'd been some kind of mistake, like I was the one who'd died and nobody wanted to admit it. Mostly I didn't know what to do.

◆ ◆ ◆

I HAVE ONLY ONE MEMORY from before. I remember walking around the ball field, the grass like a carpet under the water, and seeing small, dark fish, probably perch, shooting through the backstop fence. The East Branch had flooded. My father was there, and so was Aaron. There were clouds all around us and the bleachers had water up to the first seat and we walked around the bases with our pants rolled up looking for the white squares under the water and the fish running away from us looked like somebody pushing his finger up against the surface. My father threw me on his shoulders; he seemed big then.

I have a memory of my brother, I think, eating snow. And peeing on a worm. That's it.

IN BREWSTER there was no other side of the tracks; if there was, Ray would have lived there.

Ray lived with his dad and his baby brother, Gene, who was fifteen years younger than him, in a small, dark brown house with a big American flag nailed vertically to the wall under the porch. Ray's mom had left when he was nine—his stepmom, right after Gene was born. I could walk to his house in about ten minutes, and did, many times. The shingles had faded out in some places more than others and the stain had run in long drips you'd want to wipe off with your thumb but couldn't because they were hard as rock. Where the railing sagged you could see the screws being yanked out of the floor boards and the roof had nails like teeth coming through because somebody had had a size too big and didn't care. Inside, the ceiling always seemed lower than it should. That first year we'd sit around and little Gene, who we'd pick up after school from a woman named Carol, would crawl around and put things in his mouth and Ray would take them out.

"Hey little guy, you want a beer stein?" he'd say when Gene crawled up to the cabinet where Mr. Cappicciano kept his collection. "Whaddya say? Want a beer?" And Gene, who'd somehow pulled himself up on his rashy little legs by grabbing onto a kind of step on the front of the cabinet, would fall on his diaper with a soft, crinkly *poof* and Ray would say "Nope, not ready. Gotta be able to stand up before you can fall down." And he'd scoop him up and smell his ass, then hold him out in front of him like a heavy doll and scrunch up his face and Gene would smile like a senile old man.

I asked Ray about his mother once. His real one. He showed me a postcard of a yellow motel under a blue sky with two cars parked out front. "The Silver Dollar Lodge" was written in white script across the top. I flipped it over. The postmark was from Reno, Nevada. "Thinking of you," it said.

He took the card back. "Just not that much, right?" He shrugged. "I had a picture but my old man threw it out."

"You ever miss her?" I said.

"What's to miss?" he said. "She left."

THERE'S NO REASON we should have been friends. I didn't talk much. I wasn't popular. I wasn't good-looking or funny or tough. I was just tall enough that I didn't get into fights; when I did, I generally lost. The cool kids just ignored me. I didn't care. I read books. I wrote pissed-off poetry that I thought about showing to Mr. Wentzel who was teaching to avoid the draft and who walked around like he was demonstrating the effects of gravity on Jupiter—like the pull of the planet was just too much, man—but I never did. I did all right in school. I wasn't stupid, just fucked up.

For a while I thought that high school might change things for me; that I'd make friends, that the girls I tried not to look at who all seemed to be ripening at the same time wouldn't see the fear in my heart. By sophomore year, I knew better. The girls would look at me, then whisper to each other and laugh. I'd have nothing to say. Calling attendance, the teachers would pause when they came to my name. Mosher?

And they'd look at me over their green ledgers with their columns and squares, their pencil points waiting next to my name, and they might as well have been saying it out loud: "Silent?" Here. "Stubborn?" Here. "Difficult, troubled?" Here. I hated them all, hated them for their pinched-off little souls, their disgust with everything beautiful, and spent half my time trying to be what they wanted me to be—smiling at their stupid jokes, not correcting them when they said something wrong, working to be "normal," to be noticed—then hating them all the more. God knows what they would have called it twenty years later. Anger Surplus Syndrome. The abbreviation would have fit.

I couldn't let it go, couldn't go easy. About anything. Injustice burned in me like an ulcer and everything fed it: the sour little men and women who'd squirreled away just enough power to stick it to somebody else, who'd never been young, never laughed, whose every breath was a sneer—enthusiasm was a threat and they'd strangle it in its crib and hand you the body and smile, and the sooner you learned to bow your head and kiss their ass, the easier it would go for you. Only I couldn't do it. Fool that I was, I thought the abuse of power went against the order of things.

"To be or not to be?" It must have seemed like an interesting question. What to be. How to be who you had to be. I was sixteen, and I felt like someone had opened a door in my head—I *understood* this. I could hardly sit still. And so, forgetting I wasn't actually supposed to be *interested* in *Hamlet*, I blurted out a question. Who knows what it was? Probably something inane about identity and truth and having to be who you were or not be at all. Farber was writing something on the board.

"Just shut up, Mosher, you're not here to ask questions," he said, not turning around.

"I just—"

"Shut up."

It came out of nowhere, a quick slap to the face. A moment before we'd all been laughing.

I just sat there, the blood pounding in my head. It was the tone— the actual anger in it. I'd seen Farber walking a Puerto Rican kid to the principal's office, his hand like a meaty claw clamped on the back of the kid's neck.

"What's the matter, you don't know the answer?" It was out before I knew it.

He turned around. The room was suddenly very quiet. "What did you say?"

I could feel a small trickle of pee escape into my underwear. "I thought this was a school." I'd started to shake.

"I hear anybody ask for your opinion, smartass?"

"I thought—"

"Anybody ask for your opinion, smartass?"

"I just—"

"Anybody ask your opinion, smartass?"

"No."

"No," he mimicked in a mincing British accent. A few of the kids laughed. I wanted to drive the leg of my chair through his teeth.

"Don't you *ever* talk to me that way."

"I didn't—"

"Ever." He shifted his weight, letting me dangle. "You know what you are?"

"I—"

"A troublemaker, that's what you are," he said, his face swollen with rage and disgust. "One of those people always digging things up, turning everything around." He paused. "What's the matter, you gonna write to your congressman? You think this is some big injustice?" He leaned forward, whispered it like a secret: "Guess what—nobody cares what you think."

◆ ◆ ◆

I UNDERSTAND why being hated can make you angry; I never figured out why it should make you feel ashamed.

I didn't tell anybody. I didn't know anybody, really, and I knew better than to mention it at home. My mother wouldn't say anything, just sit there looking at her food with her head slightly to the side like it had insulted her, methodically impaling small pieces of potato. I'd listen to myself going on—in German, of course, which made everything even more ridiculous—all the time watching some other conversation passing over her face like small clouds on a windy day—a quick flinch in the cheek, the eyebrows slowly raised in a suffocated shrug, a smile like a spasm.

"Obviously you did something to provoke this man," she'd snap, talking to her plate, sick of it all, of me, which would be my father's cue to jump in and say, "And even if you didn't, what would you have us do—you think they're not going to stand up for each other?"

I started taking my tests in pen, so Farber couldn't change my answers. It didn't matter. He got me on the essays. He didn't call on me the rest of the term, just looked right through me as I sat there with my hand up like I was invisible, then gave me a D in participation. I got an F in citizenship. I didn't care. Fuck him.

That fall I started writing down things I read in a blue spiral notebook I carried in my back pocket. On the inside cover I copied out a quote from Gandhi: "First they ignore you, then they laugh at you, then they attack you, then you win."

I'd whisper it to myself walking down the hallway, sitting in class: First they ignore you, then they laugh at you, then they attack you, then you win. It was like a chant, a prayer. Christ, I was pathetic. I clung to it like a sapling in a cliff. I was no Gandhi, I had no idea what to make of myself: Half of me wanted to apologize to the world—the other half wanted to drive a stake through its heart. It didn't matter: I loved the march of it, the promise of it: first this, then that. I was nobody—a sixteen-year-old at Brewster High School. What was I going to do, organize a Salt March to the five-and-ten? It didn't matter. Nothing they said mattered. It could be done, it was inevitable. I'd *make* the world notice. My biggest fear was that I'd never make it past the first stage, that I'd suffocate inside my own skin, invisible, before the laughter had a chance to start.

I KNEW ABOUT HIM long before we were friends. Ray Cappicciano. Ray Cap.

I can hear Copeland in the teachers' room, the smoky dimple in the middle of that Petri dish of ignorance and cruelty and crap: "Cappicciano? Erratic. Unpredictable. Insane, basically. No impulse control. He'll charm you one minute—he isn't stupid, there's *somethin'* goin' on in there—shove you down the stairs the next. I'm tellin' you, twenty to life before he's thirty. Suspended? Sure, he holds the record. Old man's an ex-cop—had to leave the force. Runs in the family. Bruises? You mean *this* week's?"

And they'd all laugh and the women in their tight-across-the-ass knee-length skirts would take their stained cigarettes from between their cracked lips and lay them across their coffee cups and pick them up again and Copeland, encouraged, would do his ring announcer routine: "Ladies aaaand Gentlemen, welcome to the Fight of the Week. In this corner, wearing ripped jeans and a bad attitude, 'Raging Bull-Shit Cappicciano."

And he'd tell them about the time with Malatesta. "You'll love this," he'd say. "So you know Sal. He gets into this thing with the little punk for like, I dunno, the hundredth time for not having his homework, right? Asks him what his excuse is and the kid says his dog ate it. Seriously. So Sal loses his temper. He's got that bow tie on, he's got that one-room schoolhouse thing goin'. He's gonna make him write it two hundred times—the dog ate my homework, the dog ate my homework, then sign it "Loser."

The kid slams back to his seat. Half an hour later he walks up and hands over a piece of paper. Sal takes one look and throws a book at him but he's already out the door. He's drawn a picture—a good one, I've seen it—of a bulldog in a bow tie. Next to the dog is a bowl with the name Loser on it. Not bad, right? But here's the weird part. There's this pattern behind the pooch. You're thinkin' wallpaper, roses—wanna guess? Give up? Knuckles. He's picked the scabs off his knuckles and pressed them into the paper, over and over." And Copeland would press his fleshy fist into the air over the table, then lean back in his chair and spread his arms and throw one leg over the other to adjust his crotch. "OK?"

I don't mean to say they all hated him—at least not early on. Some did, sure, and they grabbed every chance they had to cut the legs out from under him. As if he was a real threat. As if it was personal. As if he wasn't sixteen, or seventeen. The rest were amused by him; he was the clown, the cut-up, the All-American delinquent with the reckless face and the chipped tooth who might not know much about algebra but who'd win the girl in the end and they'd turn a blind eye and shake their heads and kick him in the balls now and then just to keep things clear between them—that so long as he stayed more colorful than sullen and didn't cause them extra work, everything would be fine. Hell, if it came down to it they'd take him over the bookworms with their snotty questions any day.

Mainly only the cafeteria ladies with the plastic bags on their heads, who nobody fucked with, were different. They'd always been decent to me. Mary—who even the teachers didn't call Mary—who had big, gravy-speckled arms and no wrists and who always looked just one stupid question away from enraged—would take my tray from me and carefully spoon the macaroni and cheese on it herself instead of reaching through the metal shelves and slapping it down like with everyone else and say in that gravelly Dublin brogue, "All right, there you go," or, "More?" and even, once, "You'll 'ave to eat to keep up with all that studyin' you're doin'," which coming from her was a benediction.

But if Mary and the others were human to me, they'd flat-out adopted Ray. They loved him. He could do no wrong. He'd josh around and fool with them, compliment them on their plastic head bags and ask if he could put one on and they'd roll their eyes and pretend to be annoyed, all the while glowing like schoolgirls, and he'd tell them to stay out of trouble, that he'd been hearing some things, and then he'd push his hair back and take his heaping tray and leave.

It was how we met, sort of. I'd been waiting in line, amazed and resentful, listening to him ask for more of this and less of that and "How about a little more crust there, Mary?" and "I don't know, I gotta watch my figure," and "No, I'm serious, apple crisp helps you think," until, sick of waiting, I started toward the cashier. When he cut me off I just stared at him.

"Fuck *you* lookin' at?" he said.

I shook my head. He turned back to the cashier.

"That's a lot of apple crisp," I said.

He turned and looked at me—he seemed so much older to me then—deciding I guess if I was worth the trouble, then gave a small shrug.

"Yeah, I know," he said. He paused. "So eat shit." And he walked away.

He'd just come back from being suspended—something having to do with the back bleachers and some girl from Carmel. The halls were thick with rumors.

"Bullshit, it's fuckin' soaked under there," I heard some guy say by the juniors' lockers.

"You do it standin' up, moron," said the other.

✦ ✦ ✦

THAT FALL a thick-necked kid with big arms and acne on his neck sat across from me at lunch, ate, and left. We didn't say anything. The table was half-empty. I'd gotten tired of sitting with kids who all seemed to have something to say to each other so I usually just read a book. The next day he was back. He put his tray down, stepped over the bench and ate, pushing his food around, first one way, then the other, then into a pile, all the time shoveling like it was work and he might as well get to it. He looked like Moose Mason from Archie Comics. When he was done he picked up his tray and left.

It didn't take me long to figure out that he was sitting across from me every day because he was lonely. I didn't mind. From a distance we probably looked like we could be friends. To make it easier for him I started sitting at the same table so it would look like his sitting there every day was about the table, not me, and when a girl from my English class who was fat thirty years before everybody else asked if she could sit with me at lunch one day, I said I needed to study because I didn't want him to feel bad and so lost one of the few people I knew who would talk to me.

When he didn't show up anyway I told myself I didn't give a shit and left early. The next day he was back, the muscles twitching in his forearms, breaking the powdery buns into his chili.

It took three days to learn his name. "Sup, Frank?" some guy walking by with his tray said, and he gave a small nod, and then a few days later somebody yelled, "Hey, Krapinski, man, what did Jesus eat at the last lunch?" and he slowly raised his left arm without looking up or lifting his elbow off the table or missing a stab with the fork and gave him the finger. A week later he was gone. For a few days I looked around the cafeteria for him, then forgot about it.

✦ ✦ ✦

THAT NOVEMBER, Mr. Falvo, who taught American history, stopped me on my way out of class. It was my sophomore year. Falvo was a quick-moving, sharp-featured man with flat, razor-scraped cheeks, an Alfalfa cowlick and a shriveled right arm that looked like it belonged on an eight-year-old and felt—I knew because he insisted on shaking hands with it, hunching forward to make up the distance—exactly like a warm, dead fish. He'd gotten it in the war—Okinawa, they said.

Whatever else he was—and he was a lot of things—Étienne (Ed) Falvo was not a simple guy. First generation out of the Bronx, second out of Aosta, Italy, he was badgering, impatient, generous—hard to resist and hard to take. Everything about him seemed too much—too much curiosity, too much enthusiasm, too much energy—until you realized that you were looking at something like a happy man, a man condemned to love this world the way a father might love his convict son. Helplessly. Knowing better.

He was always talking, yelling, laughing, "NO, Barkus, by God you're an embarrassment to idiots, promise me you won't multiply except in math. NO! In the early eighteenth century, with the exception of the locals we hadn't gotten around to yet, our great land west of the Alleghenies was about as empty as Jones's head, and 'Bleedin' Kansas' was NOT bleedin' because it did not EXIST! Miss Mazzola—yes, that would be you, my dear—confirm my faith in your gender and tell me within half a century when 'Bleedin' Kansas' was actually bleedin'. NO!" And he'd throw a piece of chalk at her head. "Washburn!"

The rest of the class had filed out. "I'm going to be late," I said.

"How tall are you, Mosher?" he said. "How tall would you say?" He'd leaned back in his wooden teacher's chair and put his black shoes on his desk. I'd spent a lot of time trying to figure out what kind of quick, chattering animal he reminded me of.

"I gotta go," I said.

"How tall? Six? Six-one? Maybe one fifty-five? It's not a test, Mosher, you can't fail this one."

"I don't know," I said.

"You know what I'm asking."

"You're asking me how tall I am."

"Don't be stupid, Mosher, it doesn't suit you. I want you to try out for the track team. The brooding demeanor, the chip on your shoulder—you could be perfect."

"I really . . ."

"Four o'clock, Mosher. Legs and balls are required, the brain is optional—may in fact be a hindrance. You've got the legs, we'll see about the rest—I'm not expecting much."

"I don't really do sports," I said.

"This is America, Mosher—don't put that in writing." He lowered his voice. "In any case, foot racing is not a sport. Gladiatorial combat with the mace and the trident was not a sport. The Sun Dance of the Plains Indians was not a sport. Foot racing is a conviction, a calling. You think Geronimo would have joined the basketball team? You think Thomas Jefferson would be doing layups? No! Jefferson would have been a miler!"

He'd been scribbling something with his left hand while he talked, and now he handed me a folded note.

"For your next inquisitor. By the way, that last paper wasn't entirely hopeless though I'm still considering what grade to give it, and yes, in case you're wondering, it's completely unethical for me to blackmail you this way so if you tell anyone I'll be forced, as the tape recording says to that constipated-looking blond man in *Mission Impossible*, to disavow all knowledge of your existence." He grinned. "Dismissed, Mosher."

◆ ◆ ◆

I WAS ALREADY WALKING HOME that afternoon when I turned around. I don't know why. Half the things we do we do by accident.

I found them in the old gym that always smelled of sweat and wood and heat rub, an unimpressive-looking group of twenty or thirty whose faces I vaguely recognized from the hallways and the parking lot, stretching in a loose circle around a guy with long brown hair and a red headband. To the left, carefully lacing up his sneakers, was the kid from lunch—Frank. Nobody noticed me. They were bullshitting quietly, reaching for their toes or bicycling in the air, and I was about to leave when Falvo rushed in carrying a boxful of gray sweat pants and a clipboard which he held pinned to his chest with his shriveled right hand.

"Mr. Jefferson," he called, "I see you've abandoned your principles and listened to the voice of reason. Shoe size?"

I told him.

"Back room. Pick a pair. And put these on." A few faces looked over lazily, not smiling.

I HAD NO IDEA I was going to do what I did. Looking back, I can see the two roads dividing like in the poem but I never stopped, never considered, never looked back. I just went—and it was like opening something. Kids these days cut themselves. My way was better, but it was the same thing.

He stood propping the metal door, the stopwatch in his good hand—*Let's go, gentlemen, let's go, Mr. Jefferson*, and we jogged out into the wind which smelled like mud, across the football field and up a small rise to the dirt track. This was a time trial, he said—a one-mile time trial, four laps—not a race. It was meant to give an idea of where we stood, no more.

We'd gathered around the middle of the long side of the track, just ten or twelve of us, including three others who seemed new like me, jogging back and forth in the wind, loosening up. The rest, including Frank, had walked over to the other side of the field.

Falvo took me aside. "Warmed up? How're the shoes?"

"Fine." In the distance I could see kids walking toward the parking lot. The sun stabbed out from under the clouds, glancing off the windshields.

He raised his voice over the wind. "All right, I want you all to stay contained, stay smooth. I don't want to see anybody draining the well today—that means you, Mr. McCann." A tall, tough-looking kid with red hair and a tight face smiled like a gunslinger.

He turned to me. "I don't want you doing anything stupid, Mosher. Some of these boys have been at it for a while. Don't think about them, think about yourself."

I shrugged.

"Pace yourself. Let them do what they do. They'll be about thirty yards ahead after the first lap. Don't worry about them. Go out slow, feel your way, then bring it home as best you can. OK?"

"Sure," I said.

"Remember, it's a time trial. Not a race."

THERE WAS NO GUN. We lined up in the gusty wind, Falvo standing in the soggy infield in his dress shoes holding his clipboard like a small high table against his chest with his left hand and his stopwatch in his right and then he barked, "Runners . . . marks? Go!"

They didn't run, they flowed—the kid in the headband, the red-headed kid, and two or three others in particular—with a quiet, aggressive, sustained power that looked like nothing but felt like murder and I was with them and then halfway through the third turn they were moving away smooth as water and I could hear them talking among themselves, joking, *Bullshit—Lisa Arrone? I swear to God, she just reaches in and I'm*—and I was slowing, burning, leaning back like there was a rope around my neck. "Too fast, Mosher, too fast," I heard Falvo yelling, and his ax-sharp face came out of nowhere looking almost frantic and then it was gone and there was just the sound of my breathing and the crunch of my sneakers slapping the dirt. The group, still in a tight cluster, wasn't all that far ahead of me.

By the end of the second lap I heard someone far away yelling "Stop, Mosher, that's enough," and then at some point someone else calling "Coming through—inside," and they passed me like a single mass, all business now, and I remember staggering after them, gasping, drowning, my chest, my legs, my throat filling with lead and looking up through a fog of pain just in time to see the kid with the headband, halfway down the backstretch, accelerating into a sustained, powerful sprint.

I don't know why. I can't explain it. By the end of the third lap I was barely moving, clawing at the air, oblivious to everything except the dirt unfolding endlessly in front of me. "Let him go," I heard somebody say. They'd all finished by then, recovered, and now stood watching as I staggered past them like something shot. "C'mon . . ." I heard someone start to call out uneasily, and then, "What's his name?" and then, louder, "C'mon, Jefferson." A small crowd, I found out later, sensing something going on, had gathered by the fence to the parking lot. The last of the newcomers had passed me long ago.

I remember seeing him appear in front of me like I was coming up from underwater and trying to swerve but I was barely standing and I walked right into him and he caught me as I fell, his one good arm around my back, saying over and over, "All right, easy now, easy, you're done, keep walking, walk it off," like he was gentling a horse. I threw up on the infield grass. I could barely see. "Fuckin' Sloppy Joes, man," I heard someone say, almost respectfully.

"They look better now."

"Shit, I think I see the bun."

"Somebody go help Coach."

"Fuck you, I'm not gettin' that shit on my shoes."

"That was like *On the Waterfront*, man."

"You see him on that last hundred? Jesus!"

"Hey, Terry don't work, we don't work." A couple of people laughed.

"Keep walking, Mosher," Falvo was saying, "if you lie down it'll be twice as bad." I could feel him holding me around my waist, his arm like a steel belt above my hip. I didn't want it there. I couldn't see. I could hear myself sobbing, trying to rake air into my chest. My head felt like it was cracking from inside. I didn't know that I'd put my arm around his shoulders.

"What we have here," he was saying, "is a failure to communicate. Stay within yourself, I said. Don't drain the well, I said."

"What did I get?" I couldn't seem to hold my head up, or open my eyes—the pain kept coming in waves.

"What?"

"Time. What time did I get?"

He laughed—that bitter Falvo laugh—ha!—like he'd just been vindicated. "He wants to know what he got," he said, like there was somebody with us. "You want to know what you got? I'll tell you what you got: proof you could beat yourself senseless—something I very much doubt you needed. If I was a better man I'd report you for assault. OK, turn. And for what? Nothing. Tiny Tim could have tiptoed a faster mile. Tiny Tim, Mosher. With his ukulele. Singing."

I could feel the wind now, chilling the sweat. He was walking me back and forth like a drunk in the movies.

"Two more. No, you're an idiot, Mosher, there's no point denying it. Unfortunately for me, you may also be a miler. This won't mean anything to you, but you ran the first six hundred yards, before you died like a dog, at sixty-seven-second pace; truth is, you shouldn't have finished at all."

THE NEXT DAY my calves, my thighs, my shins—my shins most of all—felt like they'd been replaced with steel plates. I winced my way up the stairs, lowered myself to my desk with my arms. Even my father noticed. "*Was ist los?*—You have a problem with the shoes?" he said.

"You're going to be very unhappy with yourself, my boy," Falvo had told me. "I mean more than usual. You've paid the piper—you know the piper I'm talking about, the piper of pain, Mosher—and now he's going to play whether you like it or not."

Two days later he gave me my paper back—an A–.

"Seems you're only selectively stupid," he said, and walked back to his desk, cowlick bobbing, ridiculous as ever.

I was sitting at lunch with Frank later that same week—we'd started talking a bit—when I heard the cafeteria monitor yell and looked up to see Cappicciano, just past the register, shove some senior in the chest, then duck something I couldn't see, then flick something off the fingers of his right hand. He was wearing that long coat, as always—dressed to leave. From a distance he looked like a magician releasing a very small dove.

"I said knock it off," the monitor bellowed.

He ducked again, laughing, and started toward our side of the cafeteria. "Cut it out, Ray," a girl I couldn't see said as he passed behind her.

When he dropped his tray with a clatter of silverware next to Frank, he was still clowning around with her, pissing her off. I didn't know what he was doing at our table. I thought it was some kind of mistake.

"Mind if I join you two lovebirds?"

"Fuck you," said Frank.

"Not me, fella—but hey, I'm open-minded."

He started shaking his chocolate milk, singing Dusty Springfield's "Wishin' and Hopin'" under his breath: *Show him that you care, ba-ba, ba-ba . . .*"

I must have smiled.

"I seen you somewhere," he said.

I didn't say anything.

"Up on the track. Couple a weeks ago. You were like *Night of the Livin' Dead*."

I didn't say anything.

"*On the Waterfront*," Frank said.

"That's what they're callin' it?" He took a drink, then wiped his mouth with the back of his hand, smiling. "That's fucked up." He looked at me for a few seconds. "Why didn't you just stop?"

I shrugged.

He took another drink of milk. "You got a test?"

"No."

I was reading Nietzsche, or pretending to.

"That's one fucked-up mustache on that dude."

I shrugged.

IT WAS NOT LONG AFTER that he began showing up at practice, sprawled out on the bleachers in that long black coat and a sweatshirt, sometimes with a girl in a miniskirt who'd sit there freezing next to him, sometimes not. I'd look up and he'd be there, leaning on one elbow, smoking. I'd look again, he'd be gone.

Nobody said anything until McCann, who didn't give a shit and liked to prove it, walked past the bleachers with his group. "Fuck *you* doin' here, man?"

"Hey, fuck you, I can sit where I want. What're you, the bleacher cops?"

"Yeah, you'd know about them," McCann said.

"That's right, pencil dick, I would." He took a drag of his cigarette, confident, arrogant. "Tell ya what. I'll polish up your VIP box here with my ass. Leave it nice and shiny for ya."

The next day he was back. I was nowhere then, stuck in the

slowest group, burning to climb the ladder. I'd have to earn it, Falvo said.

I'd gone to see him, still hobbling, two days after the time trial. I wanted to run another, I said. I knew what I was doing now.

He didn't look up from the clipboard. "It's not that I don't admire your eagerness to throw yourself on the pyre, Mosher, and for all I know immolation *is* the sincerest form of flattery—but it won't make you a better runner."

I had no idea what he was talking about.

He looked up. "No," he said.

There were five groups, he said, slowest to fastest, divided by their times. I'd be starting with the slowest group, like everyone else.

"I'm better than that," I said.

"We'll see."

"I am."

"This will come as a shock to you, but sometimes we do more by doing less."

"What're we running today?"

"*We* are doing quarters. You're going for a light, ten-minute jog."

"But—"

"On the track, where I can see you."

"I—"

He held up his left hand like an Indian—a gesture I'd come to know well. It took me a second to realize he was actually angry.

The lesson was clear: I'd move up when he said so.

IT WASN'T A TEAM so much as a sect—a cult of individuals. Which shouldn't make sense, except it does. We had one thing in common, at least the runners did: we believed in time, pledged allegiance to it—one nation, utterly fair, under the second-hand god on Falvo's watch. You couldn't lie or talk or cheat your way in. It didn't matter if you were cool, if you looked good in a pair of jeans, if you were popular. You could be all of those or none—it didn't matter. You either covered ground or you didn't.

We'd be running quarters, he announced—what he called bread and butter—twelve quarter-mile runs with a quarter walk between each to recover. He introduced me to the group. One or two, stretching on the mats, mumbled hello, a few nodded, most didn't hear him or didn't care. McCann kept talking to the guy next to him. I went back to trying to touch my toes. I was as loose as a brick.

"What's his name again?" It was the kid with the headband—Kennedy. A dozen faces looked up, then over at me.

When Falvo told him, he nodded like he had to think about this information now that he had it, and went back to stretching.

I remember that first day. The fifth group was a sickly-looking bunch of nerds—when I walked up they were standing around awkwardly, their skinny white legs sticking out of their oversized shorts, hugging themselves in the wind and arguing about old episodes of *Time Tunnel*. They seemed nice enough. They talked to me a bit after the first interval as we walked around the outside of the track, then went back to arguing about whether by rescuing Dr. Newman from being killed at Pearl Harbor the show had broken something called the Novikov self-consistency principle. I couldn't believe it. By the time we'd finished the third interval I had bigger problems.

By the sixth I was hurting. They were still arguing. They'd run the quarter, then pick up where they'd left off. "So the Novikov self-consistency principle means you're changing recorded history." "Yeah, so?" "So 'Time Tunnel' means the past, present and future are all happening at the same time—duh!"

By the time I'd done eight I was wondering if I'd make it at all. I could still hear them, like static in my head: "They have to get a *fix* on the past." "No they don't." "Yes they do. If he's killed, you moron, then the adult Tony can't exist." "Sure he can." "Don't you remember what Dr. Swain says to Senator Clark when he's looking at the *Titanic?*" "Yeah? So?" "So he's seeing *the living past,* dufus. Ready?"

I finished last, dragging in five yards after the others. As I stood there with my hands on my knees, trying to keep my legs from buckling, a pasty-looking kid with a caved-in chest and a feathery mustache came up and patted me on the back. "Nice job," he said.

It was my answer for a while, the combination to whatever it was I'd locked inside. I liked the details, the rituals, the numbers; I liked the hot smell of the weeds in the infield, the six-mile runs in the rain around the Middle Branch Reservoir, the peepers in the muddy woods a hundred yards behind the track screaming in the spring. You could be who you were, *would* be who you were, whether you liked it or not. *First they ignore you, then they laugh at you, then they attack you, then you win.* I'd climb the chain, link by link. I'd show them all.

I wasn't the only one who brought to it more than it could bear. It had a way of doing that, of convincing you it was more than it was—not a stage but the world, not war by other means but war itself. That it mattered.

IN JANUARY 1968, just three months after I joined the team, we climbed into a bus and got out at the 168th Street Armory in New York—a great cavernous hall with a flat wooden indoor track at the center of it. I'd never been before. Down below in the huge cave-like basement where the food venders were, you could hear the runners pounding by over your head, then the roar of the crowd, and making your way through the mass of runners shoving up the stairs sticky with soda and Cracker Jacks, the air thick with heat rub and hot dogs, you'd hear the roar growing with every step and then the whole thing would burst like a multicolored shell, thunderous and overwhelming: fifty teams, six hundred runners camped out in patches of yellow and blue and maroon on the dark wooden bleachers over the track, stretching, sleeping, listening to their transistor radios, warming up, and there, only yards away, another heat ready to go, eight runners at the end of the straight shaking it out then kicking into the blocks, "Runners, set . . ." the gun like the crack of a whip, jump-starting your heart. It was like entering the Coliseum.

The Bishop Loughlin Games, the Cardinal Hayes Invitational, these were our Olympics, but nothing I saw there those three years came close to what I saw that first time.

They may have been from Boys' High—I don't remember. It doesn't matter. What I remember is the attitude, the stance. The concentration, the focus, the four of them exchanging a few words at the beginning of each heat, then the lead-off climbing into the blocks. Fifty yards away you could feel it: black, ghetto, just off the subway in mismatched sweats, they didn't own shit but by God they owned this. The mile relay. It was theirs. Six years in a row they'd beaten every team in the city: teams with money, teams with facilities, teams five times their size. Nobody else in any event had a record like it. Nobody even came close.

When the mile relay final was announced, the great hall quieted, the transistors were turned down, the crowd—two, maybe three thousand—moved as close to the rail above the track as they could. I was jammed in with Frank, Falvo, the mustached kid from my group. Kennedy and McCann were a short way down, leaning over the rail. I could see the muscles in McCann's face jumping like he was chewing something; when Kennedy looked up our eyes met over the backs of the others for a second and he nodded, barely seeing me, as if to say, "Here we go."

They said a few words, heads bent, then the lead-off walked to the blocks. Big Afro, bouncy stride, he was the last to take off his sweats. We watched him shake out the muscles in his legs, not look-ing at the others, then fold himself like a supple jackknife into the blocks, the neon-green baton between the palm and forefinger of his right hand. Everything was critical, each leg a full-out quarter-mile sprint through the track's flat, tight wooden curves where elbows flew and tangled legs regularly sent runners sprawling across the splinter-filled boards. The lead-off runners would keep their lane through the first curve, then break for the inside as best they could.

"Runners, there will be two commands, then the gun."

The place was silent. Reverent. Substitute the smell of heat rub for incense and you've got it. On the opposite side of the bleachers a tiny voice was singing something from a radio someone hadn't turned down enough.

"Marks. Set."

He rose, balanced on the thumb and three fingers of his right hand.

THREE THOUSAND RUNNERS jumped at the gun. I remem-ber being hypnotized by the controlled fury of it, swept up in the brutal, beautiful momentum of it, and then he was down, hard, his head actually banging on the boards, the green baton ricochet-ing off the guard wall like a hockey puck and a groan of shock and disbelief went up from the stands. It was over. This was a mile relay. Another runner was lying on his back in the outer lane, stunned.

I don't think he ever thought of not going. We saw him roll, scrabble onto all fours, already searching for the baton, snatch it and go. A few people laughed, embarrassed for him: There was something almost clownish in his desperation; in the first few sec-onds, disoriented, he'd looked the wrong way as the baton skittered across the track behind him. Then a polite ripple of applause rose from the stands: It was the right move, the admirable move—the reigning champions making the most of the disaster, finishing in style. All the runners in that hall knew it was over. All except four.

More than in him, alone an entire backstretch behind the pack, you could see it in the others: the second man already in position, tensed in a sprinter's half crouch, his receiving arm out, willing the baton to him still forty yards away, his teammates screaming in his ears. They'd never considered lying down; what was possible had nothing to do with it.

Nothing happened at first. He ran all alone, as if in a different race altogether. Thirty yards back in a relay usually decided by inches or feet, he gained six yards on the strongest sprinters in the city, handed off and fell to the track. By then it had begun: a growing roar like an approaching army, a thousand fists beating in unison on the metal signs that hung down from the rails circling the track. It didn't matter that it couldn't be.

Turn, straight, turn—it was like the pack was a magnet drawing him slowly back to them, shrinking the gap. Six runners, spread out now, handed off like well-oiled machines; he passed the baton, ran into the arms of some man who held him up like a limp doll—he'd closed to under twenty and the hall was in pandemonium, roaring like a shell, pounding with a single pulse.

On the third leg something changed, some magic distance was crossed: the impossible had become conceivable. Thirteen yards, eleven, ten, and he passed the sixth man, handed off, and fell like the others. I hadn't seen him. I'd been watching the anchor leg. In that sounding chamber—deafening, overwhelming—he was as still as a candle flame in a closed room. And I saw him receive the baton and go, a full eight yards down in fifth place, and he was like a scythe going through grass—gorgeous, ruthless—smooth as a razor cutting into the curves, passing the fourth, the third, out of the last turn edging into second, closing on the leader who seemed to be slowing, tying up because he had to, because by now it wasn't up to him but the gods themselves, and then he threw himself through the tape.

I'VE THOUGHT OF IT SINCE—more than once. And I've thought of Ray looking at my picture of Tommie Smith and John Carlos with their fists raised on the medal stand in Mexico City, saying, "Yeah? So what?" and I know he was right. So what? This was what they gave you—what they wanted you to have. Go ahead, boy, take it. It's yours. Take your two-fifty chunk of metal on the purple ribbon and hang it in your room and grow old; you can have the salt shaker—the pepper shaker too—'cause I own the house, the block, your dime-a-dozen soul if you really want to know.

What fools we were, spending ourselves on trinkets and symbols. We lost, all of us. And when we realized it, we took our love beads and our lyrics and sold them on the street.

But I'm not the only one who remembers that race. It meant nothing. But it didn't feel like that. For those three minutes and twenty seconds, as they handed off each to each in the heart of that roar and fell to the track, it felt like it mattered.

IN MARCH OF 1968 I ran the mile in 4:52 on an indoor track at the New York City armory, which was decent for a sophomore. Things were changing for me. A few of the guys from the track team nodded to me in the hallway now. I'd met Ray. Frank and I hung out together. He was big into Jesus and the javelin, in that order, but didn't really go on much. We'd talk about the team, or classes, or the teachers we hated, and then he'd eat and I'd go back to my book. That was pretty much it. The week I ran my mile, Lieutenant Calley and the boys from Charlie Company did what they did at My Lai. I didn't know about it. Nobody did.

People love to tell you afterward how they saw this and saw that. We didn't see a thing. We heard about Vietnam, we heard about Newark, Detroit, other things—but it was like listening in on a party line: You'd hear voices talking over each other, a man chuckling over a joke, a sound like somebody crying—and then Rowan and Martin would yell "SOCK IT TO ME!" and that woman on the show would get knocked in the head with a giant hammer.

The closer something is, the louder it sounds; hold a baseball to your nose, it's big as the earth. It takes time for things to find their distance. We misheard pretty much everything, sang words for years that no one had ever written. We confused the large and the small, what mattered, what didn't. There's somethin' happenin' here, Stephen Stills sang and we all sang along, a bunch of blind men staring off in a dozen directions, waving our canes like batons.

Even now I can't say what it was, exactly, can't separate the voices from the silence from the noise. "Plastics!" was part of it, and *Bonnie and Clyde* and "Up against the wall, motherfuckers" and two cats in the yard. Mr. Montourri was part of it, hitching up his office pants by the belt saying, "Yeah, I got a dream—pay off the goddamn mortgage, know what I'm sayin'?" and bell-bottoms and beads and Gina Falconnetti's nipples rubbing against the fabric of that peasant blouse she liked to wear and we liked her wearing, and I'd be a liar if I said that Gina's nipples meant less to us than the Tet Offensive. We were sixteen.

THAT SPRING, Ray's dad got him a dog, a brown lab named Wilma, and sometimes after practice I'd walk over to the house and Ray'd be on the porch with little Gene and Wilma would be crapping in the yard and Mr. Cappicciano would have the hood up and he'd wave me over and stand back and wipe the grease off his hands and talk to me like I knew something about cars. I don't know why. He had a tattoo of an apple with a knife in it on his arm and sometimes he'd get this look like a kid watching his goldfish being flushed down the toilet one by one, but for some reason he liked me.

"You got sense," he'd say, tossing the rag and taking the beer off the battery block with two fingers like he didn't want to get the can dirty. And I'd stand there, apprentice little man that I was, concentrating on something I knew nothing about, pretending I hadn't heard what he'd said, wasn't pleased.

I'd help him with things, hand him stuff. "C'mere, I want to show you somethin'," he'd say when I came around, "you'll get a kick out of this." And he'd stab the cigarette in his mouth, his sleeve rolled high up his veiny arm, and jam his oil-slick hand deep down, his face to the side like an Indian listening to the rails, and loosen the belt. "Come over here—no, here, see that?"

"Sure," I'd say.

"People don't understand," he'd say, the cigarette nodding between his lips. "It's all parts. You got the part, you got the whole thing. See that?"

"Sure," I'd say.

"That's what I'm talkin' about." And he'd grunt pulling his hand out, turning it this way and that, working it free. "Tight as a ten-year-old," he'd say, and I wouldn't smile or laugh, just give a little puff of air through my nose to show I'd heard, appreciated it, because that's what men did, and he'd turn to the porch: "You gonna get me that goddamn beer or what?" and Ray would pick up little Gene and go get him a beer.

IT WAS A LONG TIME comin' and I was twenty years gone before I began to see there was no difference between the big and the small, the close and the far, that the times had been playing themselves out in us—Newark and us, Vietnam and us—that in Brewster just like everywhere else you could choke or fight, but by then it was too late.

Stop, children, what's that sound? Even if we'd stopped, we wouldn't have heard a thing.

I CAN SEE IT NOW. At the time it was different. Maybe it was me. Back then the roots of why things happened always seemed deeper than I could go. It was as if half of my heart could feel, could close my throat over a line in a movie, a song, anything—while the other half was as dead as a pit in a peach.

Take my parents. I knew they'd barely made it out of Germany, that they'd escaped the worst by sheer luck and bribery, that they'd slipped sideways through the closing door with a suitcase apiece and started again. I knew my father's brother, Klaus, had disappeared into Sachsenhausen, that my mother's sister, late for a train, had simply vanished from the earth. But sitting in History watching *Night and Fog*, sick to my stomach, I didn't connect it to them, to me, and when Moira Rivken belched and ran out of the room with her hand over her mouth, I understood but I didn't, really. I felt for her of course—I figured it was about her parents, or relatives—but what had happened to mine didn't have anything to do with me because that was how they wanted it.

Whenever I asked about the war, and I did, more than once, it was as if I wasn't even in the room. "Your father died for them at the Somme and they turned on us like dogs," my mother would say to my father, as though he didn't know, and my father would sit there staring at the carpet. They'd suffered—I could never understand. It was the same with Aaron. They'd lost their firstborn, an unthinkable thing. How could they explain it to me? It was like watching somebody making dinner while blood pours from their sleeve.

We were watching a Walt Disney special about tigers one night when I was little when my mother started to cry. This happened. You weren't supposed to do anything.

"It's alright," my father said after a while. And then: "Do you want me to turn it off?"

My mother just sat there, sobbing into her hands.

"I know," my father said. "I know." He kept saying it: I know, I know. He went over to the couch and put his arm around her and she started to cough—a forced, fake-sounding cough like she was choking.

On the TV a kid my age was running across a kitchen floor with muddy shoes.

My father said he'd make a cup of tea, then looked at me and quietly shook his head, telling me something.

I didn't know what to do. On the TV a tiger was walking along a broken wall.

When I touched her hair she flinched away like I'd stuck her with a pin.

I remember bursting out crying, more with surprise than anything else, and my father rushing back in yelling, "What happened? What on earth?" as my mother ran past him and up the stairs. We heard the door slam. I was maybe five, six.

My father just stood there. "She's upset," he said, then started wiping at my face with his handkerchief which smelled like tobacco and spit. "Do you want to finish watching the show?" he said. "I'll be right back."

FOR A WHILE when I was in fourth grade I had to go talk to the school psychologist during gym class—I forget her name. She reminded me of those folding rulers you used to see—tall, straight, angles and elbows. She wore men's glasses and very red lipstick and great square stiff dresses that looked like they belonged on a large doll, and once, when she got up from her chair, I saw a long, thin stripe of black hair going up the middle of her white calf.

Who knows what she talked to me about? Coping skills, probably, or whatever they called them then. The importance of Communicating My Feelings. Some things don't change. They'd sent me there because a few weeks before, watching Scotty Steinberg tease our class guinea pig with a carrot, then knock it on the snout, I'd tapped him on the shoulder, waited till he turned around, then punched him in the stomach. I'd never hit anybody before. I was surprised how easy it was. My fist just sank in like he was pudding and then he bent over and started making weird barking noises and ran into the bathroom at the back of the class and locked himself in. I wasn't sorry.

It wasn't Scotty. Or the guinea pig. It was the way she wouldn't look at me some days when she gave me my lunch in the morning, or the way she suddenly wouldn't answer when I asked her something—when dinner would be, or what we were having. Like I'd done something. Like I'd been bad.

Some days I'd wake up and the house would feel empty like somebody had taken all the furniture out and I'd find her in bed, crying, and I'd try to talk to her to see what was wrong but she wouldn't tell me and later when I was older I'd make her scrambled eggs and she'd give me a note for school: "Please excuse Jon. He was sick." And things would be OK. And then the next day or the one after that I'd come home from school and she'd walk right by me in the hall and when I asked what was wrong she'd say in that angry, I-don't-want-to-talk-to-you voice, "Nothing's wrong. I don't know what you're talking about." Sometimes she'd keep it up for days, not answering. Other times she'd lock herself in the bedroom. Every now and then you'd hear her come out, walk to the bathroom, slam the door.

It wasn't much—I'm just saying how things were. My father didn't figure into it—he went to work, he came back. He read, he slept. He didn't get mad at me. He didn't do anything except sell shoes. For a while in seventh grade I tried to talk to him about things because I'd seen a show in which the dad was kind of quiet but cool underneath and I thought it might be the same with him. It wasn't. I had to think about my schoolwork, he'd tell me. Someday I'd understand how important it was. He didn't say when.

When I was ten I woke from a deep fever to find my mother slumped over in a chair next to my bed, sleeping, her hands neatly folded on an open book. I'd been sick for days, and Dr. Rusoff had been over again the night before. He'd given me two injections in the shoulder, felt my throat and my armpits with his soft, hairy hands, and then he and my parents had talked for a long time in the hall.

I watched her sleeping—a strand of hair had come down over her face and her mouth was open—and then the book fell off her lap. When she saw I was awake we just looked at each other for what felt like a long time and then she leaned forward and brushed the hair back from my forehead. "I should tell your father," she said, and then she smiled—an emptied-out, nothing-left-to-give smile— and for just a moment it was me and her. A few days later, when things went back to the way they were, I began to wonder if I'd imagined it. After a while I hoped I had. It would make it easier.

When I was thirteen or so I came home and she'd turned the switch off—that's how I thought of it. She was sitting up straight at the dining room table, doing the bills. And maybe because I'd had a bad day at school or because I was older now or because earlier that week she'd put a note in my lunch bag saying she hoped I'd have a nice day I asked what was the matter.

She didn't look up, didn't answer. I could see her mouth—that way it got, pulled tight, the wrinkles bunching up into her lips. She looked from one paper to another, then back.

"What's the matter?" To my surprise I could feel the tears rush under my eyelids as if they'd been waiting there, shamefully close to the surface. "Mommy?"

"I'm busy." It was that tone—slow, quiet, seething. Determined to stay calm even though she was being pushed, tested.

I started to put down my books. I could feel myself shaking.

"What did I do?"

She didn't look up.

"Mommy, what did I do?"

"Don't be ridiculous."

I started to walk away, then turned. "Why do you do that?" I said, my voice rising into an accusing whine. "Why do you do that? Why do you—"

"Don't you dare come into this house and—"

"Why do you—"

"Don't you dare. Just because some little shiksa didn't smile at you—"

"Why don't you like me?"

She stared at me like I'd cursed her to her face. Like she'd always expected it of me. In an instant, disbelief turned to rage and we were both yelling.

"You would raise your voice—?"

"I didn't, I didn't."

"Change your tone."

"*You* change your tone—why do you hate me?" I was sobbing now, furious. I remember feeling sick—like I was fighting myself somehow.

It got ridiculous. She grabbed me by the collar of my brown jacket and dragged me to the kitchen sink. I didn't know what she was doing. I didn't know what to do—you can't hit your own mother. I flapped around like a shirt on a clothesline, trying to get free but not too hard because I was worried she would slip and fall. "Change your tone, change your tone," she kept screaming, and scared as I was I kept yelling, "*You* change your tone," and, absurdly, "there *is* no girl."

It was a big, new bar, and it wouldn't go in. She tried it the other way but it wouldn't go either, just hit against my teeth. "*This* is what we raised," she kept hissing, "*this* is what we raised," and grabbing the bar she turned it in her hand a few times, then jammed her lathered hand in my mouth and turned it like she was rinsing out a small cup. I gagged and wrenched free.

Farce. Seen from the outside—and time is outside, I guess— these things are always a farce. I can picture myself standing there in the kitchen but what I see is Dopey after he swallows the soap in *Snow White*: that same surprised look—*hick! hick!*—then bubbles popping out, one after the other, and even though I'm sobbing, frothing at the mouth, yelling "I wish I was him, I wish I was him," even though I'm humiliated, stripped, the shame doesn't take away from the farce, it multiplies it.

Hick! Hick! She's burst into tears, her face in her hands.

Hick! I'm staggering around the kitchen, my shirt soaked, my jacket half pulled off. "I wish I was him," I'm screaming— melodramatic, self-indulgent, beside myself. "You blame . . ." I start to gag, cough, "You . . . you . . ."

And she looks up at me, weeping, wrecked, a bizarre calm like clear sky coming over her face, and says, "Well, you were there, weren't you?" and goes up the stairs.

I TRIED to make it up to her afterward, to say I was sorry. We ate dinner that night like nothing had happened, the three of us at the table, the little clinks of silverware—"You want more brussel sprouts? No? Potatoes?" She seemed energized somehow, controlled, sitting straight-backed and stiff, holding her silverware just so, even answering something I said while looking right through me, like some contessa who, having just received some terrible news, is determined not to let the company see her suffer.

We never said much after that. There was no going back, though thinking about it, I'm not sure there was much to go back to anyway. Truth is, there's nothing more stupid than fighting something that isn't—a *lack* of love, a *lack* of respect. It's like fighting an empty room. Nobody understands what you're doing. You punch the air, you yell, you weep, but there's nobody there—just this feeling that there's something holding you back, that there's a place outside that room that could answer everything, that could tell you, finally, who you are. And you're not allowed to go there.

IT SOUNDS TOO NEAT, I know: Literature Teaches a Lesson. Still.

I was in the library one day during free period when I decided to find a book I remembered liking as a kid. I never found it. I was going through the K's when I found Kafka. I'd heard of him. The book was called *The Trial* and it had weird little drawings like the kind a messed-up kid might make of stick figures trapped inside fences or frames or doors. The fences or windows overlapped and crossed. I sat down at one of the round tables—and I didn't get up again. I skipped gym, then lunch, then math. Nobody asked.

I didn't understand most of it. Toward the end a priest tells the story of a man who goes to the law. To get to the law he has to go through a door but there's a guard in front of it—he's not allowed in. He tries everything—he can't get by. Even if he did, he's told, he'd just find another door, and another guard, and another. So he waits. He waits for years. He grows old. Finally, dying, he calls the guard over and asks him why, if the law is supposed to be meant for everybody, he wasn't allowed in. And the guard, watching the man's eyes closing, leans over and yells: "Because this door was meant for you. I am now going to shut it."

Kafka didn't save me. He just told me I was drowning. This life, this love—was meant for you. I am now going to shut it.

Which was something.

AND SO, YES, maybe I ran to other things, shallow things. Maybe I lacked coping skills. Maybe I was weak. I cared for people for no better reason than they seemed to care for me, acknowledge me. It didn't seem so dangerous at the time.

In the spring of 1968, Ray and Frank and I had become friends. I couldn't honestly say how it happened except that it happened. Frank was funny, confused, a Boy Scout with a temper. His parents had come from Poland. Big arms, thick neck, he had a smile like a little kid's if the joke was dumb enough. He could do voices— Yosemite Sam and Nixon, Mr. Farber and Mr. Falvo and the Smothers Brothers—and the way he'd laugh, like he didn't want to, like there was somebody inside of him laughing and he couldn't keep him down, could make *you* laugh just watching him, and he'd pile it on till the two of you were bent over like drunks, holding your knees, then stop—and he'd get this look like somebody buttoning the top button of his shirt, and say he had to go.

The better you know somebody, the less you can say about them. I knew Frank. He liked Perry Como in 1968 and didn't care who knew it. His pimples bothered him, and sometimes he'd come to school with Band-Aids over the bad ones. He could annoy the shit out of you—one of those Christian squares who get all red in the face and dig in over nothing—but he wasn't mean. I think he had a hard time with things because he believed the world was a certain way—because he'd been told it was—and it wasn't, and on bad days he'd drive that javelin like there was somebody standing on the other end of the field with a target on his chest. I never figured out who. I had some ideas.

I used to like to watch him, the five or six big, bouncy steps that started the run-up, the spear already cocked behind the head, then the slight turn to the right, the legs cross-stepping, faster now, the body beginning to lean back while still moving forward, bending like a bow, then snapping forward into the release, the body balancing, the eyes following the flight of the spear, off to its work—I thought it was beautiful.

So there was no one moment. We just became friends and because of that probably fucked with and fought with each other more than we had to. I figured out early on that girls and God were an issue; if I found him reading the Bible at lunch—he'd started helping out at church the fall of sophomore year, teaching Sunday school—I'd let him alone.

IT WAS A GOOD SPRING. I'd come home late now as the days grew longer, my head full of split times, my spikes in my bag. I'd learned the code: You didn't showboat, you didn't put daylight between yourself and the group. You could set the pace, no more, and hope coach would notice. In two weeks I was in the middle of my group; in three I was leading it. It meant nothing—the slowest guy in the next group could have run me down in his sleep—but the day I got the nod and joined the fourth I felt like I'd done something. Frank came over and slapped me on the back. Ray was sitting in the stands, watching.

It had taken us a few months. We'd started slowly, a few words, a nod in the hall, a joke or two at lunch; over time it built into something. I was fascinated by him. I wasn't alone. With his long coat and his dancing brawler's walk and his black hair which he was always raking back with his fingers, he drew people like something dangerous, unstable—an actual cheetah slouching down Main. He was crazy, people said, actually crazy. He'd walk through Harlem at night. He'd been sleeping with some woman from Carmel whose husband was in the mob. Jumped by three grown men, he'd fought back with a PVC pipe and a garbage can lid, put one in the hospital and walked away. The only reason he was still alive was that he wouldn't hesitate and knew how to improvise.

I couldn't figure out why he was talking to me, why he sat at our table, why he asked me what I was reading. It had to be some kind of joke. I didn't say much, waiting for the knife, expecting it.

It never came. Ray never fucked with me, even when I deserved it. We talked about everything. He'd ask me things and I'd tell him what I knew or what I'd read and he'd listen like it was something he needed to hear. His voice was different when he was with me, with us—*he* was different. When we ran into others we understood we had to step back from the ring, let him be who he had to be, and sometimes, watching him walk into the arena, smiling, coiled, graceful as a ballet dancer who'd explode at a touch and gently lay your head down on the pavement, there'd be this sense of wonder that this other Ray, who moved like this, who everybody else knew, was him, too.

I remember the day he asked me about Wilfred Owen. He'd been sitting with us a few weeks by then, had dropped the act, pretty much. It had become a routine with us: He'd walk over, sit down, eat. Now and then he'd ask me something about what I was reading—weirdly serious, like he was wearing horn-rimmed glasses. I could see the other kids looking over at us, trying to figure out what he was doing. He ignored them. It wasn't all at once. Sometimes you'd still see him break off a piece of hamburger bun and dip it in whatever he was drinking—or we were drinking—mold it into a ball of dough, wait, pretending to be interested in whatever we were talking about—"Really? You sure?"—then shoot it with a short, sharp flick into someone's cup or tray or hair without changing his expression or missing a beat—"I don't know, sounds pretty far-fetched to me," even as the screaming started—but more and more he seemed to actually want to hear about things.

I told him. Owen was a poet, I said. He'd been fucked up in the war, in France.

"Which war?" he said.

"First."

"Pretty sure there was one before that."

"No, like first—"

"Yeah, no, I know. Jesus." He took a bite, pointed to the book with his chin. "So what's that one called?"

"You mean this one?"

"Yeah, I don't know, that one—the one you're reading."

"It's in Latin."

"What—you mean the whole poem?"

"No, just the title. And one line. At the end. "

"What for?"

"I don't know. They used to do that." I went back to reading.

"So—what's it called?"

"Really?"

"I wanna know."

"*Dulce et decorum est.*"

"The fuck does *that* mean?"

I told him.

"No shit. You talk Latin?"

"It says here at the bottom."

He nodded. "So how's it go?"

"What, you want . . . ?"

"Sure, why not?"

"I'm not going to—"

"C'mon."

"No, fuck you, I'm not—"

"C'mon, read the fuckin' poem."

"I'm not going to—"

"C'mon, quit dickin' around an' read the fuckin' poem." He looked at Frank. "Tell him to read the goddamn poem."

Frank shrugged.

"C'mon, you pussy, it's not like you have to get on the table and recite it for Christ's sake." He was tapping his plastic fork on the edge of the tray, enjoying himself.

So I read the fuckin' poem. *"Bent double, like old beggars under sacks, / knock-kneed, coughing like hags . . ."* I could hear my own voice. I felt embarrassed, nervous—I kept expecting to see him break off a piece of bun. *"Dim, through the misty panes and thick green light, / As under a green sea, I saw him drowning. / In all my dreams, before my helpless sight . . ."* Halfway through he stopped tapping. I finished up, hurrying through: *"If you could hear, at every jolt, the blood / Come gargling from the froth-corrupted lungs, / Obscene as cancer, bitter as the cud / Of vile, incurable sores on innocent tongues, / My friend, you would not tell with such high zest / To children ardent for some desperate glory, / The old Lie: Dulce et decorum est / Pro patria mori."*

I closed the book quickly. When I looked up I was surprised to see something in his face I hadn't seen before. A kind of quiet. He was leaning forward, his head slightly to the side as though listening for something. He seemed confused, troubled. I thought it was a joke.

"What's it mean again—that last part?" he said.

I told him.

He was quiet for a few seconds. "So what happened to this guy—what's his name?"

"Owen."

"Yeah."

And I told him about the mustard gas, the shell shock, how he'd been hiding in a trench next to the bodies of his friends when the shell came, how he'd been evacuated, recovered in London—the whole thing.

"Lemme see." He waved the book over. I found the page, handed it over, watched him read it again. He handed it back. "That's fucked up." He turned to Frank. "That was fucked up, right?"

Frank nodded. "That was good."

"Right?" He turned back to me. "So, what happened to the guy?"

"What do you mean?"

"I don't know, like, after the war or whatever."

"He died in the war."

"You just said he made it."

"Hey, Cap," somebody yelled from the table behind him. He ignored them.

"You just said he made it, that they got him and fixed him up and all."

"He did," I said. "He went back."

"Whaddya mean he went back?"

"He went back. Reenlisted."

"Hey, Cap," the guy yelled again.

"You mean like volunteered? After all this shit?"

"Hey, Cappicciano." It was the same guy. Some girls laughed at the table.

"I mean, I don't get that. Why the fuck would he do that?"

"Maybe he did it for his country," Frank said.

Ray turned to look at him. "What're you, stupid?"

"I'm just—"

"Didn't you just hear him read all that Latin shit about how sweet it is to die for your country and all that crap?"

"OK, fine."

"Jesus."

"I don't know why—maybe he just had to go back," I said.

"What for? He knew how fucked up it was. And it fuckin' killed him?" He shook his head. "Jesus."

"Maybe he couldn't stay away. Maybe—"

"Hey, Cappicciano! Jackie says you—"

It happened so fast it was almost like I didn't see it, didn't see him scoop the burger from my tray, turn, and with one vicious, beautiful move explode it on the other's chest like a mortar—it suddenly just *was*, a quick burst of meat and catsup like something opening and then the guy was being held back by two friends and people were screaming and the monitor was blowing his whistle and Ray, his coat flapping behind him, was already at the cafeteria doors, smashing them with a double crack against the walls like gunshots—gone.

WE STARTED HANGING OUT together, mostly just the two of us. Frank brought Jesus with him and even though he kept him to himself it made things different. For some reason when Frank was around, even though we were friends, I'd always end up pretending to be tougher than I was, to know more than I did, like I wanted to separate myself from him, to make clear I wasn't like him. When it was just me and Ray it was easier. After the first few weeks I stopped flinching, stopped worrying I'd say something stupid that would show him who I was and not who he thought I was.

That spring I'd come by the house after practice sometime and he'd be watching TV with little Gene and we'd sit on the floor with our backs against the couch talking and looking through the stacks of dirty magazines his dad kept in the utility room. He'd bring in an armful and dump them on the carpet between us. One had a story called "Cleopatra and the Snake" with pictures of some woman dressed up in an Egyptian headdress squeezing her breasts together over a boa constrictor.

I liked being there, liked sprawling on that dirty carpet with the cigarette butts and the paper bags and the still-wet towels. Half-empty but cluttered, it felt like a house in the middle of moving out, when the couch is still there so you have a place to sit but the shelves are gone and the pictures are gone and the place where the loveseat used to be is just a shadow on the wall. It's hard to explain. There was something free about the pile of dust and butts that somebody had swept into a corner. The coffee table was covered with bottle rings like the Olympics gone crazy. A broken table lamp lay on its side by the wall, the wire torn from the rim of the shade.

Early on I'd keep thinking about Ray's dad coming home from his shift at Sing Sing and finding us there. We'd be sprawled out on the floor against the couch, leafing through *Playboy* and *Swank* and I'd swear I heard his car in the driveway.

"Don't worry about my old man," he'd say—"he wouldn't give a shit anyway."

"Sounds pretty cool."

"Think so?" He handed me a magazine. "Check this one out." He went into the kitchen. "You want a beer?"

Behind me I could hear little Gene breathing. He sounded plugged up, his face stuck in the crease of the couch. A can cracked and hissed in the kitchen, then another. I reached behind me and rolled Gene over and wiped his nose with my fingers.

"So what's it like being smart?" Ray said from the kitchen.

"C'mon," I said.

"C'mon, what?—All that readin' you do, you're probably goin' to college." He came back in, handed me a beer. "Fuck, I'd go. Anything's better than this shit."

"You could go."

He laughed. "Get me out of the draft, right?" He took a drink, swallowed a belch: "Only way I'd get into fuckin' college is if I broke in through a window." He started talking along with the TV in a fake baritone: "Like sands through the hourglass . . . so are the Days of Our Lives. I can't stand this shit." He crawled over on his knees, switched the channel.

"My mom watches that crap," I said.

"Yeah?" Little Gene stirred, started to cry, then fell back asleep. "Almost time for him to eat. Ours took off."

"She just left?"

"Funny how that happens around here."

"Where to?"

"Who the fuck knows? Not my mom anyway—his." He was looking at the TV. "You ever think about takin' off?"

"Sure."

"I mean, seriously, one day just like walkin' the fuck out. Not like, you know, Philly or somethin', but different, like some place they talk a different language an' everything."

"Sure."

"I think about it all the time."

"You should go," I said. "I mean, you know, when you're ready."

"Maybe I will."

He stood up. "I gotta get his bottle."

He grabbed the empties and walked into the kitchen. "Have to take my little guy along—can't go anywhere without him. Who knows—maybe we could go out west, live off the land and shit." I heard the refrigerator open. "Fuck, we're outta milk."

He came into the doorway. "Listen, you think your folks would have some milk?"

I WAS NERVOUS when I called—I'm not sure why, exactly. We'd had a few beers, but it wasn't that. It was Ray, mostly: the coat, the walk, the broken tooth. I could see us showing up at the door, him carrying the baby. And what would he make of my parents, our house—the books, the quiet, the references to Max Brod or Camus, Versailles or Saigon—the whole thing seemed crazy.

I was relieved when I got my dad.

"Mosher residence?" he said, sounding unsure.

I explained, talking quickly. I was sorry, a friend, his baby brother, only a few minutes . . .

He didn't understand. "And you say this person is a friend from school?" he said, speaking English, grinding on the r's like he was getting up some phlegm. I could hear my mother in the background: "*Wer ist es?*"

"Only for a few minutes," I said.

"Here? Now?" I heard her say.

"And you say you are where now? And who is this baby that . . . ?"

I explained, again. "I see. One moment." My mother's voice disappeared as he put his hand over the phone. I knew what she was saying: Who was this so-called friend? They'd never heard of him. Did I think I could just call at any hour and . . .

He came back on. "Your mother says we have some milk," he said.

I KNEW what would happen. They'd be outraged, appalled. Who was this hoodlum who talked like this, who dressed like a gangster? For his part, Ray would think they were stuck-up, fucked up, weird—worse, he'd think I'd been putting on some kind of act, that I was like them.

"Listen, we could just go over to Kobacker's," I said as we walked up the street in the dark.

A cold mist was falling, just enough to wet our faces. Ray was shushing the baby, patting him on the back, making little noises to distract him: "That's right, little man, we're gonna get you somethin' to eat, yes we are." He turned to me. "Don't worry about it," he said.

MORE THAN THEM it was him—like there was another person talking through his mouth saying "Thank you, ma'am" and "Yes, sir" and "What a nice house you have." For a second, thinking he was laughing at them, I felt a confused flash of resentment. He was being polite.

My father met us in the hall holding his reading glasses. "Welcome, welcome. And your name is Raymond?"

"Yes, sir." He shook his hand.

"Would you like me to take your coat, Raymond?"

I could see him looking at the pictures, the books.

My mother had taken Gene as soon as we came in. "And so this is the baby? Here, let me see—may I?"

Ray started to apologize for bothering them.

"No bother." And she walked away with the baby cradled in her arms. When he looked at me, all I could do was shrug.

"So, people call me Ray," he said to my father, who was standing in the closet, hanging up the coat.

"I'm sorry?"

"My name. People call me Ray." The chipped tooth, the long greasy hair, the way he stood by the glassed-in bookcase, alert—he seemed charged, unstable, like a cyclone in a bottle. He scratched the back of his head, a long pink cut, half-healed and puckered, running from his wrist to a scabbed knuckle. "I'm only Raymond when I'm in trouble."

My father smiled. "And you know Jon from the classes at the high school?"

"Lunch, mostly."

"I see."

Ray smiled. "Yeah, I'm pretty sure in eating I've got him beat."

"Can this be true?"

"Absolutely."

"You eat more than Jon?"

"It's not even close."

It was unreal: my father kidding around with Ray Cappicciano in the hall, my mother feeding Gene, swaying back and forth as if remembering a dance, saying, "You have to feel the milk with your elbow so it is not too warm for the baby." I just stood there.

I watched her holding Gene on her hip, then cradle him again and work the nipple into his mouth. "There we go, that's a good baby. Did we have something to eat?"

"We gave him some banana," Ray said.

"Is this true?" she said to the baby. "Did we have some banana?" She moved the bottle to a better position. "What is the matter with you?" she snapped. "Did we raise you like this?"

She hadn't looked up. For a second I thought she was angry at the baby, that she'd gone crazy.

"Ask—your—friend if he wants something to eat or drink."

"You want something to eat or drink?" I said.

I saw him look at me, then at my mother. "No, I'm good," he said slowly, seeing something. And standing there, awkward as a teen-aged baboon pretending to be a man, pretending to be tough, pretending, I felt a spasm of gratitude and shame.

"You're quite sure?" my mother said. "Because it's no problem. You'll have to excuse my son's manners."

"I'm fine," he said. He was looking at her, an angle to his voice, almost a smile. "We ate before."

I think it wasn't until then I realized how alone I'd been.

IT'S HARD TO CHANGE what you remember. In my head I can hear Falvo trying to talk to us about the Russians going into Czechoslovakia and somebody in the back of the class saying *he'd* check *her* slovakia, no problem, and one of the girls moaning "Oooh, baby, check it," and Falvo kicking the kid out, and all that happening around the same time as Tina. And even though I know it wasn't like that, that Tina was that April and the Russian invasion of check her slovakia almost four months later, I can't unstick them. And maybe it doesn't matter. Everything was crazy then, charged up. The fact that a stupid joke like that could actually get under my skin—*Oooh, baby, check it!*—that it could make me shift around in my chair to get myself loose, tells you everything you need to know.

That spring, grabbing something in my room on the way to school, I saw Mr. Perillo walk out of his house followed by his daughter, Tina. She was wearing bell-bottoms, a halter, some kind of yellow headband. They were arguing about something.

I liked looking at Tina. She was five years older than me, in college at New Paltz, and in summer I'd watch her lying on a towel in the back yard smearing lotion on her stomach and I'd try to make things happen. I'd try until my legs were shaking but even though it felt good, nothing went anywhere. In fact, nothing had ever gone anywhere—not with Cleopatra, who I'd torn out of the magazine when Ray was in the bathroom, not with anybody. I didn't know what was wrong with me. Still, all those times watching her, trying, felt like some kind of connection between us. Sometimes I even imagined she knew I was there, was helping me out, flipping over on her stomach and letting the straps of her top fall to the towel just for me.

The windows were closed—I couldn't hear what they were saying. Mr. Perillo had the car door open and was about to get in when he turned as if to say something and Tina spun into the car and fell to the driveway. I didn't understand what had happened. I could see her lying on her side, the headband pulled down over her face. I was about to run outside when I saw Mr. Perillo get in the car and slam the door and pull out of the driveway. She was standing up, holding her face with both hands. By the time I realized he'd hit her in the face with the back of his fist, she was inside the house.

I just stood there. The whole thing—the smallness of the movement, the way she'd slammed into the roof of the car, the way she lay there like a dropped doll, her hair covering her face—it seemed acted, unreal. I'd never really seen what people could do to each other.

I didn't know what to do. Should I call the cops? Would she want me to? We'd known the Perillos all my life. Mr. Perillo had cleaned our gutters after Aaron died. Mrs. Perillo had always been kind to me. I grabbed my books. I was walking down the steps with the idea of knocking on their door to see if she was OK when she ran out of the house carrying a backpack, threw it in through the open window of her car and got in. I slowed down. I didn't want to embarrass her. Worse, she might think I was doing it for some other reason, using it somehow, that I was ridiculous, a kid.

It was too late to turn around, or hide behind the bushes. For a moment I thought of pretending I hadn't seen her but she backed up right next to me. She was crying. She'd tied the bandanna over the side of her face but you could see the blue coming out around the edge. I'd never seen a face so broken.

"Hey," I blurted. "I . . . are you OK?"

She looked up, surprised to see me there, then shook her head, her lips trembling like she was cold.

"You saw?" she said.

I nodded. I'd known her all my life.

She was shaking like someone freezing to death.

"I don't . . . he didn't mean to, he just . . ."

"It's OK." I took off my jacket and handed it to her through the window. "Here."

She just sat there holding it, the tears running down her face.

"I can drive," I said. "You want I can drive you to the hospital."

She tried to smile and I could see her reach up and catch the edge of her grief. The shuddering start to slow.

"No. Thanks. I'm OK."

"I could do it."

"No, I know you could. I'm OK, really." She cleared her right eye with her finger, her left with her thumb, then gave a small laugh. "So . . . how's school?"

I shrugged.

She lit a cigarette, her hands shaking badly. "You're, what, a junior now?"

"I'm—"

"Jesus, look at me." She glanced up the street. "You goin' to school? C'mon, get in."

IT WAS ONE of those days in spring—warm, still, dripping—that remind you of what dirt and roots smell like. The trees were just leafing out. A week earlier the hill above the station had been bare except for the maples and here and there a willow, like some painter had touched a smear of green to the brown. We didn't talk much. We took the old route down Brewster Hill Road and I watched her shift gears, holding her cigarette. She'd cut the base of her thumb and every few minutes she'd suck on it, steering with her right.

"How's my eye look?"

"I can't really see it."

She pulled back the bandanna. "Be honest."

"Not so great," I said.

"I can't see much out of it."

"It's closing up."

She shook her head, then laughed. "This is so fucked—sorry."

"It's fine," I said. "I'm not a kid anymore."

She turned to look at me. "No, I guess not."

We lined up with the other cars. "Jesus," she said, looking at the buildings, "I can't believe this place is still here."

"Me either."

"I bet."

"Well, thanks for the ride," I said.

She nodded. "Hang in there—it just gets weirder."

"Great," I said. I yanked at the door.

"It sticks—you have to pull it in."

"You goin' back to New Paltz?"

I turned around when she didn't answer.

"I'm not goin' back," she said quietly.

"What do you mean? Don't you have to—"

"I'm not goin' back. I'm leavin'. For good."

"Jesus, where?"

She laughed. "God, you're so uptight—I don't know where, someplace else. What's the difference? I heard about this commune up in Vermont where they're not all about rules, where they share everything—maybe I'll try that. Anyway, you don't need to hear about my shit, you've got a life to—"

"I don't have anything," I said.

"Oh, c'mon, sure you—"

"Really," I said.

She glanced over at me, then out through the windshield.

"It can seem like that sometimes."

"It *is* like that."

She shook her head. "I'm sorry. It's just so fucked sometimes." She smiled. "You want to know why he hit me? Because of Martin Luther King. Should have kept his mouth shut, he wouldn't've gotten shot. I say how can you say that and he starts yelling it's his house he paid for it he can say what he wants and if I don't like it I'm free to leave. King was just a nigger with a collar and an attitude, a Communist, a liar—he's surprised nobody shot him sooner, so I say, 'What are you afraid of, Daddy?' and he walks out the door. 'What are you afraid of,' I say, because I'm still tryin' to talk to him—'you afraid I'm gonna sleep with a black man? Is that it?' And you know what he says to me? I mean, I'm his little girl, I used to ride around on his shoulders, and you know what he says to me? He turns around and looks at me like he actually hates me, like he's gonna cry or something—and says, 'I'd rather see you dead.' I mean, I just couldn't believe it—I couldn't believe he'd say that to me. The next second it's all crazy and he's screamin', 'Get back in the house, get back in the goddamn house' and I'm saying, because now I want to hurt him like he's hurt me, 'What's the difference, Daddy, men are men, it's my body, I can ball who I want,' and that's when he hits me."

She was still looking out the window. "It's always like this, you know?—What they did to Martin, what they're doin' in Vietnam. It's their answer—killing. My dad's no different—if it scares you, hit it. Even if it's your daughter."

A light mist of rain—as if somebody was standing on the roof with a spray bottle—came over the windshield, then stopped. The other cars had gone.

She turned to look at me. "You're late for school, Jon Mosher."

"I don't care," I said. I was looking at the strand of hair she'd caught behind her ear, the two small freckles on her cheek, the blue-gray mound of her right eye.

"Thanks for letting me—"

"Nobody should hit you," I said.

"Sure, but until people—"

"No, I mean you."

I could see her hesitate—surprised, confused. "Thank you, I . . . Shit, we're about to get busted." A man was walking up from the school. "Shit, shit—quick, get your head down." She started the car, put it in gear. Around the side of my book bag I could see him speed up, then break into a jog, his head to the side, trying to see who was in the car.

"Hey, you! This is school property."

"Shit! He's gonna cut us off."

"Go over the grass."

She laughed. "Hold on." We bumped up and over the grassy divider and out on the road. "Did he see you?"

"No way."

"That was like Steve McQueen or somethin'."

I'd had too much coffee that morning—my stomach felt shaky. We drove on, not saying anything, the quiet thickening between us. I could feel the muscles in my legs tensing, bracing against the floorboards like they wanted to break through.

She checked the rearview, not looking at me. "Listen, I don't, you know, have to be anywhere. You want to take a walk or something?"

IT WAS THE BARN below the spillway that made us notice it. We must have seen it a thousand times before: an old-fashioned dirt road with a grassy strip running down the middle. She loved barns. Did I know where the road went? I said it went around Lost Lake.

She knew that—she meant had I ever been? "I've been driving past that road all my life," she said.

"It's private," I said.

"C'mon," she said.

We parked up along Fairfield Drive and walked down the shoulder, already thick with poison ivy, then turned in past the barn—huge, red, sagging under the oaks. A mailbox said S. Colby. Across from the barn on an overgrown lawn stood an old white house. Where the lawn narrowed, a weedy cut led to the lake. Somebody had set up a half-dozen rowboats on sawhorses.

"I don't know that we should be doing this," I said.

"C'mon—what's the worst that can happen? We'll say we're lost. It's called Lost Lake, right?"

"I don't know."

She didn't turn around, just reached back.

Before I could think, she was holding me by the hand, pulling me along like it was a kind of joke, like she had to drag me, but there was something in her voice—a little forced, a little nervous—that was like falling into warm water. I could feel the heat of her palm, her fingers wrapped around mine, slipping, tightening.

She still hadn't turned around, though she wasn't pulling as hard. As if she knew the act couldn't hold. She laughed quietly. "C'mon. What's the matter—scared?"

We saw her at the same time, a woman in a long, flowery dress walking through the woods toward the dirt road. She was carrying a basket covered with a towel.

"Shit, now what?" Tina said. She'd dropped my hand.

"Maybe she's cool," I said. I could feel my heart, slowing.

"This is a beautiful place," Tina called out.

"You guys want some mushrooms?" the woman said, like she'd known us for years. "I can't help myself—when I see 'em, I—" She saw Tina's eye. "Oh, wow—you should probably put somethin' on that."

❖ ❖ ❖

IT WAS LIKE SOMETHING out of a shampoo commercial, only real: a wooden cabin at the bottom of a stone staircase set into a hill, a small, still lake alive with the rings of fish like a slow rain. Swallows were dipping and wheeling over the water, touching their wings; a striped yellow butterfly fanned slowly on a hanging basket dripping with long-necked blooms.

A strong-looking shirtless guy with a scraggly, graying beard and a ponytail looked up from an easel as we came down. "Any luck?" he said.

"Almost more than I can carry," the woman said.

"And somebody to help us eat them—cool."

We'd just realized we'd been hearing kids screaming when two little girls, one naked, came tearing out from behind the cabin and started going back and forth around their father's legs, trying to fake each other out.

In an instant he had them both and was walking across the grass to a narrow dock, the paintbrush clamped between his teeth.

"Gotcha! Hey, shtop wiggling."

"No, Daddy, no."

"What'd I shay?"

"No, Daddy."

"Fish gotta eat."

"No, Daddy—"

"One, two—" Somehow he'd managed to move them both to the same side, a squirming bundle of kid—"three!" And with a great heave he sent them flying—a tangle of arms and legs, one upside down—out over the water.

He came walking back to us, pleased with himself, dusting off his hands. He had a smear of green paint on his temple. "Hi," he said. "Hungry?"

They made us fried mushrooms, eggs and toast, offered us a

joint, gave Tina an herb thing for her eye that smelled like licorice and manure. They made her take the hammock that hung from hooks in the wall—she was wounded, they said. I'd never been in a place so weird, so—easy. We talked about music, the war, the lake, largemouth bass and Henry Kissinger. We listened to Louis Armstrong and Jefferson Airplane and some stuff I didn't know and at some point the kids, who turned out to be a boy and a girl, led us to the kitchen and introduced us to Sacco and Vanzetti—two white rats who sat on the counter turning crusts of toast in their little red hands like corn on the cob.

We returned to the living room, ducking our heads under the bundles of drying twigs and leaves hanging from the crossbeams. A rust-colored cat lay curled in a salad bowl, a baby slept in a half-covered basket with wilting dandelions tucked into the mesh over its head.

"This is so cool," Tina said.

"Think so? You haven't met the neighbors," said the painter, who was scrunched up on the couch moving his toes around with his fingers like he had a cramp.

"We dig it," said the woman from the kitchen.

"Anyway, it's a beautiful place," Tina said.

"Bug in every bloom, take my word for it."

"Mostovsky's pretty cool," the woman called out. We could hear her talking to the rats: "Come here, sweetheart—you want an olive?"

Someone at the A&P had told her the baby looked like Moses in the Bullrushes, she said.

"Jesus."

"No—Moses."

"What did *you* say?"

"I said, 'Moses 'n' the Bullrushes'—didn't they open for Hendrix at Monterey?"

The painter chuckled. "Hey, baby, you want to bring the papers?"

"Who's driving?"

"You are." He turned to us. "Sure you won't partake?"

I shook my head.

"Sure, if it's cool," Tina said.

His wife came in and handed him a bag of weed and some papers.

"Anyway, all I was saying was, you know, it's been tried before, no ties, no guilt"—he licked the joint and lit it—"and it hasn't worked out so well. All those utopian communities in the nineteenth century—it always gets fucked up in the end."

"So then how come you guys aren't married?" Tina said.

He handed her the joint. "Marriage was invented by the church to control sex—everybody knows that."

"See, that's what I mean. All this shit that keeps us, like"—she passed it back—"tied down and miserable is changing, right? I mean, you guys are a perfect example of . . ."

"Muddling," the woman called from the kitchen. "We're a perfect example of muddling."

He took a long toke. "Anyway, don't get me wrong—I'm all for love. It's just, you know, I don't think it's free."

He started rummaging around in a pile of books. "Ever read Marcuse?" He tossed a paperback into the hammock. "It's about how—fuck, what's it about? It's about how we've been, like, pacified by stuff."

"Because affluence represses the need for liberation," the woman called out.

"Right. Exactly. It's like we're living in a big room so full of shit we can't even see that we *need* to be liberated."

Tina took a hit and passed it back. "Sure, OK, but what's that got to do with—"

"OK, so you ever see *Let's Make a Deal*? Yeah, like on TV. So they give you a prize, some medium-sized piece of crap—let's say a TV—and now you have to choose to, like, keep it, or trade it for something behind door number one—which the lovely Katie is pointing to—or door number two or whatever. If you guess right, you get to trade in your medium-sized piece of crap for a bigger one. If you guess wrong, OK, you get what's called a Zonk—which could be a llama, or a lot of food, or a room full of old furniture—and everybody laughs. After the show of course you get to trade it in for bread."

"We once met a guy who took the pig," the woman said, coming in and taking the joint.

"You what?"

She took a hit, let it out. "We met a guy who took the pig. This huge sow. He's . . ." They were all laughing by now, squeaking out "he took the pig," and "zonked with a pig." "He's supposed to trade it in after the show for, like, I don't know, whitewall tires or the *Encyclopaedia Britannica* or something—"

"It's like Joseph McCarthy with hooves."

"—and he says, like, fuck you, I want the pig. It's staring out the bars of this little Green Acres pen like it's tryin' to figure out who to kill first but they have to give it to him 'cause it's in the contract so they bring it down in the service elevator and throw it on the forklift to get it in his truck and he drives away."

She walked back to the kitchen.

The artist wiped the tears out of his eyes. "Jesus. Anyway, the machine is like *Let's Make a Deal*, man. It controls all the options. Want to know what matters? Pick a curtain. Want to figure out who you're gonna be? Pick a box. Because that's your choice: door number one or door number two. When the truth is, we're surrounded by doors, when every breath we take is a door."

Tina was sitting up in the hammock. "But that's exactly why we have to, you know, get off the show or pick the pig or whatever—"

"Sure, yeah, I'm cool with that."

"So—"

"All I'm sayin' is it's not *all* out there, OK, it's not *all* the man—that people are pretty good at poisoning their minds all by themselves. That while you're, like, fighting to get free from Big Daddy you can't forget the little daddy in your head because he's busy knocking together a cell with your name on it. It's like, I don't know, original sin or something, except God's got nothin' to do with it."

The woman came into the room, wiping her hands on a rag. "We gotta split, Mike." She looked at us. "Listen, you kids want to stay?"

THEY WERE GONE in ten minutes. They didn't care that we weren't a couple, or that they'd just met us. It was cool either way, come or go, leave or stay, one of us or both. A quick, disorganized little whirlwind—"Yeah, it's a drag we have to go into the city . . . Go, you can get dressed in the car . . . You want to bring the turtle, bring it"—and they had the rats in a cage and the cage in the car with the kids—the little girl walking up the hill naked dragging a long striped towel, the boy carrying a turtle ahead of himself like an offering—had flashed a quick peace sign through the window and split.

We just stood there in the quiet, listening to the car bumping down the dirt.

"I can't believe they'd do that," Tina said. "That's just so cool."

I could feel her there next to me—her hair, her sun-brown neck, the hollows below her hip bones just above her jeans. I could feel my stomach, tight against my belt.

She turned and started back down to the cabin. "What do you want to do? Man, I am *so* high."

"I should probably take off," I said. Something in me was shaking like those leaves you sometimes see spinning like crazy when nothing around them is moving. She was barefoot, stepping down carefully from rock to rock. When she swayed, reaching out to steady herself against a tree, her hip, like it had turned liquid, kept going till it brushed the bark.

I tried again: "It's just that it's late and all and—"

We'd reached the bottom. It was going to rain—the swallows were everywhere, flashing white, dipping, banking over the water.

"So what do we do now?" she said, turning to look at me.

I couldn't speak. Somewhere in the woods, a thousand tiny frogs were screaming at once. A fat bumblebee, drunk on pollen, bumped twice into the screen over the window and buzzed away.

"You want to go skinny-dipping?"

"I—"

She took a step toward me, beaten, beautiful, the look on her face somewhere between a smile and a dare. "Would that cool you off, you think?"

"I don't—"

"Is that what you want?" She reached behind her back, breathing through her mouth now, and the halter fell to the ground. "How about this—this what you want?" And she was in my arms, the heat of her coming through my t-shirt, her hips pressed against mine, her lips, her nose, the freckles on her cheek right there, right there. And she had me by the hand and was pulling me toward the door.

It was a blur, a haze—the tangled sheets, the way she moved, the smell of cedar and damp and her hair falling over my face—all of it unbelievable even as it was happening. She did everything—I didn't even know I was naked and she was over me, her thighs pressed against my hips, and I felt her reach under and back, her breasts spreading against my chest, and suddenly I'd broken in, was sliding up into that clutching warmth, and I just lay there—too young, too scared, to know what to do, knowing this thing was happening, feeling her moving over me but terrified that nothing would happen, that something was wrong with me. And then I felt it: a stirring, a fullness rising up in me like a wall, irresistibly, shamefully, and she sat up, feeling it too now, slowing, then slowing some more, whispering "Come on, give it to me then," and blind to the world now, desperate, I clawed higher and broke in her like a wave, then again, and again, and heard her laugh, surprised, then ride it down into stillness.

She was still moving, breathing hard, holding my face in her hands. "I guess it's been a while, huh?" She pulled back, flushed, to look at my face, and stopped. "Oh, no, you're kidding," she said.

I couldn't speak.

"Oh, my God," she said, putting her hand over her mouth. "Baby, I had no idea that—"

I'd begun to get hard in her again. I was sixteen.

She kissed me deep. "What's this?" she whispered. "We have more for Mama?"

She'd started moving again. She was looking right at me, one hand on my face, the other slipped down between us, vulnerable, beautiful. "What the fuck," she said, her words spacing to the rise and fall like someone riding a horse, "might—as well—ring it in—right."

I SKIPPED THREE DAYS in a row. The first afternoon she dropped me off a block from my house and I walked home in the rain and let myself in like I was coming home from school. I told my parents I'd be doing my homework at Frank's. I was nervous they'd notice something, see the change in my face, my voice, my life. They didn't. I found her where I'd left her, listening to the radio, her brown leg sticking out the car window. Later that night I called to say I'd be sleeping over at Frank's house. They were fine with it.

I did the same thing the next night, and the one after. Was it alright with Frank's mother? Absolutely, I said. I knew they didn't have the number, wouldn't look it up. I'd left a note with Ray, asking him not to come by the house, that I'd explain.

Every morning she'd call me in sick: I was still down with something, she'd say, looking at me, mouthing the word "me." I was running a fever, she said—my glands were swollen. She'd hang up the phone. "Well, really just the one," she'd say, "but it's *so* swollen—I don't think you can go to school like this." She'd have me out by then. "I better *not* be your mother," she'd say.

It rained, off and on, the whole time. It didn't matter. I built big smoky fires in the fireplace. We made tacos out of the stuff she bought in Putnam Lake by herself because we didn't want to chance somebody seeing me. One day the sun came through for a while and she walked naked over the steaming grass and out on the dock and dove in and I watched her moving under the surface, ghostly, familiar, parting the water like she was squeezing through a row of narrow windows. I'd never felt so free. On the other side of the lake I could see a fisherman in a rowboat, his line snaking back and forth against the trees, but he was far away.

I have no idea what we talked about. Everything, I thought. We didn't leave much undone. Whole afternoons would pass while we made love or lay in bed, the sky getting darker, and I remember sitting up while she read my palm, her fingernails tracing my lifeline which intersected with something else. It didn't make much sense to me. I wasn't really listening, anyway. I'd be a poet or a murderer, she decided finally, then whispered, "Hey, I've got something for you that I think you'll like," and slid down and took me in her mouth.

"I can't believe I'm balling little Jon Mosher," she said to me once as we lay together, her head tucked under my chin. She laughed, squeezed me around the ribs. "I didn't mean it that way, baby—

you're fine—it's just, you know, I've known you since you were a baby. I remember when your brother—" She stopped. "Oh, wow. I'm sorry."

"It's fine," I said.

She leaned up on an elbow. "I wasn't . . ."

"Really," I said, "it's fine."

It was almost dusk. "Do you remember him?" she asked.

I shook my head.

"He was a sweet kid."

"I've heard."

"You really don't remember him? You have to remember something."

I shook my head. "I mean, I was only four when it happened."

She'd been running her fingers absentmindedly up and down my chest as we talked.

"Still, you'd think—" She stopped, looked up at me. "Oh, my God," she said. She breathed out—her smile rueful, warm, suddenly protective: "You're sixteen?"

I WANTED TO GO with her, I said. I meant it. I had no reason to stay. We'd had a great time, she said.

"I want to go with you," I said.

"Where?"

"I don't care. Anywhere."

"Baby, I have no idea where I'm going."

"Fine."

She was pretty sure that was called kidnapping. She'd been planning to split, anyway, she said.

She didn't laugh when I told her I loved her. She didn't pat me on the head or patronize me or tell me she wasn't into being exclusive with a sixteen-year-old kid. She didn't make me feel bad for sitting there on the edge of the bed like some six-foot one-inch infant, wiping my eyes with my wrists, humiliated. She didn't push me away any harder than she had to—she just left. She gave me a hug and told me I was a great kid and that we'd see each other again someday and then she put me in the car and dropped me off a block from my house and drove away.

And the way I learned to think of it, I'd had my three days. Though I'd miss out on all the grooviness the next summer, I'd had my share of the promise, of Richie Havens singing "Freedom" like a cry, like that rhythm could make it so, like he was John Henry up against the machine and he'd pound those strings till he died. I'd had a taste—this is what I told myself—and cut out just before the mud and the shit came down.

MOST THINGS didn't change much—some did. Summer came and went, a heavy blanket you couldn't get out from under. School ended and they killed Bobby Kennedy and then it was the Fourth and we were watching them turn the hose on the field where the fireworks had set the weeds on fire. I took long runs around the reservoirs in the mornings before the heat came on, slapping deer flies into my hair. The afternoons I spent in my dad's store, the two of us working quietly, sorting, stacking, then walked over to Ray's, sweating up that long hill as the light changed, then died, and the first soft thunder like bombs in the distance sounded in the still air.

We didn't hang around the house much because his dad's hours had been cut back. I'd come over some days and Mr. Cappicciano'd be sitting on the couch in the heat staring at the TV like he wasn't seeing it at all, a can of beer in his hand and I'd say, "How you doin', Mr. Cappicciano?" and he'd turn his head slowly from the TV and look at me for a few seconds like he didn't know who I was, and then something would click in his eyes and he'd nod.

He always seemed, if not glad to see me, exactly, then something like it. Like it mattered to him what I thought of him. Almost like he wanted my approval. It's complicated. I knew what he was like.

I'd come over some days and there'd be a cruiser parked by the curb and I'd hear them talking through the screen.

"They're fuckin' everywhere now," I'd hear somebody say.

"Comin' up from the Bronx, from Newark. Fuckin' breedin' like rabbits."

"Tell me about it. My sister and brother-in-law got a place down in Riverdale—three bedroom apartment, river view—"

"No shit—river view?"

"Fuckin' beautiful. Families, kids . . . I used to love goin' down there, right? Ball fields, tennis courts, you-name-it. So three years ago they have to let 'em in, some fair housing bullshit—"

Somebody would fart.

"Right?"

"Same thing in the force," I'd hear Mr. Cappicciano say.

"Fuckin' Coonville now—"

"Queen of Commissioners could suck my cock, I wouldn't go back."

"—garbage in the hallways, needles—they're scared to let the kids out the door. Last time I was down there, I didn't fuckin' recognize it."

"And now he can't sell, right?" said another voice.

"Who's he gonna sell to? It's like back in Virginia. Fuckin' nigger holla down there."

"I'd make that nigga holler," Mr. Cappicciano said.

Everybody laughed. "You did, fuckin' A."

"That's right, an' look what happened to me? No, I'm tellin' ya, I'm fuckin' glad I'm out. You gotta deal with 'em runnin' loose—least where I am we got 'em in a box."

And I'd knock on the door.

"Fuck was that?" somebody would say.

"Somebody at the door."

"Jesus."

"Who is it?" Mr. Cappicciano would yell, and I'd come in and say hello and the others would grunt and Mr. Cappicciano would say, "Upstairs," and I'd walk through the quiet and up to Ray's room.

I was on the landing when I heard them that first time, though I could only hear pieces.

"—Jewish," I heard Mr. Cappicciano say.

"—talks Kraut?"

"—where they're from. Before they fuckin' killed 'em all."

Somebody said something I couldn't make out, and somebody laughed.

"Yeah, well, this one's alright," Mr. Cappicciano said. "Got a head on his shoulders, not like my moron—like to shove *him* back where he came from, know what I mean?" He belched. "Probably got a law against that too, now."

"Sounds like this one's gonna be one a them Jew lawyers, why don't you ask him?"

"I'll take a Jew lawyer over some guinea cocksucker outta Bayonne—these people'll fuckin' chew their leg off to survive."

"Chew *your* leg off's more like it."

"Hey, fuck you, Mikey."

"What's with you?"

"What's with me?"

"Yeah, what's with you. I mean, what the fuck?"

"What's with me? I'll tell you what's with me. Shit I seen in the service, what they did to those people? Un-fuckin'-believable."

"So what's your point?"

"What's my point? I'll tell you what's my point. Twenty years later, here they are, runnin' the show. That's what I'm sayin', Mikey. This kid? Fuckin' smart."

I LIKED HIS RESPECT. I did. I played up to it.

I knew what he was, but it was like he was trapped in it, like he was looking for a door out of himself. And sometimes—in the way he'd look at me, like an animal staring out of a shrinking cage—

I'd get the feeling I was that door. That he was hanging on to me somehow, asking me something. That he studied me, admired me, because I was something he'd never be. Truth is, if he hadn't been who he was, it wouldn't have meant as much.

I knew it wasn't easy on Ray, that he was embarrassed by him. Still, there were times, I think, when it made me feel like I had something over him, like maybe there was a reason why his old man noticed me, admired me, and the more he did, the more I believed it. He'd chuckle at my jokes, listen to what I said, nod. I had sense. We were different people, he seemed to be saying, but we agreed on things. It was about approval. And trust. And a strange kind of gratitude.

I knew who he was. I must have.

I came over one afternoon and didn't see him at first because the TV was off. There was a storm coming up over the tracks and the room had that look like somebody pulling a hood over the world. He was just sitting there on the sofa in his boxers and a sleeveless undershirt. When I saw him I said how I hoped I hadn't woken him up and he looked at me and said, "Well . . ." and then this look of terrible embarrassment came over his face and he sat up quickly, straight-backed, and threw up all over the coffee table. He looked at it for a moment, then got to his feet, almost tipping the table over, and walked out of the room.

The door had barely closed behind him when Ray came in from the kitchen. He had a pink towel over his shoulder, a mop and a bucket. The bucket already had water in it. He didn't say anything. He mopped up the mess on the floor, swept the table in two big swipes, tossed the bottles and the empties in the bucket along with the towel and walked out the back.

I found him in the little fenced-in back yard, washing out the bucket with the hose.

"Sorry," I said.

He worked quickly, taking the lid off the trash and dumping the empties, hosing off his hands, rinsing the mop.

"You want to go?" I said.

He turned the bucket upside down, lay the towel over the propane tank. I'd never been in the back yard before. A rotting mattress stood propped against the fence next to a mattress-sized rectangle of yellow grass. A hammer lay on the back seat of a car somebody had pushed against the house like a sofa.

He shook his head, looked around the yard.

"C'mon," I said. "Let's get out of here."

AND SO WE'D TAKE OFF, didn't matter where, running down those long summer days, the light drawing back into the trees as the night came on. Sometimes we'd walk down to the ball field, or up along the East Branch where you could see the trout like little torpedoes waiting in the shadows or out to Jimmy's where he'd always have one up on the lift and talk to us while he worked—hot days maybe out to Frank's or the reservoir for a swim, the shadows growing, the blue coming on. We had nowhere to be. Ray's dad had farmed little Gene out to some relative in Yonkers—I wasn't clear if it was a sister or an aunt—when Ray got a two-week job in construction; when it ended, Gene had stayed with the aunt. It fucked Ray up for a while. He missed his little guy, he said. He was going to hitch out to Yonkers to see him.

He seemed quieter. I thought it was the summer, or some girl. Or being out of school. Sometimes we'd go half an hour or more, me and Frank just yakking away and Ray not saying a thing, just lying there in the grass by the reservoir listening, smoking. Frank talked a lot about California that summer. He'd read some article in *Life* or something—couldn't get out of his head how beautiful it was.

He was going to go, he said. In California you could get a little place on the beach for, like, nothing, grow your own food . . . And Ray, instead of saying you couldn't get a kick in the balls for nothin' never mind a house, would just sit there, listening, then toss the butt in the lake and dive in after it.

Sometimes he'd just disappear for two, three days, even more. I'd walk up to the house after work and the car would be there but there'd be nobody home. Other times I'd find Mr. Cappicciano talking to his friends or banging away at something in the yard with his shirt open and he'd straighten up and take the cigarette out of his mouth and say, "How do I know? Not my fuckin' problem, know what I mean?"

OK, I'd say.

"I don't mean to yell at you, kid," he'd say. "Look, why don't you try back tomorrow—he's bound to turn up eventually."

I'd start to go.

"How's school?" he'd say.

"Good," I'd say. He'd be leaning on some piece of lumber with one knee, a couple of nails sticking out of his mouth, the cigarette propped up across a pencil.

"Still bringin' home those A's?" he'd say, pounding in a nail.

"Some."

"Well keep it up," he'd say, setting up another nail. "Make your parents proud someday."

I KNEW THE DRILL. Ray would show up the next day or the one after that with a fat lip or sore ribs like a tom that's been under the porch for a week and he'd bullshit with Mary on the lunch line then let us drag the story out of him about the ride he'd caught down to the shore and the guys in the bar and what they'd said and what she'd looked like. We should come with him next time. "Sometimes you just gotta get the fuck out, know what I mean?"

It was a good idea, we'd say.

Bunch of pussies, he'd say.

Really, we'd say, next time we would. We'd heard there'd been talks with the school superintendent about him. They were trying to have him suspended again. For good this time.

His eyes would bug out—mock terrified. "Well, fuck me—that mean I'm not gonna get into Harvard?"

"Seriously."

"Don't worry about it."

"Yeah, but what're you gonna do?"

"I'm gonna eat my lunch, that's what I'm gonna do. Fuck do I know—maybe I'll join the Army."

"What about your dad?" I asked once.

He looked at me for a while, probing the inside of his swollen lip with his tongue: "Do me a favor, Jon," he said, and it was one of the few times I heard him use my name: "Don't worry about my dad."

I CAN HEAR IT NOW—I didn't then. Or maybe I did and just didn't say anything. Didn't ask. I knew something was wrong long before that kid from the projects said what he did or Karen started asking, long before that January a year and a half later when we sat freezing in the middle of Bog Brook Reservoir in all that snow and he pulled up that perch and started to cry—but in my mind it's like I didn't know it until then. We borrowed the augur from Jimmy at the garage, carried it down the tracks, slipping around on the ties, then a quarter mile out into the middle of that huge, flat snowy field along with our poles and two folding chairs, dug the blade in and corkscrewed down through a foot of ice. It was one of the last things we did together, me working the augur, Ray on his knees in the snow, scooping out the slush with his hands, blowing on them, scooping some more. The sky that day was like an old gray blanket with the stuffing coming out in the west. The blade broke through into the water and I screwed it back up and Ray got out the last of the slush. It was beautiful, perfect, black as a bullet hole.

And he pulled out a small yellow perch and unhooked it and slipped it back down the hole and began to cry, just sitting there on the chair with his face in his hands saying "Fuck, oh fuck," his voice shaking like somebody looking at something he doesn't really believe and knows he'll never forget. And it was only then, I swear, that I felt it, that I saw the line that had looped around our legs, our arms, our throats, fed on our not-saying, our not-asking, stretching back through the seasons, the years, back to the time I first sensed it there in the cafeteria when he looked up at me and said, "Do me a favor, Jon."

That day I'd had no idea what I'd heard, or if I'd heard anything at all. Ray had come back from the shore. He'd had a thing with his old man. So what? I wasn't really listening. It was early October. I was running cross-country that fall, not because I liked pounding up hills and over marshy golf courses for two and a half miles eating mud kicked up by the spikes of the runners in front of me but because I was good at it. In a three-team meet the week before, Brewster had pulled out an unexpected win mostly because of me.

Cross-country meets were won on depth, something we didn't have. Week after week it was the same thing. Kennedy would take first—nobody could touch him. McCann would come in somewhere in the top five. After that, except for a tight-skinned, nasty-looking farm kid named Brian Moore, who might sneak into the top ten, we had nobody. Which was where I came in. The week before, in twentieth place or so with a half-mile to go, I'd found myself, in a haze of pain, passing runners who seemed to be pushing through thicker air. I ran them down, one after the other, and was coming up on Moore's skinny back when he crossed the line. We finished eighth and ninth. McCann came up and slapped my back as I staggered around, clutching my knees. "Banzai, Mosher," Falvo yelled from the sidelines, doing his Japanese kamikaze. Kennedy was already in his sweats, talking to his dad, a friendly guy in a Teamster's jacket who came to all our meets. "Way to go, Jon," his dad called out.

"Nice run," Kennedy said.

I repeated it to myself as I sorted boxes of men's shoes in the storeroom, as I ate my liverwurst sandwich against the back wall in the sun, as I sat in biology learning about the double helix: Nice run. I'd fantasize about the races I'd run in the Armory that winter, how I'd come out of nowhere in the final lap, untouchable, how I'd put my hand out in front of my chest and part the tape the way I'd seen Kennedy do the season before—gently, like it didn't matter. He'd notice the gesture, acknowledge it with a simple nod.

No, Ray was a good guy, a friend of mine, but I wasn't about to go chasing after his ass down to the shore, or sit around on his porch waiting for him to get home, or waste my time trying to figure out his particular deal with his old man. I had my own life. Everybody had their shit. Frank's sister had disappeared. My mom was going nuts. We didn't have to go looking for problems.

WE'D BEEN SITTING on the railing over the East Branch one evening in August when Frank told me about it. How his sister had gotten knocked up, then refused to tell them who the father was. How his parents had thrown her out of the house, thinking to scare some sense into her, only to find out she'd had money saved and had gotten on a bus for God knows where. It had been a month and they hadn't heard a thing. I had no idea how fucked up it was in his house right now. Nobody talked about it.

"Sounds familiar," I said.

"Serious."

"Me, too."

He broke off a piece of stick and threw it in the current. "It's like, I don't know—I don't even know what. Like they took a pair of scissors and just cut her out, you know?" He started working his shoulder in small circles. "My Dad actually went through the house and took down every picture with her in it, which was basically all of 'em. We came home from school and there were all these spaces on the wall. Megan went nuts."

"How's the shoulder doin'?" I said.

"Good. Should be able to throw tomorrow."

I nodded. "So what'd he do with 'em?"

"I don't know—stuck 'em in a box, burned 'em, I don't know." He shook his head. "It's just I don't get it, you know? I mean, Jesus is all about forgiveness, right?"

"Sure, I guess."

"I mean, I know you're not into it and all, but that's what Jesus is all about. I mean, that's the whole point—forgiveness. He forgave us our sins"—he slapped at a mosquito, then flicked it off his arm with his finger—"so we're supposed to forgive others. It's not like he said, you know, 'Forgive everybody except your own family.' "

"Maybe it's easier that way."

"Easy's not supposed to be part of it either."

I slapped at my face. "Lots of things aren't supposed to be parts of things—but they are, you know?"

"Maybe, but then they shouldn't say they're not."

"Sure."

The light was going fast. I watched the current, pulled endlessly from beneath us. A short way down, where it kept bulging over something, the water looked like syrup about to boil.

"I mean, my folks went to talk to Father Donnelly after—"

"Who?"

"Our priest, good guy, known us all our lives—'cause, you know,

Mom's all messed up, Dad's not talkin'. They want to know what's the right thing to do, right?"

"OK."

"So he tells 'em"—he slapped himself—"we should probably get outta here. So he tells 'em, basically, to put her behind them, that she's slipped from the path of righteousness and only she can save her soul and they've been blessed with two other children—to concentrate on that. To cast her from their hearts."

The mosquitoes were coming in thicker now. It was almost dark. The water had turned to ink.

"I'm gettin' eaten up," I said.

"Yeah."

We got off the rail and started walking back to town in the near-dark—there were no lights on Sodom Road.

"He said that?" I said.

"I mean, that's crazy, right?"

"Crazy's goin' around, what can I tell you?"

"Mom?"

I shrugged. "So listen to this. I come home from practice last week and nobody's home, right? It's around seven—the house is dark. I'm taking off my shoes when I hear this guy's voice comin' from upstairs—this fucked-up, high-pitched voice, almost like a kid's. Scares the crap out of me. I'm halfway up the stairs holding my spikes in my hand when the voice starts goin' up and there's this sound like somebody knocking on a coconut and suddenly I'm listening to Squirrel Nutkin—don't laugh—I'm listening to Squirrel Nutkin singin', *'I've got a tail, I've got a tail, I hold it high as a sail . . .'* Mom's in Aaron's room, playin' these little kids' records we used to listen to before he fuckin' killed himself."

"Weird."

"Think?"

"Gotta admit, though, it's kinda funny too—in its way."

"Yeah, no, I know."

"More weird than funny, I guess."

"I mean, she hasn't listened to these things in twelve years. It's like she's been savin' them up—like a last piece of birthday cake or something."

"I'm sorry, man—that's rough."

We were quiet for a while.

"You'd have kicked that squirrel's ass, though."

"Yeah, I think so," I said.

"Especially with the spikes."

"I liked my chances."

"What size—pin or half-inch?"

"Half-inch—I wasn't fuckin' around."

"So what'd you do?"

"How do ya mean?"

"I mean, you know, after you figured it out."

"No law against playing records—went back to the kitchen, made myself a sandwich. When my old man got home she had *The Prince and the Pauper* on."

"The prince and the pauper?"

"We used to listen to that stuff."

"What'd your dad do?"

"Same thing he always does. Put his shit down, asked me about my day, the two of us talkin' like this, like we don't want to bother her—nothin'. The thing is, she's set up shop up there. Sometimes she doesn't come down all night and it's just me and my old man eatin' dinner listening to Peter Rabbit."

"That's messed up," he said.

"No shit. *You* try listening to Peter Rabbit."

"Soon as I get home."

A car went by and somebody yelled something I couldn't make out.

* * *

I'D BEEN STANDING in the stairwell in the dark, listening to the needle click, when I realized she might open the door and find me there. I can't explain the fear I felt at that moment; for some reason I suddenly imagined a stranger coming out of that room and opening his mouth and my mother's voice coming out. I could hardly move—it was like my blood had gone thick. I'd almost made it to the bottom of the stairs, walking on the sides to keep the boards from creaking, when I heard her voice, gentle as a touch. "*Guten Abend*," I heard her say, and then something I couldn't make out.

"I see," my dad said when I met him at the door. The music was on again, muffled by doors.

He washed his hands at the kitchen sink, shook them twice, then dried them on the dish towel.

We ate leftovers, sitting at the dinner table. Far above us a duck quacked, a midget answered. I watched him cut a slice of dumpling, his shirtsleeves folded neatly above his wrists. He chewed thoughtfully, his eyes moving from the woodcut over the dresser to the empty vase to the streetlight outside the window, then back again. "This is not so bad," he said.

"No," I said.

I saw his eyes stop at the vase, not seeing it, his knife and fork making a roof over his plate.

"You want to watch the news?" I said.

"That's a good idea," he said.

ABOVE US the rowhouses set into the hill stuck out against the sky. I saw a drifting spot of light—a firefly, I thought, though it didn't make sense in September—then realized it was somebody sitting on their porch in the dark. I wondered what their life was like, if they could see us passing.

We walked on past where the rocks bulged out from the retaining wall. The warm smell of somebody's garden, a quick hit of rot. The firefly glowed and fell.

"I'm goin' to take the back way," Frank said.

"See you at practice," I said.

I was coming up Oak when I saw someone on the other side of the street just ahead of me. He was walking along the stone wall that climbed up the embankment but it was dark so I waited until he passed in front of a light from a window before I called his name.

He didn't ask who it was, just turned, dropped the cigarette, ground it slowly under his shoe.

"S'up?" I said.

He didn't answer.

"Thought you were gone," I said.

"Back."

"Came by the house."

"Yeah?"

"Sure."

"Have a good talk with my old man?"

"What?"

"Forget it."

"Wait a minute, I don't—"

"Forget it."

"I don't—"

"Just fuckin' drop it, alright?"

"Fine."

For a second I thought he was going to walk away but he just stood there and lit another cigarette.

"So how's Jesus?" he said.

"How'd you know I—?"

"Your mom told me. Wanted to see if you wanted to hang out."

"I don't know—you know Frank. Usual shit."

I couldn't see it but I could hear it—a smile like a sigh. "Yeah." He sounded tired suddenly, like a soldier sinking down into a foxhole. "I guess some people's usual shit is just nastier than other people's."

I didn't say anything.

"Sorry about—you know," he said. "I didn't mean—"

"It's OK," I said.

"It's been kind of fucked up lately."

"OK."

He nodded. "Listen, there's some stuff goin' on at the house— any chance I could crash at your place?"

I DON'T KNOW how late we stayed up that night. Late. It wouldn't be the last time.

Nobody came downstairs. I figured they were asleep. Everything was quiet. Anyway, my parents never minded—they bought all his bullshit stories about having to fumigate the house and the aunt who didn't have room and after a while he stopped bothering. It's like they needed the noise, the distraction, the extra set of feet creaking the floorboards. Maybe we all did. He'd go downstairs sometimes and stand out on the front porch to have a cigarette, even when it was cold, and sometimes my father would walk out and hand him a jacket. Mom would be upstairs somewhere.

He slept on a mattress on my floor. We'd sit up late, listening to records, then turn off the light and go right on talking— about school, about girls, about life. I'd hear his voice coming out of the dark and I'd drift off and come back and he'd pause and I'd say, "Yeah, that's fucked up," because that covered pretty much everything.

It's like he was hungry for it—to sit in a room just playing records, talking—like he'd never done it before. Sometimes we'd get silly—even for me—and I'd have to remind myself that this was Ray Cappicciano sitting against the wall leafing through a magazine with my stuffed gorilla behind him for a backrest, its paws draped over his shoulders, its huge dark feet propped up on either side of his hips. I don't think I thought less of him for it. I understood it was important, that some part of him needed it. I even felt proud of having him there, a little tamed, not quite so dangerous now, like an actual leopard curled at the foot of the bed.

The first time we walked up the stairs he pointed to Aaron's room and mouthed the question and I nodded and said, "Yeah," and he said, "*That* can't be easy," and I said, "Yeah."

It's been years. I still hear his voice, talking to me out of the dark. It was as close to having a brother as I'll ever get.

THAT WAS THE FALL that Karen came and changed everything.

It's hard to explain about her. It's like trying to describe the smell of fresh-cut grass on those evenings in June when everything stands out from everything else, when the shadows moving up the trees are as sharp as the leaves that made them. You can compare it to something else, you can break it down into parts and hope they add up, but really it's about how it makes you feel.

That's the way it was with her. She was beautiful, sure, but it wasn't that alone—other girls had the hair, the face, the parts. It wasn't just the way she moved, kind of loose and laughing and natural, her arm trailing her body when she turned, or the way she'd suddenly duck and twirl away like a little girl for no reason at all. It wasn't even how smart she was, though she understood things, put them together the right way, better than anyone I ever knew. It wasn't any of these things—or maybe all of them plus something that made them different, that made them her.

It was the life in her. The courage you felt in her. It was the way she'd look at you—straight, compassionate, listening—actually *seeing* you. It's hard to explain. When she looked at you, you liked yourself better. You stood up straighter. Whatever act you had, disappeared. It's ridiculous, I know, she was a sixteen-year-old kid from Hartford, but it was like a current. An honesty current. You could feel it. And you'd know—as if somebody had cracked open your chest and shined a light in on your heart and said, calmly, matter-of-factly: "Look, see what you've got here? And here?"—that you had something to give, strength you hadn't known you had, and that if she ever took your side there wouldn't be anything in this world you couldn't put down.

It should have been so easy to ridicule: another High School Romance, the delinquent and the debutante, darkness and light, the hair-trigger brawler bleeding in the mud and the girl who sees the heart in him. It wasn't. It's not just that she was tougher than any of us, or that Ray didn't always fit his part; the truth is, he'd fit it well enough before her, and for all I know it was only knowing him that made her who she was.

No, it was the two of them together. To see it was to feel it. To be forced to acknowledge it, like light, or hunger. So what if they looked the part, black hair and blond, olive skin and pale, if they seemed to have been shaped to complete each other: his body, like hers, slim, loose, but charged, pent, meant to hurt, not heal—it didn't matter. The more evidence you piled up, the less it seemed to weigh. To see them holding each other, her body worked into his, her head tucked against his chest, her hair like a sheet of light cut by the sleeve of his coat, was to understand that some things simply were what they were—intended, inevitable—that they might end someday like everything else but that while they were here we couldn't deny them.

I SAW HER FIRST, fell in love with her first. There was always something there. She came into English class looking like the hippie cheerleader she should have been—the jeans, the face, the long blond hair tucked behind her ears—and promptly got into an argument over a poem we were reading. It was the second week of

October. I don't remember who the poem was by. It was about loss, she said.

Leventis had been pulling teeth, like always—I was pretty much the only one who ever spoke. When her hand went up right after I'd said something you could see the surprise on his face. "Yes . . . ?"

"Why can't it be about death in *this* life, like he said?" she said. "I mean, isn't forgetting a kind of death?"

Leventis was amused. "Well, you're certainly hitting the ground running on your first day. Perhaps after you've had a chance to—"

"I've read it."

And they were off. Some of the students rolled their eyes, others slumped down in their chairs. She didn't seem to care or notice.

Certainly, yes, forgetting could be a metaphor for death, Leventis tried to argue, but surely the third line of the second stanza suggested physical death. The poet was looking back from the afterlife, having gained a certain perspective on . . .

Why did it have to be one or the other? Memory . . . She didn't give an inch. Leventis sat down on the edge of his desk, pulled out all his guns, more charmed than annoyed. Ten minutes later they called it a draw.

I was walking down the hall when she came up next to me. "So you ever read Neruda?"

"What?"

She smiled. "I'm sorry, I didn't mean to jump you like that. It's Jon, right?"

"Yeah, no, it's fine," I said.

"It's just that you seemed to like poetry."

"It's OK," I said.

"It's OK?"

"No, it's, you know—I like it."

She laughed, dropped her voice like Dick Butkus. "Poetry? Well I don't know, Bob—I like football. I mean, I've read some poetry, mostly by accident—"

"I don't like football," I said.

"Say it: I like poetry."

"I don't—"

"I won't tell a soul, I swear."

"It's not—"

"C'mon. You can give somebody a bloody nose right after."

"I like poetry."

"See? Was that so bad?"

"Pretty bad," I said.

"How about, 'I'm a guy and I like poetry?' What do you think— too much?"

"I think so, yeah."

"That's OK, keep breathing—deep in, deep out. We'll try again tomorrow. Build up more slowly."

"Can't wait," I said.

And she was gone.

We talked again the next day, and the day after that. How could I have *not* misunderstood? In my world there was no room for a girl to just say what she said and have it mean no more than that. To walk up to a guy, to laugh, to be herself, and have it be that alone.

No, I fell for her for all the right reasons. There was nothing to get past with her. She was exactly who she was—not uncomplicated, just herself—and it made you feel like you could be, too. That you had permission. In two days I felt like I could talk to her about anything. She didn't run hot and cold, smile at me one day, ignore me the next.

All the right reasons. All but one.

RAY WAS GONE those first three days, so it had time to set. When he came back he came back hurt, a big bandage on his right temple, another on his neck. A basement club in the Bronx, he said. Ten-dollar pay-in. He'd picked up a quick fifty.

He seemed worn down, sleepy—quieter than usual. He'd been out to see Gene, he said. The little guy was doin' good—pretty much out of diapers, babbling up a storm. He was OK with him being there. For now, anyway.

He looked at his tray. "I can't fuckin' eat this. You want some of this?"

I shook my head. I was thinking about how she'd looked at me when I'd walked into class that morning. Frank reached over and took the milk.

"Get this—I'm Way now," Ray said. He felt the bandage with his fingers. "That's what he calls me."

"Like Elmer Fudd," Frank said.

"Every time he sees me it's 'Hi, Way' this an' 'Hi, Way' that."

"Wascally wabbit," Frank said. "Go womp and fwowick in the fowest."

Ray lay his head on his arms. "Figure if I get dead I'll be like 'No Way.'"

"No Fuckin' Way," Frank said.

"Or Sub Way," I said.

For a second he was gone somewhere. "Or maybe Free Way, who knows?"

I laughed. "Could be. Maybe you could—"

I saw him raise his head, then slowly push his hair off the bandage with his right hand. The look on his face was like a surprised wince.

I knew before I turned around.

WE NEVER KNEW how they actually met, only that it was impossible that they wouldn't. Or what they'd have to talk about. Everything, it turned out.

It says a lot about her that even after I realized I was wrong I didn't feel stupid. She'd made her choice—no explanations, no apologies. She continued to talk with me, with Frank, with everyone else exactly the way she had before and expected the same. The few girls who couldn't handle it she just ignored.

She asked me if I had time to talk with her the day after they met. That guy, the dark-haired one—his name was Ray, right? What was he like? We were walking next to each other down the hallway to the gym. I remember thinking how I could never feel self-conscious walking next to her.

I told her the truth. Ray? He was my friend. A good guy. Angry, maybe.

He had that look, she said. She'd heard he was a fighter, a bully. He scared her a little.

"Listen," I said, "I don't know what the opposite of a bully is, but whatever it is—Ray's that."

She looked at me. "You like him."

I shrugged.

"OK," she said.

✦ ✦ ✦

WHAT I DIDN'T TELL HER, because I didn't want to risk the respect she might have for me—because I wanted to take *something* away from this—was that Ray had already talked to me about her. I'd known it was over for me. I had nothing to lose by telling her what I did. By being a friend.

He'd found me up by the track. It was one of those October days—still, waiting, sharp with the cidery smell of things dying. I watched him walk up from the school, that easy, fighter's stride—unmistakable. I had a pretty good idea what he wanted to talk to me about.

I'd never seen him nervous before.

They'd talked a little in the hall, he said—just a smile, a few words. He didn't know what to do. She was smart—what would she ever want with him?

You're not dumb, I said.

"I have to talk to her," he said. "You get that, right?"

"Yeah," I said.

He looked up the track like there was something there, the wind blowing his hair around, the small white scar through his upper lip showing in the sunlight. I didn't say anything. I already knew what I was going to do—in a strange kind of way, it gave me the upper hand.

"Listen, it's just that, you know, she's in your class . . . I mean, you're my friend and all." He looked at me. "You OK with this?"

"Yeah," I said.

"Sure?"

"Why not?" I said.

"I keep thinkin' about her." He shook his head. "Listen to me, I sound like a fuckin' idiot."

"Nothin' new."

He blinked but let it go. "It's just—it's like I can hear her voice even when she's not around."

"Yeah," I said.

"I have to try."

"So, OK."

"OK," he said. "Listen . . . thanks." He looked up. "What's goin' on, you have a meet?" The Carmel High school bus had pulled into the upper parking lot.

I nodded.

"Shit, I didn't realize."

The rest of the team had begun to straggle out, dressed in their good sweats and hoods.

"Maybe I'll hang around, watch you kick some Carmel bootie."

I nodded.

He looked at me. "You OK?"

"Sure," I said. Falvo was walking toward us with his pointy shoes and his cowlick, carrying his little arm across his chest as if in an invisible sling—enthusiastic as death. "Mr. Jefferson"—it was the same old schtick—"are we ready to remind these people they're just a vowel away from toffee-colored candies that stick in your teeth? That's a rhetorical question. Mr. Cappicciano, we seem to be seeing a lot of you lately. Thinking of joining up?"

Ray didn't smile. "Why would I wanna do that?"

"Inspirational pep talks, moral fiber, regular bowel movements— the benefits are legion."

Ray scratched his ear, bored, waiting it out.

"Might be an improvement on your current activities. I was going to say extracurricular, but it seemed redundant."

Ray looked away, and I understood why people were scared of him.

Falvo was looking right at him. "No? Not interested? You could fight with your feet for a change."

"I'll pass."

Falvo took the stopwatch out of his pocket, looked at it like he was checking the time. "Well, you know what Dorothy Parker said about horses and water." He put the watch away, paused. "Let me tell you something, son—nobody fights for the reason they think."

"I'm not your son."

"Imagine my disappointment. Still, it's true, you know."

"What?"

"About it always being about something else. People, nations— interesting, wouldn't you say?"

"You done?"

Falvo looked at him a second, then made a lazy sign of the cross in the air. "*In nomine Patris, et filii, amen.*"

He turned to me. "As for you, my friend, you should beware of what you wish for." He indicated Kennedy, loosening up alone on the backstretch. "You see that young man with the unnecessarily long hair and the red headband? He seems to think you belong in the first group, starting Monday. I'm inclined to agree with him."

He paused. "Trust me, it's not a favor."

I RAN THE RACE that day—too long, too dreary, the hills killing my rhythm, the mud sucking my strength—hearing her voice, see-ing her face, the piper of pain screaming in my ears, and I took his price and doubled it, then doubled it again and paid in full—in rage not at him, or her, or fate, but the muscles and tendons of those ahead of me—because it was easier. I had my weapon. I'd suffer my way to grace. I took Moore in the final two hundred, seeing Ray, the bandage white against his face, leaning in a blur of tears or sweat against the bleachers. I was coming up on McCann's back when I ran out of rope. If I had nothing else, I had this. I had this.

The following Monday I joined the first group, more nervous

than I'd ever been before an actual race. A quick pat on the back
from Kennedy, a nod from McCann, and we were lining up in front
of Falvo standing on the bottom step of the bleachers in his rain-
coat saying, "Gentlemen, I'd like three dollars in quarters, please.
I'd like them smooth, I'd like them shiny, and I'd like you to drop
each one in my hand as you come through. On your marks?"

I'd been running quarters in 68 seconds with a walk to recover
and working hard. They went through the first in 64, moving to the
outside to drop an invisible quarter in Falvo's palm like everyone
else, then slowed to a jog and went again. By the third I couldn't
talk, couldn't keep my hand steady at the finish to drop the coin.
"Sixty-three, five," I heard Falvo say behind us, and then: "Mr. Kennedy, a dollar's worth from Mr. Jefferson will do fine today."

Kennedy dropped back alongside me. "How we doin'?" he said.

I didn't say anything.

"I know you don't like it, but coach knows what he's doin'."

I nodded.

"Andy, I'm gonna take this next one," he said to McCann.

He turned back to me. "Don't worry—I'm gonna let you spend
a little somethin' before you're done."

I nodded. It was all I could do. We were almost at the half and
I still hadn't pulled a full breath.

"Just follow me. We're gonna go smooth through the two twenty,
then kick it up a notch—not a sprint, just a gear change."

I nodded.

I'd watched it before—the easiness, the deceptive gliding flow of
it, but I'd never understood it until I was behind him on the curve,
tucked inside the slipstream of his body, stride matching stride. I'd
never seen anyone move with such terrible economy, such balance,
the arms, held high, powering that long reach like thought. I could
hear him talking to me as we flew: "How we doin'—we doin' OK?
Remember: Keep it sweet, don't press. When we hit the mark, just

slip it into third—no change, nothin' different, we're just movin' away from where we were. Ready?" And we were off, not so much sprinting as extending, unfolding, the rhythm shifting, tightening, and he was still talking to me as we came out of the curve into the straight, saying "Good, good, smooth, that's it, don't press, just keep it down—good," and it wasn't until I heard Falvo's voice saying "fifty-eight, five, gentlemen, that's a dollar's worth" that I remembered seeing him swerve to the outside and neatly drop an invisible coin in Falvo's outstretched hand.

It carried me that fall, that winter. I could feel my body changing, altering, my stride extending. I could feel the muscles in my thighs slipping and clenching like ropes when I jogged up the stairs. I didn't think about how much it meant—or how little. I had this. If I had nothing else, I had this.

I EXPECTED TO SEE less of them now and I did. Or maybe I was just busy. Anyway it was only natural. I remember seeing them one afternoon on the far end of the football field by the woods—his coat, her hair, a steady rain turning to sleet—just standing there holding each other the way you see people at the airport, like they'd been told one of them had to leave.

There was nothing you could say to that. It was one of the most beautiful things I'd ever seen. It reminded me of a cartoon I'd seen once—it might have been in *MAD Magazine*, I don't know—of a guy who's just been punched in the chest—the fist is just stuck inside him, his skin has closed around it—and he's saying, "You didn't punch me in the chest—I trapped your fist with my heart."

THEY WERE THERE, of course—the beauties and the thugs, the royalty and their serfs, acting out their parts those seven hundred days or so—but even though I can remember their faces, their names, it's like they never existed, really, like even though they filled those years, flexing and posing, cringing, kicked, they were just holding up their end until they could drop the sneer, wink at the company and walk out the door. Become who they were—who they'd been all along. Only the desperate ones, who were playing for keeps, seem real to me now.

I used to watch him sometimes, to see how he did it. How he managed it. I wanted to be like him, move like him. I wanted that James Dean cool. For a while I thought it was in the clothes, the hair, the timing: the cigarette tossed at exactly the right moment, the look, the nod. He had a gift for cutting away early. From everything. It took a while for me to understand it was who he was, what he did—cut it short, toss the butt, walk away—because nothing had lasted, nobody had stayed. Didn't matter how strong it felt, the ledge would always crumble. So walk away. Just shrug and walk away.

And he did. Until Gene was born. Gene changed things—forced him to stay. As did Karen. As did I, for a while.

We were like three people pulling on a rope, dragging him back to who he'd been before he became who he was. Back to who he wanted to be.

THE WINTER AFTER he met Karen was a good one for Ray, though he had to do more around the house because Mr. Cappicciano broke his arm and his jaw when he missed a step near the top of the staircase. Little Gene was still in Yonkers. Ray would hitch out twice a week to see him. He seemed more confident, less tired that winter. He stayed in school. He'd backed off the fighting, he said.

Others hadn't. Since the beginning of the school year, two buses of kids from Yonkers, all black, had started coming to Brewster. Nobody knew what they did with them during the day—they seemed to have separate classes. We'd see them in the cafeteria, clustered around one table listening to a transistor, nodding to the music, silver Afro picks stuck in their hair. Ignoring us. Nobody knew how to talk to them—not even the two black kids we had at Brewster. It's like they were in an invisible room that went wherever they did. We could tap on the walls, yell shit at each other, make threatening gestures—but nobody could break through.

That afternoon a few of us were stretching in the gym with the throwers after practice when the big metal door to the outside opened with a crash and a gust of wet air, and one of the bused kids walked in. It had been pouring all afternoon—the windows were dark with it. He was wearing what looked like a half-dozen sweatshirts, just one on top of the other, hood on hood, as if he thought that by piling them on he could keep from getting soaked. No more than five-six, five-seven, he looked like something drowned.

"Hey, asshole, you want to shut the door?"

It hadn't been meant one way or the other—Trachosis hadn't even looked over his shoulder. Even then it could have passed—Harry was just being Harry—except that someone whispered that it was one of the new kids, which made it sound like Harry should have kept his mouth shut, which changed things.

"So the fuck what?"

"So nothin'."

"What, they're so fuckin' sensitive you can't even tell them to shut the door?"

"No, I—"

"Hey?" Harry yelled across the gym. "Are you very sensitive? Did I hurt your feelings?"

The kid didn't answer. He'd yanked the door shut. We watched him walk to the water fountain, his sneakers slap-squelshing on the wooden floor.

"Forget it, Harry," somebody said.

"What, fuck you, I'm not allowed to ask a question? Hey, you," he yelled, laying down the sixteen-pound shot he liked to mess with and getting to his feet, "they talk where you people come from?"

The quiet probably made it worse; normally everybody would have been bullshitting, laughing. As it was, nobody said a thing. We could hear the rain against the metal doors.

The kid had bent down to the water fountain. He was still wearing his sweatshirts, his face almost invisible inside the hoods. At that point he still could have pulled the plug on it. A simple "sorry" when he first closed the door, a wave, a joke—anything would have done it. But he didn't. Either he was deaf or he just didn't feel like it that day. It was something new to us.

"Hey, *paisano, habla inglés?*"

The kid didn't move, which was strange. Harry was a very big guy, 225, no fat—hard to miss. I'd seen him lift Chris McClement by the ankles with one hand, take the lid off a garbage can and drop him in.

"Hello. Anybody inside all that shit?"

It wasn't until he was right there, maybe three feet away, that the kid turned and unloaded a mouthful of water in Harry's face, then slowly moved a few steps back and waited.

Everything stopped, like in freeze tag when somebody touches you and you can't move. I can still see the room at that moment: the lights with the protective wire cages over them, the dark windows, the wooden floor with the kid's footprints going across it, the group of us in dumb stretching positions on the mats. It was a big mouthful.

I think if there had been another way, Harry would have taken it. Even if it had been just the two of them, he might have turned and walked away. He didn't want this now. He wasn't a bad guy. He had no choice. I saw his face when he turned to wipe the water off with his hand. He looked confused, panicked; he hadn't known there'd be a test. Then he flicked the water and charged.

It was only afterward, playing it over and over in our heads, that we were able to break it down into parts, understand what we saw. At the time it was just one movement, an explosion—the bullet going through the egg. A slight pivot and the left flicked out to the face, once, twice, snapping Harry's head back, a hard right to the gut bent him forward, a knee to the face flipped him back. From the side he seemed to be bowing at terrible speed. We'd never seen anything like it.

In the quiet you could hear the kid's sneakers squelching across the floor, then the clank of the door handles.

IT STARTED PROBLEMS. Nobody wanted to touch it, but that didn't stop the talk from running. Hear what happened to Harry? Some nigger—the word would always come out with a little pause on the *n* like they were running up to it—some nigger broke his nose. Sucker-punched him.

We'd fuck 'em up. It was always "we," always "them." Somebody's mother had called the office. Somebody had called the cops. It didn't matter that Harry didn't want to talk about it, that he showed up at practice a couple of days later with a hill of tape over his nose, threw the shot and left, that the rest of us avoided it like we'd seen something unnatural, embarrassing—the rumor mill had started grinding. They were this, they were that. They'd been in juvenile detention homes, committed crimes. Some kid had been pulled off the bus with a gun.

Nothing big happened. A few near–fist fights—"That's right mutha-fucka, you just keep starin' . . . Anywhere, anytime, asshole, hear what I'm sayin?"—and the thing settled into a low boil. The lid rattled but stayed on the pot.

Ray moved through it all like the invisible man. A heaping cafeteria tray would float down the line, carried by a coat. He could give a shit. So Harry got a nose job from some kid who knew how to handle himself—so what?

It wasn't just that, Frank would say, bringing him up to speed. One of 'em had a gun.

"Show me how to do this," Ray would say, pushing his algebra book over to me.

"Seriously," Frank would say.

"See, I don't fuckin' get that," he'd say, watching me cancel factors.

"Seriously."

"Who says?"

"Who says what?"

"Who says he had a gun?"

"Everybody. The cops took it off him."

"You can just do that?" he'd say to me.

"Sure."

"Seriously," Frank would say. "There's gonna be a war."

And Ray would look up like he was hearing him for the first time and just look at him a while.

"You're an idiot," he'd say. "Seriously. Now can you shut the fuck up so I can learn this shit?" And he'd turn to me: "Do it again, slow."

Fine, Frank would say, but people were sayin' that Champbell was gonna bring in his old man's gun.

And Ray wouldn't even look up. Maybe they could just cancel each other out, like in math.

HE'D TALK TO ME about Karen: what she'd said, how she'd looked—it never occurred to him. I was his friend. It was a whole new thing, he'd say. And he'd have this look on his face that would have been ridiculous on anybody else—like he was looking at himself in a mirror, changed, and liked what he saw, and didn't quite believe it.

We didn't either. It felt like a betrayal of some kind, like he was turning his back on us, on who he was. It was like in *Cool Hand Luke*, when Paul Newman, his mind finally right, starts sucking up to the bosses—we kept expecting him to grab the shotgun and jump in the truck.

Maybe he'd changed, Ray said. Where did it say he had to fight every moron in Putnam County? Let somebody else take out the garbage for a while. He'd gone to talk to O'Reilly, who'd said he could come back and shoot a little pool. It felt good being back.

We didn't buy it, we said, and told each other stories to prove it. Ray was Ray, Frank said, leaning toward us over the cafeteria table. He'd been in the locker room when Champbell and Copeland and Jonas had started up their usual shit. Who knew what they were thinking—maybe they'd heard he'd gone soft.

I smiled in anticipation.

"Anyway, I'm there, McCann, a couple of others," Frank said. "We figure maybe ten seconds before the deodorant and the bottles and shit start flying, but nothing happens. I mean, Champbell's just slingin' it—really personal shit—and Ray's just standin' there like in *Billy Jack* when they pour the flour on the kids' heads, just *dum, da-dum, da-dum*, tie your shoes, tuck in your shirt. Champbell doesn't know what to do. Calls him a faggot, punches a locker, say's he's gonna fuck him up and Ray picks up his shit and just walks right up to him. Doesn't say a thing. He's right in his face, his coat over his shoulder—wide open. 'Go ahead, fuck me up,' he says. He turns his head for him. 'C'mon, right here.'"

"Jesus."

"Just humiliating. Champbell doesn't know what to do, so he goes like, 'Why don't you put your books down, you pussy,' so Ray lays his stuff down on the bench and puts his hands in his pockets and says, 'OK? So go ahead—hit me. C'mon, what're you waitin' for?' and when Champbell still doesn't do anything he nods, picks up his shit and leaves."

Frank grinned. "Am I right? I mean, you know Champbell. That's gotta be crazier than anything I've seen our boy do."

We agreed with each other, reassured. No, you could sing along with the Mamas and the Papas all you liked—the world would bring you in line soon enough. It was all around you. Forget "be who you want to be"—you'd be who you were.

BREWSTER HILL ROAD. It might have been December because the leaves had been down a while and you could see things in the woods that you'd forgotten were there: a rusted junker that had been there longer than the small trees that had grown up around it, an old house you'd swear you'd never seen before. It was after practice. We were trudging home. Ray was going on about Karen. He'd been takin' it slow, he said, trying not to fuck it up. They'd gone for a walk down the tracks all the way to Jimmy's and back. She'd walked across the trestle with him.

Somebody had taken the front wheels off—it was resting on its engine like something brought to its knees.

"You know how freaky it is," he was saying, "especially in winter when you can't really move that fast. I mean, you're listenin' all the time."

"Sure," I said. A car went by.

She didn't even think about it, he said, didn't hesitate—just asked him if he thought it was OK, then walked right out. They couldn't talk, he said, so they could hear. What would they do if a train came? she asked. It can't come, he said. Halfway across she took his hand.

He didn't know why he decided to push it—maybe it was because she trusted him. It was on the way back. Did she want to try something? It was almost dusk now—the trestle was just ahead. It was safe, he said, as long as she did what he said—scary but safe. He hadn't thought she'd say yes.

I could have told him different.

Holding on to the railing, they'd sidestepped out on the tie ends that stuck out over the gorge and the river. Ray went first, kicking the snow, watching it curtain off into the air. It was slow going—forty feet out, clearing the wood with his right boot, he started hitting ice. Maybe they should head back, he said. She smiled and shook her head. They were almost halfway across when he heard the whistle.

The fear wasn't something you could hide. She had to listen to him, he said. They'd be OK. Was she listening? She nodded.

Just tell me what to do, she said.

They had time, a minute, maybe a little more. They weren't on the tracks, no part of the train could touch them, but it would be close—very close. How close? she said. A foot, not even. It wouldn't be going that fast, thirty, thirty-five, but it would feel fast. Very fast.

They could feel it in the timbers now, in the steel under their hands—that deep thrum as if the earth were vibrating.

She'd feel a jolt, he said—like getting hit hard by a pillow.

She nodded, tried to smile.

"You OK? I've got you—warm up your hands."

"I'm OK."

"We'll be all right—all we gotta do is hang on."

"I'm OK."

They could hear the huff of the engines, approaching through the woods.

The noise would be bad, he said. They'd probably blow the whistle coming up to the trestle. She had to be ready. And the snow coming off the ties. They'd be standing in a blizzard for a few seconds. She had to turn away from it, close her eyes.

It was loud now—very loud. They could see the light cutting quickly through the trees.

"OK?" he yelled.

She nodded, then pressed herself to the railing. She'd turned her head away, was looking at him.

It was only then he saw it was a freight, and in the shock of that first blasting scream of the whistle, the steel vibrating under his hands, he swung around and across her, pinning her to the rail, his arms around her body, his head pushed against her hair and then they were lost, buried in a blizzard of screeching steel that went on without breath or pause for a minute, then two, then three because it was a freight, a mile-long wall, and when his hands began to go he pushed them through the rail and locked them like a belt on the other side and then it was gone and they didn't move—just stayed there until he could feel her breathing underneath him.

They didn't say much making their way across to the other side—it was almost dark now but you could see because of the snow—and when they stepped off the trestle they brushed the snow off themselves. He asked her if she was OK. She nodded.

"Listen," he said, "I'm—"

And she stepped up and kissed him. "I'm not," she said.

A CAR CAME BY, flaring Ray's coat like someone dragging him by the lapels.

"I mean, I've almost just got her killed, it's dark, I'm going to have to walk her home 'cause we've missed the last bus . . . *You* know how far it is to Putnam Lake—I didn't get her home till eight."

"A.M. or P.M.?"

He didn't hear me. "I can't stop thinking about her."

I could see the patches of snow in the woods, thicker on the hillside. I wasn't used to winter yet.

"I mean, it's crazy." He shook his head. "It's just bein' with her, listenin' to her talk—" A gust whipped the snow over the road like hair. "I don't know, it's like you put your arm around her and you just feel, I don't know . . ."

"What?"

"Forget it—I'm just talkin' outta my ass now."

"What?"

He laughed, yelled it into the woods: "Fuck, I don't know! Jesus, listen to me. I'm tellin' you, man, she could just walk out of those woods right now an'—"

He'd stopped, was walking into the road.

"What're you doin?"

He lay down across the dotted line, his arms out like Jesus.

"—tell me to lie down in the middle of the road—"

"What the hell you doin?"

"—and I'd say fine, let 'em run over my sorry ass."

"C'mon, Ray, quit fuckin' around."

"Just run me over."

"Fine."

He was smacking the snow off his coat when he caught up to me. "What?"

"Nothin'. Just gotta get home, that's all."

He nodded. We walked quietly for a few seconds.

"You met her folks yet?" I said.

He shook his head.

"Why not?"

"I don't know. Not like I'm—"

He stopped.

"What?"

"I don't know, you know—not like I'm you."

"Don't be a jerk."

"I'm serious—you know what I'm sayin'. Anyway, I will—just not yet."

"She met your dad?"

He looked at me like he didn't understand. "Why would I do that?"

"I don't know, you know—he's your dad."

He nodded. "Yeah," he said quietly, and then: "No. She hasn't."

"Guess that makes sense," I said, because I didn't know what else to say.

"Really? Why?"

"I don't know, if it was my dad—"

"It's not."

"No, I know that. I was just thinkin', you know, if it was me—"

"It's not you."

"OK, fine."

"Hang on, wait." He stopped. "You think it's because I'm fuckin' ashamed of him?"

"No, I . . . what're you doin'? I just meant—"

There was a look on his face, almost like a smile. "That what you think? That I'm ashamed of him?"

"No, I just meant—"

"—because he puts away a fifth of Jack Daniels and throws up all over himself an' shit—that what you think?"

"I don't know, fuck. What do you want me to say? I just thought—"

"What?"

"I don't know, you know—I'm ashamed of *my* old man, sometimes."

He looked at me for a second. "Really? I didn't know that."

"Sometimes, you know . . ."

We walked around a woman's high-heel shoe standing up in the road like it was waiting for a foot.

"Why?"

"Fuck, I don't know."

"Seriously."

"I don't know. Colonel Klink—you know. Hardly knows I exist."

"Lucky you."

"Look, all I was sayin' is you don't have to be ashamed of him," I said.

"Thanks," he said.

"I mean, he's done some good stuff, too, right? Like during the war? Or when he was a cop?"

"Sure."

"I mean, that's somethin'."

"No. You're right." We'd started walking again. The wind moved the tail on a squirrel somebody had run over in the road.

"There's one should have looked both ways," he said.

We passed the beautiful white house with the green shutters. Set back from the road, cozy and clean, it always looked like the kind of house you'd have to be happy in.

"I ever show you that stuff?" he said.

"What stuff?"

"The stuff he brought back from the war."

"Don't think so."

"Wanna see it? C'mon, you'll get a kick out of it."

He could see me hesitate. "Don't worry about it, he's back at work, doin' his bit for society. Bein' the man."

IT ALWAYS LOOKED WORSE in winter: the rim of snow along the crease of the wall where the sun couldn't reach, the broken chair, the nails coming through the roof. When we walked in Wilma was bobbing up and down behind the loveseat which somebody had dragged in front of the kitchen door. Ray picked up the lamp by the couch, then went over and knocked her gently on the nose between her eyes with his knuckles. It made a hollow sound that used to make us laugh.

"Home sweet home. You want a beer?"

"Sure."

It was the usual mess, only colder, damper. The lamp was out. Bits of some kind of shiny paper covered the sofa, the carpet, the table.

He stepped up on the loveseat and over the back into the kitchen. "Father had company last night. I just put her in here so she wouldn't fuck up her paws."

"What *is* this stuff?"

"Glass—what's it look like?" He turned on the radio.

I looked closer. A tiny bolt of lightning curled to a point. The couch glistened, dusted with fangs and needles. On the table, next to a shard on its back like a cartoon egg was a glass half-filled with beer. Somebody had dropped the screw-in parts of three lightbulbs into it.

Ray stepped back over the loveseat, carrying a couple of beers in his right hand. "Maybe I'll leave it—let him clean it up."

"What the fuck were they doin'?"

"Batting practice."

"With light bulbs?"

"Cheaper than glasses."

He leaned over and picked up a plastic stick with a fist-sized horse's head on the end of it. The head had long orange strands coming out of its skull the color you sometimes see on old men who dye their hair.

From the kitchen I could hear Harry Harrison saying something about *The Ed Sullivan Show* and the Doors.

"Yeah, it was a real happenin'." He swung the horse stick like Mantle lining one to third. "Around two in the morning my old man's just talkin' shit an' swingin' Trigger here when I hear Tommy yell 'Hey, batta batta' and then a pop and everybody goes nuts and my old man yells, 'Yeah, bring it—I'll put your lights *out*, baby.'

After that it's basically just pitch, swing and duck." He took a sip of his beer, wiped his mouth on his sleeve. "Took 'em a while to run out 'cause they're so fuckin' drunk they keep missin'."

"So where were you?"

He shook the horse's head at me. "Well, Wilbur, I didn't care for it," he said in the voice of Mister Ed. I looked at the horse. Up close, its yellow marble eyes looked oddly terrified.

He tossed it on the couch, handed me his beer. "No big deal. Do me a favor—sweep that shit off the couch. I'll be right back."

I started cleaning the glass off the armrests and the table with the horse. WABC was on. Harry Harrison was saying something about the Knicks in that great, gravelly voice that made him sound like the uncle you never had, the one who'd always understand, who could talk you through anything.

Ray came back carrying a wooden crate filled with something wrapped in garbage bags. The Beatles' "All You Need Is Love" had just finished. He'd never understood that song, Harry was saying—what gloves? He needed galoshes, too. And a hat.

"He worries about this shit so he keeps it in plastic," Ray said.

Some of it was in small tins, some wrapped in newspapers going back to 1949 and taped up with masking tape. We unwrapped it piece by piece like it was Christmas: torn-off uniform patches with side-by-side S's like bolts of lightning, a set of silver dinner forks with "Waffen SS" engraved on the handles, a blue-velvet sack with four gold rings that spilled heavy and cool into my palm. One ring had a jawless skull with tiny red jewels for eyes.

"Cool, right?" Ray said.

"Fuckin' amazing," I said, not knowing what I was feeling, exactly.

He popped the tape on a thick packet of newspaper and pulled out a small dagger in a silver-tipped scabbard. Like everything else it was intricately worked—the guard engraved, the blade slim and straight. It sat in my hand like it had been made for it. I slipped it back in the scabbard, then pulled it out.

"Where'd he get this stuff?"

"Fuck knows. Overseas."

Two oak leaves had been engraved into the blade. Next to them, like an artist's signature, was a tiny oval with a squirrel in it. I turned the blade over. Engraved in the steel were the words *Meine Ehre heist Treue*. My honor is loyalty.

Your father died for them at the Somme and they turned on us like dogs, my mother had said.

"Wonder who this belonged to," I said.

Ray was prying the lid off a tin of Prince Albert with his fingernails.

"Yeah? I wonder who *these* fuckin' belonged to." He spilled a hill of gray, dried-out cigars on the newspaper.

I was looking at the tin. On the front was a picture of a bald man with a beard, leaning on a cane. Underneath were the words "Crimp Cut. Long Burning Pipe and Cigarette Tobacco."

Then I saw the fingernails.

Ray chuckled. "Every man needs a hobby, right?" He picked one up and the hill slid down a little like in a game of pick-up sticks. "There's twenty-seven of them—used to be twenty-eight. Only fifteen of these, though."

He spilled out another tin.

They looked smaller than they should have, like dried apple slices, but you could see the ridges, the lobes, the curled-in edges where the cut skin had dried.

He held two up to his forehead. "He's all ears," he said.

The guy with the cane had a white rose in his lapel. His head looked strangely small for his body.

"Twenty-eight. How do you figure *that* worked?" He was scooping them up with two hands, dumping them back in their tins. "C'mon, you're good in math—divide by five."

Your father died for them at the Somme and they turned on us like dogs.

"Remainder of two, right? What'd ya think—got bored, maybe? Sounds like Dad. Still, anyway you cut it there's some two-fingered German out there havin' trouble holdin' his beer stein.

I picked up a strip of cloth. It was about as wide as a man's belt—a rich gray-black with white borders. Near the center was something I couldn't make out: a head-like shape, but disordered—something like a jaw, a hole like a single eye.

"Flip it." He pointed to the cloth. "Go ahead—turn it over."

It should have been nothing—you see a thousand every Halloween—but I started to shake. I could feel myself breathing shallow so I wouldn't be sick; my forehead was wet.

"Anyway, it's not like fifteen is any better," Ray was saying. "I mean, it's like that painter, right?"

This skull had been made by an adult, I kept thinking. An adult—a grown man or woman. Carefully, lovingly sewn to look like it was made of ropes: frayed, cut-off ropes for the eye sockets, the nose, each decaying tooth a thin double-strand of rope. It wasn't a joke—it was an expression of faith, an assertion of principle. *Like dogs. They turned on us like dogs.* A straight black cut ran down the middle of its forehead, another passed over its left eye, a third sliced the left cheek. It looked like it was in pain, like it had been killed with a cleaver and was proud of it. Like it was staring you down.

"Funny, my old man beat the shit out of me once when I was in second grade," Ray was saying. "Said I took one of his fingers—that he had counted 'em." He taped up the dagger, put it in the box. "Fuck, I'd rather give him the finger than take one."

There was something about the hole that used to be the left eye that affected me like a smell, that forced my face to the side like a hit of carrion. I couldn't look away. I kept trying but it was like being in a crowded room, knowing someone's looking at you. I could feel it, drawing me like a pit, a Niagara in the earth; I could hear the roar rising up from the dark. One morning I'd walk out across that field, the ropes like hardened gopher mounds under my feet, step carefully over that strange, straight canyon—and disappear.

Then I saw it, the detail that tipped it from nothing to nightmare. A single stitch, drawn too tight by the skull's maker, had accidentally made the left eye human—given the pit an expression, like a slight spasm of compassion, or regret. The right, unflawed, showed nothing.

Ray took the cloth from my hand, put it in the garbage bag, tied it off. "I mean, he was right—I took it. The finger."

"Why?" I said stupidly.

"I don't know—guess I just wanted to show somebody. Wilma, sit! Funny thing is, nobody believed it—they thought it was fake. Even after they'd touched it."

"Why didn't you just put it back?" I said, pulling myself up, following his voice.

"I don't know—got scared. I was showin' it to this bunch of kids during recess when the teacher started walkin' over so I threw it over the fence. She wanted to know what it was, so everybody started yelling that I'd thrown away my finger. She wanted to know what that meant. Didn't mean anything, they said.

Anyway, it turned into this big deal. She threatened 'em with all kinds of stuff, said she'd call their parents if they didn't tell the truth—some of 'em started to cry. Then she took 'em aside, one by one. After a while they figured out the truth wasn't gonna work so they started makin' shit up: it was a cigarette lighter, a pocketknife, I don't know what. A box of Raisinets—that was my favorite."

"Did it work?" I said.

"People only believe what they already believe."

"Weird story."

"You know what's really weird? Somewhere across from the

Shell station is a Nazi's finger with flowers and shit growing out of it in the spring."

I didn't say anything.

He chuckled. "I mean, you talk German. What do you think he would have said if you'd walked up to him in some beer hall and said, 'Guess what, you Nazi fuck. That finger you're pickin' your nose with is gonna end up in the weeds in fuckin' America a thousand miles from the rest of your ass and there's not a goddamn thing you can do about it—Heil Hitler."

He picked up the box.

"Whaddya think, time to put away Dad's good deeds—all those medals from the war?" he said.

It was a good time, that winter, spring, most of that summer—the best we'd have. The four of us down by the frozen reservoir making big gurgling holes in the ice with rocks, listening to that hollow *tock* and *chunk* echo off into the dark. In the spring the lights from the cars disappeared and then it was hot and we'd stay out late, swimming, and I'd see Ray with his arm around her sitting on the bank, his t-shirt tan like brown, shoulder-length gloves. We'd horse around, throw each other in, lie in the grass and talk about what we were going to do. Ray had met Karen's parents.

It's the music that brings it back, brings it alive. Dylan and Creedence, the Beatles and the Stones. It would take us back down where cool water flows, Karen smiling, the three of us nodding to the beat, doing our best John Fogerty imitations, Ray stalking the embankment in his cutoffs, leaning back to play that invisible lick, then whipping forward, wet hair falling in his face—*Let me remember things I don't know.* In July there would always be that one night when the air was warm as the water and the water like velvet and you'd swim out and dive and come up into the dark and a soft wave of fields and honeysuckle would wash over you and you'd say to yourself, because you could, because you were young, I could die right now and it wouldn't matter. It would be years before I learned that the actual words weren't *things I don't know*, but *things I love*, but by then the barefoot girl dancing in the moonlight had moved on, and the right words seemed wrong.

It's funny how we fit her into the things we used to do before, how the two of them being together didn't matter as much as it should have—how easy she made it. She'd kid around with us, give us a hard time for being guys, for being gross, for making fart jokes when our trunks filled up with air, but somehow make it clear that Ray was Ray—separate, hers—and that it shouldn't matter. And it wouldn't, really. Or less, anyway. She'd talk to Frank about his sister, who we'd heard had lost the baby, who it didn't look like was coming back, and he'd tell her things he couldn't say to us.

You'd see them sitting next to each other on the cement block by the dam, arguing about Jesus. She used to go to church but she couldn't do it anymore, she said. And Frank would tell her about Jesus' love and being forgiven for your sins and she'd say she wasn't sure what a sin was any more, and that love was fine but what did it say that in the whole Bible Jesus never laughed, or even smiled. And the two of them would sit there, their legs dangling over the side, actually listening to each other. She had that. She'd listen, and it would make you do the same.

It was the same with me and Leonard Cohen. I couldn't stand him—that beatnik-poet thing annoyed me—and we'd go back and forth about him and about *Candy* and ecology and acid and Vietnam and Joni Mitchell and everything else but whether we agreed or not—and nobody could hold her own like she could—it didn't matter. It was respect—I've never known it so uncluttered. Or call it generosity. You had your beliefs. She might think you were wrong—and say so—but you were you. Only when it came to cruelty did she draw the line—there she was immovable. It was wrong. It would always be wrong. Particularly when it was unnecessary, in which case it was unforgivable.

So of course I was in love with her, though if she knew, she didn't show it. And after a while I could live with that. For a few weeks I went out with a girl, Abby Fisher, who had beautiful dark bangs that shone like wood in old houses and big, serious eyes and who always seemed to be trying to hear something whenever I put my hand up her shirt. It seemed to bother her that she couldn't make it out, and sometimes it felt like it was just me and her breasts. She was nice enough. Karen said I should invite her out with us sometime, but we didn't last long—I kept expecting her to say "You hear that? What *is* that?"—and I never did.

Anyway, it was good the way it was: the heat, the summer, the smell of Off! and beer, the black-eyed Susans in the weeds along the dam and the four of us diving to get away from the horseflies that came down from the farms, gray and long as the joint of your thumb—I didn't want to change it, risk it. We were like that CSNY song, which didn't make sense but kind of did: " . . . *one person* . . . *two alone* . . . *three together* . . . *four* . . . "—and for a while we were—"*each other*." If confusion had its cost—if it *was* confusion— we didn't know that then.

There were other times, of course, times when they wanted to be alone, times when other things—parents, work—got in the way. Who knows how many afternoons and nights there really were, how many times we really sat on that embankment watching the moon lift clear of the trees, so perfect it seemed to be daring us to laugh. Maybe it's like with little kids, who you do something with twice and who remember it as a thousand. Take movies: I remember hitching down to Carmel with Frank a dozen times—the crickets and the heat on that open stretch along the lake, the dark of the theater until your eyes got used to it, the Good & Plenty I'd always get—but the only movie I can remember us seeing is *Easy Rider* the week Karen went with her family to the shore and Ray started living at our house again.

Who knows? Maybe *Easy Rider* was all there was, just Fonda and

Hopper tooling across America, looking for that shotgun. Maybe there'd only been one winter day with the four of us stumbling along the shore and Frank shot-putting small boulders through the ice, and just one day in April when the sun was suddenly warm enough to risk getting in that water still dark with winter, and just one night with our bonfire on the embankment and the moths and the moon and the radio playing that corny Dusty Springfield song we had an excuse to listen to because we couldn't pick up the alternative stations, Karen sitting there next to Ray with her arm around him, swaying back and forth, teasing, *"The only boy who could ever reach me . . ."* and I just multiplied them in my head to fill the seasons. If so, that's OK—they were worth it.

It makes sense that she didn't understand, that the more time she spent with him, or with us—the four of us out by the reservoir or up in my room, listening to records—the more she'd start wondering. What doesn't make sense is that *we* didn't. She'd ask me sometimes—more often as things went on—and I'd tell her what I could. About Gene, who was still living in Yonkers that summer, about Ray's parents. Of course he'd want her to meet his father, I'd say—it was just that his dad was kind of a rough guy. His mom? She'd split for Reno when Ray was nine—nothin' in the contract said a mother had to love her kid. Ditto with his stepmom, five years later. No, Gene was great—we used to take care of him together sophomore year.

She didn't get it, she said to me one time as we sat next to each other in the hall—how could a man just send off his three-year-old kid? It was complicated, I said. What was he like? she asked—Ray's dad. Complicated, I said.

Complicated good or complicated bad?

Not so good, I said, but everybody had something.

We were supposed to be preparing a report on Steinbeck's *The Red Pony*. People were turning in their textbooks, the windows were open—everything had that end-of-the-year feeling.

"Ray won't talk to me about him," she said.

"I don't blame him."

"That bad?"

"Look at it this way—when people yell 'Kill the pigs,' he's the one they're thinking about."

She didn't smile. "Why does he get into fights all the time?"

"Maybe it's easier," I said.

"You don't fight. Frank doesn't fight."

"Ray's got a temper," I said. "Anyway, he's stopped."

"Because of me?"

"I don't know. Maybe. Listen, we should probably do this thing."

She shook her head, looked down at our assignment, read aloud: " 'There's nothing so monstrous that people won't believe it of themselves. Discuss.' God, that's such bullshit."

"That what we're gonna say?" I said.

"Why not? Maybe we can talk about how he left out the word 'some'—'Nothing so monstrous that *some* people won't believe it of themselves.' Most people it's the opposite."

"You think?"

"You kidding?—Manson, Calley, Oswald, Sirhan, Joseph Stalin, Chiang Kai-shek—"

"OK, OK."

"—every Nazi that ever breathed, that general that Falvo keeps talking about—LeMay?"

"Half of 'em were crazy."

"The point is you couldn't *get* them to believe it."

"Maybe we could go with that." I scribbled it down. When I leaned forward the air felt cool against my shirt.

She went back to Ray. "Thing is, it just doesn't seem like him. I mean, he's not a fighter."

I smiled. "You think so?"

"I do—don't you?"

"I think Ray's a lot of things."

"Let me guess—you think he's complicated."

"I guess I do."

"Like you?"

"Different."

"Really?"

"Yeah," I said.

She paused. "Ray told me about your brother."

"It's not a secret," I said.

"I can't—I mean, there are some things you can't even imagine."

"Pretty much all of 'em." I smiled. "Hey, maybe we could work that into our report somehow, whaddya think?"

She was looking at me. "I'm sorry, Jon. I'm sorry you had to go through that."

"Long time ago," I said.

THAT AUGUST 15TH she borrowed her dad's car and we drove down to Yonkers—Ray had said he'd probably be hitching down and she said, why didn't we all go? She'd never met Gene. Frank and I hadn't seen him in over a year—it would get our minds off where we weren't.

We didn't know then how big it would be, who would be there. Nobody did. Anyway, it wasn't really an option for us. It wasn't just the twenty-four bucks—though the thought of spending twenty movie tickets for three days even if we'd *had* the money was hard to get around—it was everything: money, work, Karen's parents and Frank's, even mine. How could *we* have known they'd cave and let everybody in for free? Anyway, we were seventeen. We could no more say to our parents "Hey, man, we're heading up to Woodstock for three or four days to get our soul free" than we could ask them for bread so we could score some acid.

So we went to Yonkers. It wasn't far, less than an hour, just a poor-looking place with hot, twisty little roads and houses stacked tight like in Monopoly before you trade them in for a hotel. Some parts, with scraggly trees wilting in the heat and rows of small brick stores, made even Brewster look good. We got turned around and lost and wound up bumping over railroad tracks with weeds growing knee-high between the ties, then driving along chain-link fences protecting huge, cracking parking lots turning back into fields and factories with black stars where the windows used to be until we finally came to some run-down buildings with laundry hanging limp between the windows and people sitting on stoops in the shade.

Ray said it looked familiar, but he'd always hitched so he couldn't be sure. He was riding shotgun, his hand out on the roof. Music from people's radios came in on the hot air. You could hear people yelling to each other, kids screaming. Summer.

We were stopped at a light when he called out to a black guy wearing shades who was coming out of a store. "What the fuck, might as well ask," he said.

The guy stopped, his head wobbling a little on his neck and looked around like he couldn't figure out where the voice was coming from. It was only then we saw the bottle sticking out of the paper bag, the pants, the shoes flapping apart.

"Lock the doors," Frank said.

"Hey, can you help us out?" Ray called, leaning out of the car. "Excuse me."

He turned—in parts, like a driver making a three-point turn—then came toward us on that gently rolling boat. A big man in an open shirt.

"Sorry to bother you—can you help us out?"

Frank reached over and pushed down the lock buttons.

"Don't do that," Ray said.

"I'm not gonna sit here and—"

"Charles Street?" Ray said. "Any idea?" He'd turned around, pulled up the nobs. "I know it's around here somewhere."

He blocked the sun when he came up to the car, so close I could see the sweat gleaming in the hollows of his stomach muscles. He didn't say anything. We could hear him breathing through his mouth.

"Charles Street?" Ray said again.

He swallowed, then set the bottle carefully on the sidewalk. He straightened up and leaned on the car.

"Charles Street," he said, in a voice like Sidney Portier's. "Well, you just all wrong here."

"Yeah, I know," Ray said.

He scratched his stomach. "Charles Street," he said again, then pointed up the road. I'd never really seen a black man's hands up close before. "Y'all go straight up here two, no, three lights, then right on Foster. Charles'll be"—you could see him counting in his head—"your fourth on the right. That way you don't have to go 'round 'cause it bein' one-way."

"Thanks," Ray said.

The man leaned down, swaying slightly, and picked up the bottle.

"You folks have a nice day," he said.

RAY'S AUNT, Suze, turned out to be his dad's cousin, a blond woman with a kind, tired face and big red hands who walked like her knees had frozen or her shoes were made of iron. The house, small and wooden with a front lawn the size of a table, was crammed between split-levels with brick steps and short white railings. It smelled like Ajax and paint, and when the four of us piled into the small, hot living room with Suze and her grown son, Vinnie, and then little Gene came tearing in yelling Ray's name, I felt like maybe we should keep it short.

"I'm sorry I got nuttin' to offa youse," she kept saying, her accent big as Brooklyn. "Vinnie, go on down to the sto-ah and get some bee-ah."

We wouldn't hear of it, we said. Besides, Frank could go. Anyway, we'd only be staying a minute. It was just that it'd been so long since we'd seen little Gene, and Karen had never met him.

Well here he was, Suze said, meanwhile looking at Vinnie and pushing the air in front of herself with both hands and mouthing the words "Go, go!" like we were blind and wouldn't notice, "Growin' like a Gene-bean not that it surprises me the way he eats, I keep sayin' I need that goose with . . . sit, sit, here, make yourselves at home," and then, to Vinnie, "Go! What? In the drawer."

He disappeared into the kitchen and came out stuffing something in his pocket, a Mets cap on his head.

"You mind if I come with?" Frank said. He nodded toward the cap: "The Mets, huh? Tell me the truth—you think they can take the Cubs?"

The screen slammed behind them.

"And some cold cuts," Suze yelled after them.

"I want some co-cuts," Gene yelled from the couch.

"Whaddya say?" Ray said, tickling him on the sofa.

"An' Cheez Doodles."

"An' Cheez Doodles," Suze yelled.

Ray pulled up Gene's t-shirt and made a long flubbery mouth fart on his belly. "Whaddya say?"

"Pleeease."

"We had a poop party for his second," Suze said. "Filled some diapers with chocolate pudding—remember that? The kids loved that."

"Sure," Ray said.

"This kid from three over starts crying, 'I wanna eat Gene's poopy diapers,' remember?"

Ray laughed.

She glanced out through the screen door. "You think he heard about the Cheez Doodles?"

"You have to let us help out," Karen said.

"Please, you didn't come all the way down here to buy your own lunch." She was sitting on the edge of the kitchen chair, her knees together like a socialite. "So you're Ray's girl?" she said, pushing a long strand of hair behind her ear.

Ray was showing Gene how he could take his thumb off and put it back on.

"I guess I am."

Suze nodded, something unreadable in her face. "Well I'm pleased to make your acquaintance."

"And I'm pleased to make yours, ma'am."

"And so polite," she said to nobody in particular.

"Smart, too," Ray said.

"Smart, too? A face like that an' smart too? Well, it's like I been sayin', it's about time you found yourself a nice girl."

"Suze . . ."

"What?—I'm just sayin'." Gene was holding Ray's hand, turning it over. "Gene, sweetie, why don't you show your brother that picture you made."

WE STAYED FOR AN HOUR, maybe two. Frank and Vinnie came back with two six-packs and cold cuts and bread and we sat around the coffee table that was made of strips of wood-colored plastic and at some point Suze sent Vinnie back out for some Entenmann's. She had a daughter, too, she said, older than Vinnie, both happy to help their mother, not like most kids these days you suffer for 'em they wipe their hands a' you. She was sorry we couldn't make her acquaintance.

We said we were too. A Good Humor truck came up the street, the jingle growing, turned, faded.

Gene was a good boy, she didn't mind watching him for a while. The neighborhood was something else again. "Can you smell that?" she asked.

"What?" Frank said politely.

The breeze had been bringing in the hot smell of garbage for a while. There were three fans going. They didn't help much.

"All I'm sayin' is, two weeks they don't take out the garbage. S'not the blacks, I got enough trouble, anyway I ain't prejudice—it's our own people. I tried talkin' to 'em, I'm ashamed to repeat what they said to me. Was everything I could do to keep Vinnie from goin' over there. Here, have some more."

"You want I'll go talk to 'em," Ray said. Gene had fallen asleep, his head on a pillow on Ray's lap.

She gave him a kind look. "What, you don't have enough trouble?"

"Easier for me—I don't live here."

"Like they wouldn't figure it out?"

"Nothin' to figure out—just talk."

"Talk is never just talk." She looked around the room at us. "So you all heard about this thing upstate? Radio's sayin' it could be half a million people, traffic jams far as the eye can see . . ."

We smiled weakly. We couldn't go—parents, money.

"Why would you want to?"

I asked Vinnie if he'd thought about going.

He snorted. "I look like a hippie to you?"

"Better off tryin' to get a job 'stead of protesting all this stuff you don't know nothin' about," Suze said. She'd heard they'd had to move it, that some town wouldn't let 'em in. "Here, have some more," she said, pushing the box of Entenmann's my way. "I like to see a boy eat, specially one like you needs some meat on his bones."

Ray told them about the running. "This one's gonna be state champion," he said. "You watch."

They seemed confused.

"You know, like the track team," Ray said. "The mile run, stuff like that."

"Better finish it off, then," Suze said, pushing the box over.

"I would've liked to go," Karen said suddenly.

Nobody said anything. Ray covered up by pulling on his nose. "Well, I should put up some coffee," Suze said.

The Good Humor truck was coming back around.

"So you're a runner, huh?" Vinnie said. "Where do you run?"

I told him.

He nodded. "Be glad you live up in Brewster," he said, and winked. "Round here they see you runnin', they shoot you," and everybody laughed.

I DON'T KNOW when we first started going down to Jimmy's. Early. It seemed like he'd always been there at the bottom of the hill—the workshop, the office, the garage crammed against the woods. I don't think he ever left. I'd see his light when I ran by in the winter, use it to see the ice ahead of me on the road. In the summer if you came by at six in the morning he'd walk out of the shop wiping his hands on his overalls and you'd tell him the problem and pop the hood and he wouldn't even say anything, just start sniffing around like a doctor—touching, tapping, pulling on the belts, yanking a spark plug, then putting on his glasses and checking the gap. People would yak away, make stupid jokes, wonder about this or that. He'd ignore them. Every now and then somebody would say they remembered his father. "That so?" he'd say.

People wanted him to like them, maybe because they never knew what he thought. Of them. Men, mostly. Thin, wiry, the stubble coming in mostly white now, he might have been good-looking once except for a nose that looked like it had been stuck on at the last minute when the right one went missing. It seemed to pull everything toward itself, like a small planet. He was always messing with it, thinking, yanking on the holes as if his fingers were a ring and he was planning to lead himself away, and then he'd smile at something and suddenly, balanced out with the big teeth and the tight, sweaty hair that fit his head like a cap, the nose would find its place.

Ray and I would just hang around and watch him work. If it was after hours, whoever he had helping out would be gone and it would be just us and him and the radio and we'd get ourselves a Coke from the machine and sit on whatever there was to sit on where we wouldn't be in the way and talk about whatever there was to talk about.

Or not. I never knew anyone more comfortable with not than Jimmy. He talked, or didn't, like he stood: square as a milk carton, not leaning forward or away from you, just considering what was there ahead of him, seeing it for what it was. Reserving judgment. When something needed to be said, he said it. Mostly it didn't.

"Tightened the belts," he might say, and the other guy would be off like something rolling down a hill: The belts? Really? He hadn't thought it was the belts. He'd talked to his neighbor who said it was the steering fluid—the belts, huh? He'd had 'em replaced not that long ago—that was the only reason he was sayin', still, served him right listening to a guy with a '67 Caddy. Probably never worked on a car a day in his life. That screeching sound—belts, huh?

"That'll be twelve-fifty," Jimmy would say.

In the beginning we'd stop by his place because it was near the tracks, because there was nothing else around, because he'd have the kerosene heater going in the winter and we could stand around it, blocking the heat. After a while it just became a thing. He never asked. Sometimes five minutes would go by when pretty much all you'd hear was whatever the weather was doing outside, the clink of the tools when he threw them on the bench, maybe the sound of pages turning as we leafed through a magazine, passing it back and forth, and at some point we'd jump off the tires we'd been sitting on and say we probably had to get going and he'd say "OK."

Over time it thawed. Slowly. Just enough.

"Read about your race in the paper," he might say to me half an hour in, his head up inside some car, and I'd say, "Must have been a small paper," and maybe he'd chuckle and that would be that. Mostly me and Ray would talk to each other—about running, about school, about the people we knew, about Muhammad Ali, who'd said he didn't have nothin' against them Vietcong and gone to jail—and he'd listen.

We'd heard there was a bank in the city now where you could put a card in a machine to take out money. "That right?" he'd say. We'd rattle on, pitching to ourselves. Every now and then he'd take a swing. Yeah, he'd read about Manson. Walkin' on the moon— now that had to be somethin'. He knew four kids had gone over to Vietnam the past year—good kids—local kids. He didn't know about the draft—supposed if it had to be, it had to be.

"But what if it doesn't?" I said.

"Wouldn't be the first time."

"Would you go?" Ray said.

He grunted, tightening something. "I did. Different."

WE TALKED to make up for him. We'd say "How can you say that?" or "Don't you think . . . ?" and all you'd hear would be the sprocket wrench clicking and winding and then he'd step out from under the car and walk over to the bench and find what he needed and only then say, "Don't see that it matters much either way," or "Nobody else gonna live your life," or "Sounds like he's got a lot on his mind." After a time, he knew most of what there was to know.

Not that he had any advice for us. A shrug, a shake of the head, the thumb and the forefinger working the inside of the nose, not with intent, just meditating, then a Jimmyism: "Couldn't tell you," "Hard to say," "Hadn't heard that." If we'd come for enlightenment, we'd come to the wrong place. We didn't care. That place—the smell of gasoline and hot weeds in the summer, the '59 Playboy calendar curling up from the bottom ("Beautiful, but camera shy. / Jayne Mansfield, can we coax you / Into being Miss July?")—was home to us.

Only once do I remember Jimmy going on—mostly he'd just let us work things out on our own. It was just before school started, not long after we'd come back from Yonkers. Late August, hot, but with something in the air—a feel, a smell—that told you summer was on its last legs and knew it.

Ray had been talking about some hippie who'd gotten himself beat up down in Ardsley in the park they had there by the freeway. Every time the kid got his ass knocked down, before he'd stand up again he'd take a comb out of his back pocket and run it through his hair.

"What for?" I said.

"Who knows?—probably a pacifist. Or a hairdresser. Anyway, this goes on a while—he's not even tryin' to defend himself. Every time he gets to his feet the other guy just whales on him. Couple a shots an' his nose is all fucked up, he's doin' that thing you do with your mouth when you've lost some teeth, but it's the same thing all over again—before he gets up he takes the comb out of his pocket, smoothes his hair real nice, feels the part, puts it back in his pocket, stands up . . . wham! After a while the other guy just gets disgusted and walks away."

"Like in *Cool Hand Luke*," I said.

"Different—Luke keeps swinging."

"So what happens?"

"I told you—the guy walks away."

"I mean with the one with the hair."

"Nothin'. Just kneels there in the dirt for a while, droolin' blood, then takes out his comb, does his thing, and leaves."

"That's nuts," I said.

"Right? What'd ya think, Jimmy?"

Jimmy was standing by the bench with his glasses propped on the end of his nose, running his finger down the columns in a book. He flipped the page and started at the top. "About what?"

"About this kid lettin' himself get the shit beaten out of him."

Jimmy didn't look up. "Stuff you're doin' to other people you're mostly doin' to yourself." He flipped the page.

"You're sayin' this guy's beatin' his own ass, you mean."

"Sure, that's why he walks away," I said. "He can't take any more."

Holding his finger to the page, Jimmy reached behind his ear, wrote something down, put the pencil back. "Could be. I was talkin' about the other one."

"The pacifist? How do you figure that?"

Jimmy was still looking through the book. "I don't know. This kid thinks he's teaching the other guy some kinda lesson, right? Well, maybe he is—but he's also getting' the crap beaten out of him."

"So what's he supposed to do?" I said.

"Tough call." He wrote something else down, flipped the page, then lay a file across the open book and walked to the soda machine. "How's your Mom doin'?"

"Comes and goes—you know."

"She has some good days," Ray said.

"In 1955," I said.

"How 'bout your Dad?"

I shrugged. "Alright I guess."

Jimmy put in a dime and a soda thumped down the chute. He popped it with the opener tied to the wall with a string and the bottle top clanked in the bottom of the can. "You want one? I don't know why I don't use the key—my machine." He leaned back against the workbench. "I remember hearin' about your brother," he said.

"Long time ago," I said.

He took a drink, pulled on his nose holes, looked at the car up on the lift. "I had a brother, died. I was what, fifteen I guess."

He didn't say anything else.

"You miss him?" Ray said.

Jimmy took a while. "I don't know. Not that much." He nodded. "He used to smack me around but he was older so my old man would take his shit out on him. Missed that."

"So you were next in line?" Ray said.

"Didn't stop till I was twenty."

We stared at him. "Twenty?"

"Wasn't like it was all the time." He looked out the window. "Think I wanted him to see me. Instead of this thing he was hittin'."

"So what happened?"

"Busted him with a hose." He nodded to himself: "Saw me then."

We just sat there listening to the crickets. A bullfrog started up somewhere in the distance.

"So it got better?" I said.

He tipped up his chin toward the back of the garage. "Came in one day an' he's face down in a sandwich like he's lookin' for somethin'. Got better after that."

"Was me, I woulda left," Ray said. "Not just keep comin' back like this guy Owen he told me about. Just split, you know? Fuck him. Sorry," he said, catching himself.

"This ain't church," Jimmy said.

"Just stop it, you know what I'm sayin'? Right there. No more me and you, no more tryin' to figure it the fuck out—you want to beat my ass, come find me in California."

Jimmy looked at him. "That what you'd do—you and that girl you keep talkin' about?"

"Why not? Grow your own food an' shit? California, you can get a place on the beach for almost nothin'."

Jimmy was looking at him. "How you gonna get there?"

"Where? You mean—"

"You gonna walk?"

"I don't know—bus, maybe? Get a job, make some money—what?"

"Nothin'."

"You don't think I'd do it?"

Jimmy walked to a big metal cabinet and took a flashlight out of the top drawer. "C'mon," he said.

We could hear the mosquitoes whining on the screen. A couple of moths were beating themselves against the bulb under the eave.

"Where's he goin'?" I whispered. We could see the beam jumping across the lot to the back trees.

When we came up behind him he was playing the light over a blue Pontiac with a brown hood, its trunk buried so deep in the ivy it looked like it had grown out of the woods. "She's been here a while," he said. "LeMans—V-8. Two sixty."

"Bucks?"

"Horses."

"Nice."

"Yours."

In the quiet you could hear the mosquitoes coming to the light.

"You serious?" Ray said.

"Wouldn't mind gettin' it off the lot."

"Jesus, Jimmy."

"Needs work."

The bullfrog had started up again. It reminded me of those noise boxes kids used to play with—like somebody was turning it upside down, over and over.

He popped the hood, shined the light over the engine. "I don't know about California. Carmel, anyway."

"Jesus."

"—got nothin' to do with it."

"Thing is, I don't really know about cars."

Jimmy took a pull of his soda. "Yeah, me either." He closed the hood. "You learn." He looked at me. "You, too. Never know—this girl doesn't work out, you two jokers can go together. Have some fun. Now get outta here, I got work to do."

He raised his head. The smell of skunk was filling up the dark—rank and new.

"There's one didn't make it," he said.

MOST OF THE TIME when something goes bad—a marriage, a war, a run of good luck—you don't know it. It's like in the cartoons, only less funny. You run off the cliff and just keep going—talking, listening to music, making plans, for years sometimes—except no announcer interrupts to say "Excuse me, collect call for Mr. Coyote" to make you notice and make us laugh. You just wake up and fall.

It was a beautiful September, stunned and perfect, like the world had been hit on the head: chill mornings, a warm mist over the cold grass, now and then a leaf dropping down like it was being lowered on a string, sparking in the sun, then going out. Maybe a single jay, laughing. For weeks the four of us talked about someday opening a book and record shop together, arguing about the details, drawing up lists—Where would it be? What kind of records?—like it was actually possible. Karen said we'd have to have places to sit, maybe coffee and tea.

We were walking down Foggintown Road one afternoon, talking about how we'd all have to get jobs first to pay for the furniture, when we came across the frogs. They were jumping across the road from one marsh to another just like it. Dozens of them, thick with cold. There wasn't much traffic but a couple had gotten squashed anyway. You'd flip the live ones over like a piece of meat and they'd lie there, their white bellies breathing, then start kicking and turn themselves over with one arm and leap off—usually in the wrong direction. We were there a long time, slowing down the traffic, carrying them off to the side. Strange what makes you happy.

That was around the time my father started making me sandwiches for lunch. He didn't say anything. I'd come downstairs in the dark and the sandwich would be lying on the counter like an aluminum torpedo, Italian bread stuffed with cold cuts and cheese and just about everything else. Every day something different. I didn't know what had gotten into him. I took some shit for it at school, everybody leaning over like I was unwrapping the *Mona Lisa*, Frank humming that part from *2001: A Space Odyssey* where the monkey brains the other one with a rock, but the truth is they were good, so a couple of nights later when I saw him reading in his chair in the living room after my mother had gone to bed, I said thanks.

He closed the book on his finger. "It's nothing—you need to eat."

"Anyway, thanks—they're good."

"Pshh," he said, waving it away.

I couldn't think of anything else to say so I asked what he was reading. He told me—somebody I'd never heard of. I could see him in a room at the end of the world, under a small light, reading.

"Good?"

He thought about it. "Too finished. Everything is, how would you say . . . ?"

"Say it in German."

He shook his head. "Too closed, too . . ." He put the book down on his lap and pulled his hands apart as if tightening a giant shoelace.

"*Zu einfach*," I said.

He nodded. "*Zu einfach. Genau.*" Exactly. He glanced around the room, at the shelves of books, the heavy blue curtains, the framed pictures on the mantel, then shrugged. *"Das Leben ist nicht einfach. Die Literatur, sollte, es auch nicht sein.* How would you say that?"

"Life isn't simple. Literature shouldn't be either."

The clock kicked in, saving us.

"So . . ."

"You staying up?" I said.

He raised his book.

HE WAS RIGHT, life wasn't simple. Parts of it were—a frog scratching its head like a dog, the clean, heavy weight of a bolt in your hand, certain songs—and you'd try to hold on to these but you couldn't hold on for long. Things would get complicated, and the more you thought about them, the more complicated they got. It was like the SAT. That October a few dozen of us had taken it in the school cafeteria. Work quickly but carefully, they told us. Eliminate wrong answers. If you can eliminate more than two, guess.

Eliminate wrong answers. When it came to my life, I couldn't seem to eliminate anything. Karen tried to talk me through it, joking around, moving her hands around my head like it was a crystal ball, saying, "I can see it, it's getting clearer—he's about to speak!"—but I put her off. I could tell she and Ray had been sleeping together. I just could. *Work quickly but carefully*: 'Cruelty is to pain as love is to blank': (a) suffering, (b) joy, (c) shame, (d) fear. *If you can eliminate more than two, guess.*

It was like that with everything. I'd walk past Aaron's room and see my mother looking out his window with a folded blanket in her arms and I'd suddenly remember her laughing, throwing sheets of light over our heads, saying, "Where are the boys? Samuel, have you seen the boys?" Or I'd be sitting in the guidance office watching Marschner cup his hands in front of him on the desk, setting out my options like invisible bowls—"Well, what do you *think* you'd want to do?" And I wouldn't know what to say.

The war was part of it, coloring everything like a bad taste in your mouth. There was no one to talk to, really. For Karen it was simple. Vietnam was wrong. The only choice was resistance. With guys you'd start making jokes about joining the Nation of Islam. You'd start clowning, fucking around. Better than being bored to death, you'd say, shuffling your feet around in the cold like there was some law said you could say anything at all except what you were thinking—What did it mean to kill somebody? What did it mean to die? We were all standing on a conveyer belt gliding toward a cliff, smoking, laughing, and nobody wanted to be the first to say it.

OF ALL OF US, John Kennedy was the only one who'd talk about it. He was thinking about quitting the team—with everything going on, he said, running just didn't seem that important anymore. He'd gone to Woodstock, heard Country Joe and the Fish. What were we fightin' for? It was a good question. I told him my SAT theory and he said that was it exactly: We didn't have time to eliminate the wrong answers. The problem was if you were going to die—or live—it shouldn't be for *"all of the above."*

"Seriously, what would *you* do if your number got called?" he asked me one afternoon as we walked around the track.

I said I didn't know.

"Really?"

"I don't know," I said.

"You talked to your folks about it?"

I shook my head.

He'd talked to his dad, he said. His dad still went down to the VFW twice a week. He agreed—Vietnam was a goddamn mess.

Still, if your country called you . . . If John was called, he said, it would be the hardest day in his life but he'd understand and pray for him to come home safe.

We were walking down the backstretch, the gusts flattening our sweats to our legs.

"Your dad said that?" I said.

"I mean, would *you* go to Canada?"

"I don't know. Maybe."

"I talked to Coach about it. Did I tell you that?"

"What'd he say?"

"You know how Coach is. He quoted some poem about how nations were invented so bullets would have the chests of men to sleep in or something."

"That's it?"

"Asked about college—said Villanova would probably give me a half-scholarship. I said how that's great but it's just me and my dad and he can't really afford for me not to work right now so I was thinkin' I might put it off for a year—plus he's my dad and *he* served, so there's that. I kept tryin' to explain it's not like I agree with it but, you know, it's my country. Right or wrong, he says. That's not what I'm sayin', I said. An' the beat goes on, he says."

"You know Coach," I said.

"Yeah. Anyway at some point I just say it. I don't want to be a coward, I tell him, and he nods for a long time and then he says, 'Look, I'm not going to tell you that word doesn't mean anything because it does. I'm just saying look at who's using it, and why. If somebody said you were a coward for not jumping off a cliff, would you do it?' You did, I tell him. He was an idiot, he says. At least you can live with yourself, I say, and Coach just looks at me and smiles and shakes his head. He has a lot of work to do, he says."

We'd jogged into the backstretch again, leaning into the wind. We talked some more but I didn't know what to tell him. The times they were a-changin', but this was different. In the song the windows and walls we'd shake were somebody else's. In Brewster half the walls were your own.

In CROSS-COUNTRY that fall we lost and lost again: McCann had graduated, leaving us with only three in the top ten—Kennedy, me and Moore, with one of the Time Tunnel kids a sorry fourth. It wasn't pretty. Then Kennedy, who had always seemed untouchable to me—like Ray, except with feet—lost to a squeaky-voiced junior named Balger from North Salem, staggering across the line ten yards behind, his face contorted with pain. It threw me. It was like nothing would hold, nothing was sure—like the world was turning in your hands for its own reasons and you couldn't hold it. The car? We were almost there, and all I could think of was what would I do if they got in it and drove away. It was supposed to be a good thing, a blow against the man, and it filled me with a loneliness I'd only known in dreams.

That slipping feeling—it was like that with everything.

On SEPTEMBER 23rd I'd come home drunk. It was Aaron's birthday—traditionally not a good day in our house.

The night before, I'd come downstairs after my dad had gone to bed to find my mother sleeping with her head on her arms on the kitchen table. I hadn't seen her like that for a long time. She looked old and sad—but she looked like my mother. It was like I hadn't really looked at her in years. I could feel this thickness tightening my chest, my throat—and suddenly it all seemed so ridiculous, this thing we'd been doing—so unnecessary. We were both getting older. It didn't matter who was right or wrong in the end. Somebody had to take the first step.

Once I'd thought of it, it wouldn't go away—like a dare I'd set myself. It began to seem less crazy. I'd leap that gap like the guy in that famous picture jumping from one cliff to the other. I'd do it for her. She was my mother, after all, and she was suffering. I'd rise above myself, like Gandhi. I could see myself walking into that kitchen, asking her forgiveness. I'd tell her I was sorry, that I'd been thinking of myself too much, that I loved her. I'd take her in my arms and say, "I'm here—I'm your son, too. We're in this thing together." I'd be a man about it. I'd bring a cake.

The next afternoon I bought the cake. After that I bought a six-pack from Jerry-who-looks-the-other-way and took it to the ballpark down by the river. It was overgrown. I drank the beer sitting on the bleachers, the cake in its white box next to me. I don't know why I bought the beer. The usual reasons, probably. The cake didn't seem crazy. It seemed noble, necessary. Even right. We'd celebrate together. It would be like those scenes in the movies when everyone suddenly understands a character's strengths. I sat there until it was almost dark. When I couldn't see the trees against the sky any more, I left.

For some reason I expected to find her in the kitchen again but it didn't matter—it gave me a chance to take the cake out and put in the yellow candles I'd bought to go with it. I thought for a while about whether I should do five, which he'd been when he died, or nineteen, which he'd be now if he hadn't. I decided on nineteen. The extra one for good luck seemed wrong.

It took a while but I got them all lit, then started up the stairs. I could walk fine. It was OK that Dad wasn't home yet—this would be just between the two of us. By the time he came home we'd be talking. I imagined the look on her face, her sudden understanding that the time had come, that enough was enough, that her *other* son, grown now, had taken the first step, jumped the gap. I would do that for her—show her how much I loved her. There would be tears, I knew that—but there was no way around it. I walked up the stairs, concentrating on not stumbling. After all this time, all this anger, we'd make it right—for all of us, including my brother. I had to concentrate because there were tears in my eyes.

"What do you want?" she said.

The tone of her voice didn't stop me—how could I expect her to know what I'd planned?

"Mommy?" I said.

I'd thought about that. I hadn't called her Mommy in years. It would tell her I was willing to go back, start over. I put on the expression I'd practiced in the downstairs bathroom—loving, open, mature. "Mommy?"

I don't think I've ever seen a look of such horror as when she opened the door to that dark landing and saw me, the cake, those nineteen gently flickering candles.

"It's me," I said, stupidly, with what I thought was a brave smile. "It's for—" And I stopped.

"Why would you do this?" she whispered.

"I want—"

"Why?"

"I just—"

"You counted them?" She looked at me, appalled, as if her heart were actually breaking.

"I just—"

"You're cruel—there's no other explanation."

"No, no, I meant—"

"I have a cruel son." She smiled at me, full of hate. It was her battle smile—the smile she'd walk into hell with. "So this is what I have left—I see."

I stood there holding that cake like I was room service making an eccentric delivery. I could see the guy in the photograph, hanging over the gap. I was still trying to smile. I didn't understand what had happened.

She leaned closer to see my face over the flames, and thinking she would catch her hair on fire, I stepped back.

"You're drunk."

"No, I—"

She shook her head, her voice so small it seemed emptied of everything, like the last air escaping a balloon: "My God, what a life."

"Mommy," I said, like a child in the snow holding up his hands for his mittens.

"That you could do this."

"No, I—"

"Deliberately do this to me."

"I'm your goddamn son," I said. "Why do you—?"

"You're not my son."

"How can you say that?"

"Because it's how I feel."

I just stared at her. "I'm glad he's dead," I said.

"I know," she said, and went back into Aaron's room and closed the door.

I left the cake on the hallway dresser where I found it the next morning, spotted with dime-sized circles of wax like ringworm.

By mid-september it was as if the summer—the nights we'd spent up on the embankment or listening to records in my room, our trip out to Yonkers, the four of us making plans—was something we'd left behind, like we'd been forced into a car and were watching it grow smaller behind us. We had no choice but to keep going.

That October I started applying to schools. Sitting at the kitchen table, late, I'd hear the chair creak in the living room and my father would come up behind me with his book closed on his finger, pat me on the shoulder and walk back. College was the answer, everyone said; it would keep you out of the draft. I was thinking more "out of the house." Karen had applied all over, to schools I'd barely heard of: Wellesley, Barnard, Radcliffe. She'd told her parents that she and Ray might take off the next summer. Maybe I could come along, she said. Frank was thinking about junior college.

Ray and I worked on the car, scrounging parts all the way out to Trenton. This was his shot, Ray said. Jimmy said it was comin' along, that Ray had a feel for it—that we both did. He said there were some parts would take time to find, but we might get it done by Thanksgiving—Christmas at the outside.

✦ ✦ ✦

Maybe it's because of everything else, because we could feel things suddenly changing, that we decided to do Halloween that year. Be kids for a night. It makes sense. I forget who I was. Frank was the Hulk, I think. Ray was a pirate, which is always cheap. Karen was Glinda the Good Witch of the North with a cardboard crown and a plastic wand with a tin foil star at the end. We did Prospect and some of the smaller streets around it, schools of little devils and ghosts and Snow Whites crowding through the gates and tripping over the curbs, splitting around us like we were boulders in a stream. "Now make a wish," I remember Karen saying in Glinda's weird voice, "then tap your sneakers three times." And she'd whack me on the head with the star: "One—two—three!"

It felt good walking in the misty rain between the hanging skeletons and the spooks made out of hats with sheets hung over them, making fun of the people who opened the doors. It had been warm, so the pumpkins had softened and sagged, making them scarier. We got a couple of pounds of candy even though we were older because people didn't want to risk pissing us off, then went to my room and ate it, listening to Dylan's *Blonde on Blonde*, which Karen had brought from home. She'd memorized half of Glinda's lines, which should have been annoying, but wasn't. "You always had the power to go back to Kansas," she'd say, and lying on the floor of my room on my elbow, I'd smile and give her the finger and she'd do that horrible Glinda laugh and say, "You have no power here! Be gone, before somebody drops a house on you, too!" and we'd hear Dylan singing in that stoned-duck voice of his about how she breaks just like a little girl and she'd smile and say, "Don't bet on it."

It was a good Halloween. The rain started to come down and we could hear it drumming on the gutter and we sang "Rainy Day

Women #12 and 35" and "Stuck Inside of Mobile with the Memphis Blues Again," changing Memphis to Brewster, and I remember looking around at one point and thinking if I could just stay in this room, in this moment, I'd never want anything else, just the four of us lying around stuffing Milky Ways and candy corn and Sugar Daddys, laughing, talking about what we'd do next summer and how we'd always be friends. No more.

They left after one. It had stopped raining, but a mist was falling thick enough to make your face wet. Some people had forgotten to blow their pumpkins out and looking up the block you'd see spots of flame like pinholes in construction paper. Karen said she'd drop Frank at his house. I asked Ray if he wanted to crash in my room. He said he might as well head back, see if the place was still standing—check if anybody was feeding Wilma.

We were standing around the car when an exhausted clown and a guy in an Elvis mask came out of the dark walking down the middle of the shiny street and we said something about how it was the King and who was the other one supposed to be—Richard Nixon? and they said, "How's it goin'?" A little ways back a third guy in a frilled jacket with a plastic guitar over his shoulder had stopped to light a cigarette under the streetlight. "Who're you?" Ray said, "the Lone Ranger?" and the guy grinned and leaned the plastic guitar against his stomach, then pulled on a giant Afro wig he'd tucked under his belt like a scalp. "Jimi Hendrix, man," he said, then did a couple of silent licks on the guitar and we laughed and they walked on.

A PERFECT NIGHT, in some ways, the rain getting louder between songs, the four of us together—right down to white Jimmy with his frilled jacket and plastic guitar. Nobody wanted to be the first to say it was late. We talked about how we'd never be like our parents with all their sadness and bullshit—how we'd make it count.

It was three days later we heard that a woman in Poughkeepsie had hung herself along Route 55. She'd been there for two days, quietly creaking in the rain, but nobody had realized it until the decorations were being cut down for another year.

WE WERE SITTING by the lockers that morning when he came striding down the hall like nothing had happened, like everything was cool. Like his eye wasn't shut and he didn't have a stained bandage above his ear and a corner of his lip wasn't raised off his teeth.

She saw him before I did, was up on her feet before I knew what was going on. He held her for a long time, petting her hair. "Hey, hey, hey, c'mon—it's OK, it's OK," he kept saying. "Guy just got a little lucky, is all."

She pulled back to look at him, touched his face with her fingertips like she was afraid he'd break. "Oh, my God, Ray," she said.

"It's fine, it's nothin'." He tried to smile at me over her shoulder. "Little late for Halloween, right?" he said.

"What the fuck happened, Ray?" I said.

"Nothin' happened. Laced me in the second round, that's all."

"They didn't stop it?"

"This ain't the Garden we're talkin' about."

People had begun to gather around.

"Fuck, what happened to you, man?"

"Hey, Chris, get over here—look at this!"

"Bad day, huh?"

He ignored them. "Looks a lot worse than it is, baby. Just got away from me a little, that's all."

"A little?" Karen said. "You call this a little? Ray, I don't—"

"Just wanted to pick up some bucks, help with the car." He held a cloth to his lip, tried to smile. "How the fuck was *I* supposed to know he was eight and one? Make that nine and one."

"Danbury?" I said.

A couple of the bused kids walked by, looked, kept walking.

"Yeah, that's right."

I saw him look over my shoulder. Farber, who was on duty that morning, was standing a few feet behind me. He had his head to the side like he was studying something confusing. "Again?" he said.

"What do you want?" Ray said, his words slurred by the lip.

"What do I want?"

"That's right."

"What do *I* want?"

"I'm just standin' here—I'm not makin' any trouble."

"I would think it's about what *you* want."

"We're not doing anything wrong, we're just—" Karen began.

"Not your concern, honey."

"Actually, it *is* my concern."

"Excuse me?"

"I said, I think it is my concern."

"Hey, hold on, wait, wait," Ray said. He pulled some small folded papers out of his pocket. "Look, I got a note—two notes. From the nurse, an' another one from home." He saw the look on my face and looked away, pushing his hair back off his face. "OK? C'mon."

Farber was still staring at Karen. "Keep 'em," he said to Ray.

I could see Karen's face tighten. "I don't see what—"

"I'm going to have to ask you to keep your mouth shut."

"We have a right to know what we're—"

"Shut your mouth."

"You got no reason to talk to her that way," I said.

Farber turned around, slowly. "I remember you," he said.

"I remember you, too," I said.

I could feel the crazy shaking starting in my stomach.

He smiled. "Oh, you're gonna remember me all right."

"Look, he's my friend," Karen said. "I'm just—"

"Friend?" He let it hang in the air—a taunt, a leer.

I stepped in front of Ray.

"Everything alright here, Vince?" It was Falvo.

Farber didn't turn around. "Ed."

"Anything I can do—help subdue the natives?"

"I'm just—"

"I'm joking, Vince."

"Nothin' O'Hara's office can't straighten out."

Falvo wasn't moving. He nodded toward me. "Well, this one's one of mine."

"Then you know he's got a mouth on him."

"Actually, I'm surprised to hear it." He turned to Ray, whistled. "Another altercation?"

"So what?" Ray said.

"You see what I'm dealin' with here?" Farber said.

"Why don't you tell me what happened here, Vince?"

Karen and I started to say something but he held up his finger. Farber told him.

"That's unacceptable," Falvo said.

"Yes it is."

"Unacceptable."

"Glad you agree," Farber said.

"I'm telling you, it's this climate of permissiveness, Vince. No standards, no discipline . . . If this was the army we'd be talking rank insubordination."

Farber glanced over quickly.

"And you have to deal with this in class, too?"

"I wouldn't put up with it."

"Well, I'm sorry you had to put up with it this time."

"Not as sorry—"

"Especially considering they're my kids."

Farber looked confused. "What—all three of 'em?"

"Been working with him on the side." He looked at Ray. "How long have I been working with you?"

"I don't—"

"All right, Vince—I'll take care of this."

"Thanks—I've got it."

"I know you do. But it's my watch. I was supposed to have an assessment in on this one a week ago."

"Well—"

"The three of you—let's go." He took me and Ray by the elbows, started walking us away. "I don't need this coming back to bite me, Vince, know what I mean?"

WE'D BARELY TURNED THE CORNER when he stopped. He seemed tired. "Don't you people have somewhere to go?" he said.

"What're you going to say?" I said.

"I'm sure I'll think of something." He looked at Ray. "You've been to the nurse with that?"

"You want to see my note?"

Falvo looked at him for a while. "You OK?"

Ray nodded.

"Come here—let me see."

I was surprised when Ray went over to him. Falvo took his chin in his hand, turned his head to the side, touched around the outside of the bandage. "This hurt?" He felt around the closed eye socket, gently. "How about that?"

"I'm fine—really," Ray said.

"Sure?"

"I know what I'm doin'."

"OK," Falvo said, and walked away.

+ + +

"WHAT'S GOING ON?" he said to me that morning after class. "Close the door, have a seat."

"What do you mean?" I said.

"With your friend—what's going on?"

"You mean—"

"The bruises, the eye, the lip—these fights I keep hearing about, the whole thing. No bullshit."

"He gets into fights," I said. "He's got a temper."

"He's got a temper."

"Yeah."

Somebody knocked on the door.

"I'm busy," Falvo called. "What about home—how're things at home?"

For a second I thought he was talking about me.

"I don't . . . ?"

"At home, with his dad. How're things with his dad?"

"Listen, he's my best friend—he gets into fights, that's all. And he knows these clubs—where you can make some money."

"You mean like boxing? You know this?"

Somebody knocked on the door again.

"He fights middleweight," I said. "Really, it's not like that."

"Alright," Falvo said. "Come back at four."

"Don't we have practice?"

"It can wait."

I DIDN'T SAY ANYTHING to Karen or Frank. We ate our lunch like we always did when it wasn't raining—convicts in the exercise yard, huddled out of the wind. Pushing the season. Ray was lying down in the nurse's office, Karen said—his side was hurting pretty bad. He'd said he didn't mind missing lunch anyway since he couldn't really eat or talk. The nurse wanted him to get an X-ray.

"What for?" I said.

She shook her head.

"Why would he need an X-ray?" Frank said.

It was only then we noticed her eyes.

"Hey. Hey—c'mon," Frank said, putting his arm around her shoulders. "He'll be fine. Really."

"Tell me," she said.

"Tell you what?" I said.

"It's OK," Frank said.

"Tell me what's going on."

"I swear to God, there's nothing to tell. Look, he doesn't talk about it because he knows you wouldn't like it. He goes to this club. In Danbury."

"Where in Danbury?"

"What?"

"Where in Danbury?"

"How do I know where? In Danbury. Look, it's not like I'm sittin' there holdin' his spit bucket or whatever. He's been doin' it a while, I don't know, a year, maybe more."

She was just looking at me, her mouth pressed together.

"Karen, I swear—"

"I thought we were friends," she said.

"I am, we are—I swear . . ."

She wiped her cheek with the base of her thumb. "Never mind," she said. "Forget it."

I FOUND FALVO writing on the chalkboard, talking over his shoulder to one of the black kids who was sitting at a desk in the front row. "Read it out loud," he said.

"Again?" the kid asked.

"You want me to come back?" I said.

"Again. Come in," he said, waving me in.

It was the kid from the gym. I hadn't recognized him without all the sweatshirts.

He read the sentence—something about Kurt Vonnegut's *Cat's Cradle*—and Falvo wrote it on the board, little bits of chalk dribbling down like rain on a window. "OK—subject, object, verb," he said, the chalk knocking against the board. "Better. Now do the rest of them the same way for tomorrow."

The kid closed his notebook.

"You two know each other?"

"S'up?" I said.

The kid nodded.

"I've been trying to get Mr. Jones here to consider joining the track team," Falvo said.

"Great idea," I said.

The kid started gathering his stuff.

"The bus isn't leaving for another fifteen minutes," Falvo said. He turned to me. "Larry and I have had a very interesting conversation about your friend."

"Is that right?" I said.

"Go ahead. Tell him what you told me."

"Ain't nothin' to tell." He had a slow, drawn-out way of talking, like he was bored, that got on my nerves.

"Go ahead," Falvo said. "Off the record—for the next ten minutes, you're not in school."

"Tell me what?" I said.

The kid shrugged.

"Tell me what?"

"Friend a yours ain't no boxer," he said.

"What're you talkin' about?" I said.

"I'm telling you. All street. Way he uses his feet, that slidin' thing he does—he just makin' it up.

"I don't—"

"Larry's Golden Gloves," Falvo said.

"So what?"

"Try to listen to what he's saying."

"I ain't sayin' he can't fight," the kid said.

"So what *are* you sayin'?"

"Look at where he holds his hands, man. Look at his knuckles— you think he got those wearin' gloves? An' all that shit all up around his neck?"

"I don't know what're you tryin' to say. So he fights on the street, so what? Everybody knows that."

He was sprawled back in his chair, looking at me. I wanted to hit him. "Lemme ask you somethin', smart man. How many times you seen him fight?"

"Hundred twenty-three."

"All that time, anybody touch him?"

I didn't say anything.

"Yeah, now you listenin'."

"Listenin' to what? I don't—"

"Listen to what he's saying, Jon."

"Listen, man, he ain't my brother, I don't care who's takin' him down. All I'm sayin' is he ain't gettin' that shit in the ring *or* the street." He leaned forward, said it slow like it might sink in better that way: "Muthafucka beatin' on that boy knows what he doin',— an' all this other shit here, he just doin' that to cover his Eye-talian ass up."

IT's NOT LIKE I didn't do anything. I did. I talked to him—or tried. More than once.

There was nothing. His old man? Ray laughed. His old man was his old man—probably a good bet he wasn't going to find the cure for cancer. Every now and then he'd tie one on, get a little crazy—what else was new? It was like that thing about the leopard—asshole wasn't gonna change his spots.

For two days after he came in to school that morning he mostly slept. On the third I walked over to his house. It was one of those yellow, quiet fall days that feels like a memory of something else. I found him raking leaves in the front yard. Wilma was sleeping in the sun, fat as a tick.

I asked about his dad.

He was OK, he said. The two of them pretty much had it worked out where they stayed out of each other's way. Especially now.

I gathered an armful of leaves in a loose hug and walked to the chicken-wire cage standing in the shade and threw them in the fire.

"Why's that?" I said.

"Pissed about the X-ray, I guess."

"You got the X-ray?"

"Sure."

"When?"

He stopped raking, looked at me. "I don't know—couple days ago. Why?"

"No reason—just Karen said your side hurt, that's all."

He handed over the rake, picked up a pile. "Yeah, you know. But hey, check it out," he said, turning his face left and right like a man in a shaving commercial—"lookin' better, right?"

"Fuckin' Joe Namath."

"See? All good."

I took off my jacket, threw it on the fence. There was no wind. The smoke rose straight up, thinning out.

"God, I love that smell," he said, dumping a bunch of leaves in the cage.

◆ ◆ ◆

I TRIED AGAIN. It was always the same. He told me everything—about the Mexican guy, something Calderon, who put him down, about how he'd realized he was in trouble but figured he could snake his way out of it, about the look on his dad's face when he came home. Lucky for him the old man had his own shit to deal with—a week before he'd broken two fingers busting up a fight, had to wipe his ass left-handed.

"Your old man had to bust up a fight?"

"Regular family of brawlers, what can I tell ya? Not what you'd call your upstanding citizens."

We were sitting on the steps of the porch in the weak sun. Ray was picking shit out of the treads of his boot with a twig. Somewhere up the street somebody choked off a lawn mower—the last mow of the season. The bugs had died with the frost.

He pulled his boot closer. "I hate these squares," he said, flicking a spot of shit into the bushes.

"You were lucky," I said.

"Yeah, that's me—Mr. Lucky." Anyway, he was done with it, he said—he'd promised. He was studying for his license—the car was almost ready. Karen was giving him driving lessons.

I watched him push a small wall of shit down a groove like a twisting road. "Smells like shit," he said.

"No way."

"Yeah, some things you just can't explain."

The lawn mower coughed once, twice, then caught and rose.

"Keep thinking it's gonna get hot again," I said.

"Kiss it goodbye."

He banged his boot against the side of the steps, snapped off the end of the twig against the floorboard and went back to work. "Time to start thinkin' cold, your feet frozen, dick like an olive—"

"Not my dick."

"Olive *pit*."

He banged the boot. "There. Think I got it."

"So he's back on full-time?"

"Who?"

"Your old man."

"Guess so."

"So that's good, right?"

"I don't know. Probably not gonna be takin' me out to the ball-game as much, no more father and son talks—"

"—camping trips—"

"—playin' chess, hangin' out together . . . gonna be a bitch."

THE BURNING SMELL of the leaves, that cool dirt smell before you threw them in—sometimes it was like you could smell the sun. It smelled like stone, or wind.

I can see us there, Ray still moving a little slow—raking, piling, burning. I can see Wilma sleeping on the walk, the shadow of the porch cutting her across the shoulder—already pregnant, though we didn't know it then.

When you're used to something, it's hard to see it another way.

I could have asked him straight out. I didn't. I didn't want to embarrass him, I think.

I DIDN'T GO over to Ray's house much on the weekends, so it's a coincidence I was even there. I'd stopped coming by since we'd looked through his dad's stuff from the war. The few times I ran into Mr. Cappicciano now he'd act hurt that I didn't come around anymore. I'd been busy, I'd say—between school, track. He'd kid around with me, ask me about my parents, about school, what kind of car we were driving now. "Nice of you to grace us with your presence," he'd say, winking, then turn back to the TV.

I'd come by that day because I thought we could go to Bob's, or maybe grab a game of pool now that Ray had fixed things up at O'Reilly's. A windy day, small white clouds chasing themselves across the sky, leaves half-gone. I was restless—I'd been writing a paper on the First Amendment, figured I pretty much had it. So I grabbed my jacket and walked over.

They were already there—the cruiser parked by the curb as usual. I jumped up on the porch. "Better things to do," I heard one of the regulars say.

I'd knocked on the door before I realized it wasn't them.

They were standing in the living room, Mr. Cappicciano in a sleeveless t-shirt and pajama pants leaning against the case with the beer steins. I'd never seen these cops before. There were two, an older one with eyes like a cat's just before it goes to sleep or nails you, and a younger guy who looked like he'd had rocks for breakfast, with quick rabbity muscles in his cheeks. It wasn't a social call: they had their whole thing on—uniforms, sticks, guns, the whole bit.

"So who's this?" said the older one, turning to me.

"Friend a' Ray's," Mr. Cappicciano said. He had his arms folded across his chest, the apple with the knife wrapped across the muscle like a flag in the wind.

"What's your name, son?"

I told him.

"You a friend of his son's?"

"Just said that," Mr. Cappicciano said.

The cop looked at him.

I nodded.

He turned to Mr. Cappicciano. "Sir, could you ask your son to come down here, please?"

"What for?"

"We'd like to talk to him."

"What's he done?"

"Don't know he's done anything yet."

"Why do you want to talk to him, then?"

The cop smiled to himself.

"Ray? Come down here," Mr. Cappicciano yelled.

Ray paused when he saw the cops, then came down the rest of the way. He still looked pretty bad.

"Your name Ray Cappicciano?" the cop asked.

"That's right."

"Ray, I'm Officer Mayo, how you doin'?"

"I'm fine."

"You sure?"

"Yeah."

"You don't look so fine."

Ray shrugged.

"Where'd you get that is what we're askin'," the younger cop said.

"Some guys from Carmel," Ray said. "I don't know their names." He didn't look at me.

"Some guys from Carmel," the older cop said.

"Yeah."

"And you don't know their names."

"That's right."

"You do that a lot, am I right?"

Ray shrugged.

"You get along with your dad, here?"

"Sure, you know."

"I don't know."

"Sure."

The cop turned to me. "Your friend get along with his dad, would you say?"

"Sure," I said.

The cop looked at them for a while. "Alright," he said.

"Can I go?" Ray said.

"Yeah. You—stick around," he said to me. "Hey," he said when Ray was halfway up the stairs, "I hear about any more fights we're gonna have to talk again, you understand what I'm sayin'?"

"Yeah," Ray said, and went up the stairs.

The cop stood there a while, tapping a pen on a pad, and again I was reminded of a cat, its eyes half-closed, tail twitching.

"I'm gonna give you some advice, though I don't know why," he said to Mr. Cappicciano. "Talk to your kid—I don't want to have to come out here again." He nodded toward the stairs. "Kid goes to school lookin' like that, people are gonna jump to conclusions."

"None of their fuckin' business."

"People like me."

Mr. Cappicciano stared at him.

The cop smiled, except it wasn't a smile. "Somethin' I just say offend you?"

Mr. Cappicciano looked at me for a second, then shook his head.

"I'm sayin' reel in your kid—it looks bad." He turned to me. "Mosher, right? All right, why don't we step outside for a few minutes, get some fresh air?"

"He got nothin' to do with this," Mr. Cappicciano said.

The cop shook his head, turned around. "You know why God gave us shoulders? So you can only get your head up your ass so far. Don't push it."

Mr. Cappicciano's face had gone tight like somebody was pulling it from behind.

I looked at the cop. The cat had woken up. "What's the matter, Cappicciano—miss the good old days? What's it like not bein' a cop anymore?"

I glanced over at the younger one. He was hunched slightly forward, watching them, his hand near his stick.

"Nothin' to say?"

Mr. Cappicciano stared at him. You could see the skull under his skin.

"No? Nothin'? Let me explain somethin' to you, 'case you had any doubts. Far as I'm concerned, ex is out—I don't give a shit *how* many friends you got."

"You can't—"

"I can't? What country you livin' in?" He grinned and tapped the badge on his chest three times. "I can pretty much do whatever the fuck I want." He paused. "But you know that."

THEY'D JUST PULLED AWAY when Ray came out of the house. "Let's go," he said.

"Everything OK?"

"Didn't feel like stickin' around to find out. Fuck, it's cold."

We slowed down after we'd turned the corner.

"Where we goin'?" I said.

He stopped, turned his back to the wind, lit a cigarette.

"I don't know. You have practice today?"

"What're you—my coach now?"

"Sure, if I have to." He looked at me, not smiling. "What?"

"Nothin'. What?"

"Look, I'm not gonna let you fuck this up. I'm serious."

"Stop—"

"This is your year—you know that."

"Knock it off."

"You're gonna take that Belcher kid apart."

"C'mon—"

"C'mon what? What all the time?"

"Just—stop, OK? This guy's four seconds off the state record."

"So what?"

"So I don't want to talk about it, OK?"

"Fine."

We'd started walking again.

"We're all gonna do somethin' big this year. Karen's gonna get into some great fuckin' college, you're gonna be goddamn state champ . . ."

"What about Frank?"

"Frank's gonna stop playin' with himself . . ."

"Think?"

"I don't know—might be askin' too much."

"So what're you gonna do?"

"Me? I'm gonna get the fuck outta here, that's what I'm gonna do. Be like my whatcha call it, life's work." He smiled. "I can see it. Fifty years from now, some guy chippin' it outta the rock: 'Ray Cappicciano, RIP: Got the fuck outta Brewster.' "

"It's not all bad," I said.

"Think?—Everything good is leavin'."

We walked across the elementary school parking lot, empty for the weekend, then along the classrooms. It was quiet out of the wind. Ray stopped to look at the windows, which were covered with brown turkeys and stick figures with black hats.

"Remember doin' this shit?" he said.

"Sure."

"That smell?"

"I remember the crayons."

"Crayons, paints—all that shit. Those buckets of white paste they made us use . . ."

"Yeah," I said.

"Weird. I mean, that was us, too." He shook his head. "Nobody ever tells you stuff."

"Maybe they don't know."

He walked to the next window like it was a museum. "Check out this dog, man—it's like a potato with teeth."

I walked over. "I like the tail," I said.

He was still looking at the dog. "Listen, do me a favor—don't tell Karen about the thing today, OK? With my old man. I don't want to be puttin' a lot of ideas in her head."

"You sure? I mean, nothin' happened."

"No, I know. Still."

He moved over to another window.

"What'd you tell 'em, anyway?"

"The cops? I don't know, I told 'em what you told 'em."

He nodded slowly, like it was something to get his mind around. "OK," he said, and we headed off toward the Borden Bridge.

HE'D JUMPED from the weedy bank to a tire stuck in the mud when I asked him why he hadn't told the cops about Danbury. He didn't miss a beat. Wasn't legit. If he told them about it, they'd close it down.

Made sense, I said.

He jumped back to the shore and we pushed up through the bushes decorated with trash from the spring floods, holding our arms up like boxers covering up. It was almost dark.

I'VE NEVER LIKED PARTIES, never been good in groups. All those voices talking at the same time. I came to a party early once and there were only eight or ten people there and it was fine but as each new person came in you had to talk a little louder, and because you were talking louder everybody else had to and soon everybody was yelling and you could hardly hear a thing.

That fall was like that—all these people screaming about college applications and the League of Nations and "*Señor Mosher, hágame el favor de darme su libro,*" and me in the middle not really hearing any of it. By the time Thanksgiving came around, the only thing I would have been thankful for was a little peace.

I didn't find any. Now and then a voice, a line, would float up out of the racket and hang in the air where you could see it. That November I'd talked to my parents—we still ate dinner most nights, it wasn't always crazy—and told them I was thinking about traveling around with some friends the next summer. My father wanted to know where we'd be going, how we'd pay for it.

"With that girl you're always with?" my mother said.

"She's not my girl," I said.

"Suit yourself," she said.

◆ ◆ ◆

THAT WAS ONE. That "suit yourself" rose above the noise. It wasn't much, but it made me furious and weak like a kick in the balls and I played it over and over in my head, turning it into speed, into pain, into fifteen 220s one after the other like a chain saw coming down, pushing Kennedy through the curves, making him earn it, forcing him to bring it out because he was the only one who could make me hurt anymore.

We trained together now, just the two of us. Moore would do what he could for the first few, then drop back to the second group. We didn't talk much. We were all in. I'd think about it, plan for it. I'd go in hungry. If I ate anything after twelve o'clock, it would end up on the infield grass.

I never knew what drove him. Never asked. I accepted the beatings he gave me on that cinder track—and they *were* beatings, leaving me retching, staggering around—like a younger brother who's proud to be noticed and *knows* he's growing. He didn't think he could take Balger alone, he told me one night as we jogged back past the science classrooms because the track had turned into a quarter mile of mud—the bastard was nationally ranked now. But we could beat North Salem *and* Balger in the two-mile relay.

How did he figure? I said. We were both working hard, talking between breaths. "Moore, OK," I said, "but—we don't have—anybody for fourth."

"Kid—mustache," he said.

"You're kidding—Peter?"

"He's comin' up," he said. "Their fourth is slow, too—Peter's close—two, three seconds."

We were approaching the line. Falvo stood to the side in the lab room doorway holding a stopwatch and a clipboard.

"Anyway doesn't matter—if we spot 'em a few seconds. Ready?—I know what you can do."

"Suit yourself" and "I know what you can do." There were others that came through the blur of tests and papers, the ten-milers along the roads at dusk with the sweat freezing the ends of my hair into mats and some moron driving alongside offering me a ride because it looked like I was in a hurry, har-har, but those two stood out because they fed and fought each other in my skull: "Suit yourself" because I wasn't worth talking to, because I was pathetic, because I wasn't even man enough to admit what I felt, because no matter what I did I would never be what he could have been. "I know what you can do" because maybe there *was* something I could do, because it was my only answer, because if he'd lived I'd still be faster than him.

I'd think about it when I ran, feed on that mix of shame and rage, draw on it like a straw. I'd run him down like a wounded deer. I'd run him down as easily as sleeping. I'd chase him till his heart burst like a popped balloon and kids sucked bubbles out of the rags and popped those too, and I'd do it, gliding away like air, just to see the look on her face.

What a perfect noise those two made in my head. Even now it's amazing to think I managed to do anything at all those few months, to answer questions about Ezra Pound's black branch and the nitrogen cycle and what kind of corrective cookie I'd recommend for those fallen arches as if all the time a storm wasn't raging in my skull. Only Ray and Karen understood, Karen because she could hear what you were saying even when you weren't, because she could see exactly how fucked up you were and care for you anyway, Ray because he had his own storm, twice as black and twice as loud, and recognized the look.

It's why we were friends. I'd disappeared the day my brother died. He dreamed of nothing more.

Ray and I started walking again that fall, not as much as we used to, but close. I don't know where I found the energy. Sometimes on the weekends or if it wasn't too late Frank would come with us, or Karen if she didn't have work to do. All those miles we walked, I don't remember much. Stay somewhere long enough, you don't see it at all.

Mostly I remember the two of us pretending it was still summer, casting for bass off the spillway into the wind, our fingers too numb to flip the bail. The June before, Ray'd found a couple of spinning rods in the weeds that some drunks had left and the first time he felt that tap and his line started making those crazy figure eights you'd have thought he was ten. "Oh shit, oh shit—I got one," he yelled, then jumped to his feet and started walking backward till the fish flopped in the weeds. It was a perch, I remember, black bars across its sides, fins edged with orange. They always were beautiful. I got a kick out of his excitement. The way he held it, you'd have thought it was made of glass—or gold.

We got into it pretty heavy, picking up tips from the old guys at the tackle shop, exploring along the shores of the reservoirs whenever Karen had something going on. It was an escape, like most things—we didn't pretend it was anything else. We had some times, some laughs, climbing into the trees along the shore to get the lures others had broken off because we couldn't afford a buck for a hula popper—even caught a few fish in the bargain. It was good. Makes sense we'd want to hold on to it.

It didn't work. With the leaves down you could see the headlights from the traffic winding through the woods and the sky would be like it gets in winter and it just didn't work. One weirdly warm day the four of us went back to the embankment like we used to, but the water was too cold to swim and the fish had stopped biting and we just sat around on the bank in our sweatshirts till we decided to leave. There was no point in pushing it, we said. You had to know when to let it go. There'd always be another summer.

The last time Ray and I went out to the reservoir casting for bass in the coves must have been around the 10th because we talked about how we only had two weeks left of school before Christmas.

They didn't do Christmas at his house anymore, Ray said. Used to be he and his old man would give each other something, and of course Gene when he was home—there'd always be something for him. He was thinking he might go out to Yonkers this year.

I told him that we used to have a tree and he was surprised because he'd never seen one at our house. Not often, I said. Once before Aaron died, another time when I was seven or eight. For a couple of years my dad had hung up lights on the bushes until he stopped.

"But you're Jewish," Ray said.

"We're not really anything," I said.

A cold fog was hanging over the reservoir. The water looked black. Ray reeled in and tucked the pole under his arm and blew on his fingers.

"These fish aren't stupid, man. They're probably all hangin' out down there, sittin' around their fish fires—"

Talking kept my teeth from chattering.

"—tails sticking out of their electric blankets, eating fondue . . ."

"What the fuck is fondue?"

"This cheese stuff you dip bread in—saw it in *Playboy*."

"Shit, we should be using that—stick some fondue on a hook."

"Or a good book."

"That's it—a big, fat book with a fishhook through it."

He cast out. The lure made a little white circle in the water. "Fuck, you cold?"

"I was cold an hour ago," I said.

A FEW DAYS before the end of school he came up to me in the hall. He was trying not to smile. I should come by the house, he said, he had something to show me.

She was lying in a corner of the living room on a blanket, five puppies the size of hamsters nosed up to her belly. Ray sat down cross-legged on the floor in front of her and Wilma thumped her tail twice on the boards without lifting her head. I'd never seen newborn puppies before.

"Can you believe this shit?" he said.

When he gently popped one off a nipple it started to mew like a kitten. He put it in my hand. It lay rocking back and forth in my palm, its tiny legs sticking out to the side.

"Amazing, right?"

"Unbelievable."

He took it back and gave it the tip of his pinkie and it began to try to nurse. He smiled. "Not much comin' outta there, little guy."

I turned around.

He was leaning against the kitchen doorway, wearing only a pair of boxers. I was surprised how white his body was, the thick thighs, the neck wrinkled like some kind of animal hide, the tight gut with its broad stripe of hair, the reddened nipples. When he moved his weight I could see his dick shift under the cloth.

"Didn't think we'd be seein' *you* again," he said. "Now I know what it takes."

Ray took the puppy back and pushed it up to Wilma's belly, wiggling it back and forth like he was fitting a rubber pipe on a nozzle.

"How you doin', Mr. Cappicciano?" I said.

"Somethin', huh?" he said, nodding toward Wilma and the pups.

"Sure is," I said.

"Sure is," he said, smiling like a man clawing his way out of a well, "sure is. Hey, but that reminds me, you're such a stranger these days, I didn't know when we'd see you again. Gimme a sec—I got somethin' for ya."

"What's *that* about?" I whispered when he was out of the room.

Ray didn't answer. He'd stood up as soon as he'd put the puppy back.

Mr. Cappicciano came back in the room holding a hand-sized box. It was wrapped in deep blue wrapping paper with a small, silver ribbon.

I just stood there.

"Now I know you Jews don't celebrate Christmas—"

"You didn't have to—" I began.

"—and I don't really know about Hanukkah—"

"—Really, you—"

"—but I figured, you know, 'Season's Greetings' is kinda everybody, right?"

"Sure, yeah, thank you," I said, taking the package. The wrapping paper had tiny silver lettering on it that said "Season's Greetings" over and over.

"Figured 'Season's Greetings' might be all right."

"Sure," I said, "thank you."

"So, fine—go ahead, open it."

I glanced at Ray.

"Don't look at him—he had fuck-all to do with it."

I looked at the package.

"This is just from me to you—outta respect to you and your family."

"You sure? I mean—"

"Go ahead."

I started to pry under the scotch-taped flap like a girl.

"Go ahead. Plenty more where that came from," he said.

Wrapped in tissue paper I found a velvety black cloth embroidered with a skull and the letters SS like silver lightning bolts.

I didn't know what to say, how to act. He seemed sincere, sober—he wanted me to like it. I remember standing there, my face burning like I was embarrassed.

"I don't . . . thank you," I said.

"You're not offended?"

"Me? No. Thank you, it's . . ."

"I figured, you know, who better than you people to have it? Take a little of your own back."

"Sure, no—thank you," I said again.

He smiled, then turned to go back into the kitchen. "Give my regards to your parents. Oh, and Merry Christmas—or whatever."

WE TALKED THAT YEAR about going down to Times Square, the four of us watching the ball drop. Or the hammer, maybe. Paul Grecco's brother Tommy had come home dead for Christmas, and even though I hadn't known him, just like I hadn't known Jim Sinclair or Mark Gonzales's older brother who we heard was learning how to use a fork again in some VA hospital in Virginia, it got to you anyway. Everywhere you looked there were pictures of sweaty reporters with helmets on their heads and GIs sliding stretchers into helicopters like they were feeding something. We wanted to be done with '69.

In the end Ray and I watched it on TV with the puppies teething on our sneakers. Frank had told his parents he didn't want to teach Sunday school anymore and they'd grounded him for vacation. Karen had gone with her parents to Pittsburgh. She called just before midnight and Ray talked to her as the ball went down. "Me, too," he said. "Really," and then "Yeah, he's right here," and handed me the phone and we clanked beer cans and I talked to her for a while as the year 1970 flashed quietly on the TV. It looked strange, almost unnatural, like everything could be different now. She wanted to know how Ray was doing and I said he was good, and then she said, How're *you* doing? and I laughed and said I'm fine, everybody's fine and she said, Really? and I said, Yeah—really truly. She'd had a bad dream the night before, she said—it was like all day she'd been carrying it around, and I said not to worry about it, it was just a dream. I never asked.

We sat and watched the TV for a while. Ray's dad wasn't coming home that night and I hadn't felt like sitting at the dinner table with mom and dad listening to Walter Cronkite tell me how it was. Anyway, in my house there were no new years.

I don't remember a lot of what we talked about that night. We messed around with the puppies for a while, piling them on top of each other, flipping them on their backs. Their fur had come in. One was brown like Wilma, one was black and the other three were in-between. At some point we heard sleet on the window, dry, like sand, like somebody was trying to get our attention.

Maybe it was the beer but somehow we got onto Frank and from him to God and from God to what happened when you died. It was hard to think of people actually being gone, Ray said—you expected them to just be somewhere else, like on vacation. Like any day they could just pop up. And he told me about a farm they used to go to when he was a kid that had been run by an old lady with warts like pencil erasers on her cheeks named Mrs. Kelly. She'd been dead for years and the farm sold and gone, but some part of him still expected her to be where he'd seen her last, twisting the dirt balls off the lettuce or coming up from the root cellar. Even weirder, he expected it to be summer—a chilly morning, everything still wet. It was like she was fixed there—like in a snow globe.

"Except summer," I said.

"Maybe that's what heaven's like," he said. "Just being stuck in somebody else's head."

I said I didn't know.

We thought about it for a while. The beer had slowed us down.

He looked at the TV. We'd turned the sound off. You could hear the wind shaking the windows, rattling the walls. "Yeah, I don't know, you know?—The way I figure, if nobody thinks about your ass after you're gone, that's pretty much it."

"Guess so," I said.

The sleet hissed against the glass.

He shook his head. "Fuckin' Tommy Grecco, man. Never liked that clown."

SOMETIMES, sitting on my bed in my room, I'd take my stop-watch and press the button just to watch that second hand fly. Imagining it, seeing it. Sometimes I'd be running lead-off, standing with five or six others in the miler's half crouch, the lane narrowing like a dagger. A little unsteady, bumping shoulders—listening for the gun. Other times I'd be running anchor, waiting for the baton as the third man hit the straight, that mask of pain on his face, feeling the tickle of pee escaping into my jockstrap.

I'd press the button, explode off the line, heart pounding, hands slippery with sweat, watching that needle sweeping with terrible swiftness around the face, twenty seconds, thirty seconds, fifty, a minute. Stop. Press again. All I thought about was time.

The half-mile, a controlled sprint. If you didn't have speed, you didn't run it. Every race had something—the half-mile was special because it was right in the middle. You could be a quarter-miler, stepping up, and lose to a miler with speed who'd wear you down. You could be a miler coming down, trespassing, and get eaten up by the velocity of it.

Time—what we could do with it, how we could make it add up at the end. A two-mile relay meant four runners running a half-mile apiece. If all four ran their half in two minutes—a bragging time in high school back then—it would make an eight-minute two-mile relay. Except that hardly anyone had four runners who could run a two-minute half. They might have one guy. Or two. Maybe. And then there was the question of where to put the star—at the start, in the hope that he could break it open, gain such a lead that the other teams would fold? Or at the end, as anchor, figuring that if all was lost and you were ten yards behind at the handoff, or twenty, he could somehow bring it home?

Peter Michaelis, Mr. Time Tunnel, had run a 2:10 that December, hopeless except for the fact that North Adams's fourth guy was only a second faster. Moore could pull a 2:04 on a good day, giving away another second to their third. The summer before, I'd slipped under 2:00 for the first time, which matched me up pretty well with their second-best. Kennedy was our answer. He'd run 1:57 flat, could do it again. Balger might have the power in the mile, but Kennedy had the speed.

Numbers, split times—it was my obsession. We became a club, a unit, the four of us pushing each other, yelling to each other in the early dark as we came around the curve, the wind cutting through our sweats. When Peter ran 2:09 at an early indoor meet, stumbling around afterward like a cut puppet, you'd have thought we'd won gold in Mexico City what with all the hugging and back-slapping and Falvo yelling "Banzai!" from the sidelines. Moore lifted the poor kid clear off the ground. It seemed to matter then. It seemed to matter a lot.

THE HOLIDAYS SLID BY like a stone over ice, leaving nothing much to remember. A couple of cloudless days so cold it hurt the inside of your nose to breathe, a couple more of wet snow when Karen left for Pittsburgh. At night you'd see the porches standing out like colored frames in the dark.

I ran, I listened to music, I sold some shoes in my dad's store.

We worked quietly, handing each other things; when we talked it was usually in code—shank and footbed, tongue and throat—one of us calling, "Can you get me a ten and a half double E in the Stacy Adams Ox black piping?" or suggesting, straight-faced, sitting next to each other on the fitting stools, that maybe old Mr. Hennessey might like to see the Florsheim Mods. I was surprised to see the respect my dad's customers had for him—I'd never really noticed it. It was like he was some visiting ambassador selling shoes on a whim; he'd smile and offer the kids a lollipop out of the jar he kept by the register, and the parents, who'd been smacking the little brats a second ago, would beam like a lollipop was some old world rarity and say, "Isn't that nice? Now what do you say to Mr. Mosher, honey?" and when they were leaving he'd say, "Lovely to see you again" and, "Thank you so much for coming" and see them to the door with a smile and a nod—almost a bow—and they'd try to do the same back.

"Why do you always do that?" I asked him once.

"It is the way I was raised," he said. He was putting some shoes back in their boxes, checking the labels to get it right.

"Can I ask you something?" I said.

"Of course. Ask."

"Do you like doing this?"

He smiled at the penny loafer in his hand, then laid it next to its twin and covered it with tissue paper.

"It is what it is," he said. He put the lid on the box, then stacked it and stood up. "You have homework this weekend?"

"Some, yeah."

He nodded. "Go. I can finish up."

AS OFTEN AS WE COULD that winter the three of us would go visit Frank—he was allowed to have visitors—watching our language, stepping carefully. Frank's mother would always wipe her hands on her apron and apologize about everything like you were the Pope but if you said something wrong you'd see her wince and she'd stop talking. Frank's dad was a short guy with little veins in his nose who always seemed pissed, like everything you said tried his patience. He'd set up a manger on the front lawn, a small wooden house with a wall missing, three Wise Men, a donkey, a horse, and a bunch of plastic sheep. The Christ child, a doll with a tinfoil halo, lay in a wicker basket on real straw. The Three Wise Men were set up on the side, two of them standing, one on his knees like he'd been kicked. They didn't look surprised or happy. They just looked blank. We said something to Mr. Krapinski about the manger, how it must have taken a lot of work, and he said, what if it did, Christ had died for our sins after all, and we agreed.

That winter Karen gave me a copy of Albert Camus's *The Stranger* which floored me when I read it though I only half understood it. "Mother died today, or, maybe, yesterday, I can't be sure." That's how it started. It was about this Algerian guy who kills some Arab for no real reason. We kept talking about it, the two of us, trying to figure it out, but my feeling was there was nothing to figure out. This guy, Meursault, was who he was. He was like a sack that's been filled up with certain things—just like all of us. When he couldn't take it anymore, he killed somebody. And it didn't matter to him. It was like some kind of natural law—sooner or later it would have its say.

She was with Ray a lot so I didn't see her much, but when I did, that's what we talked about. How you stood things, or not. Like Hemingway, we said. He'd stood things as long as he could. Some things were so bad you couldn't laugh at them. Others were so bad you had to—or shoot yourself, like he did. Or somebody else, like the guy in *The Stranger* did. The worst things, we agreed, were the things you couldn't touch.

+ + +

THAT JANUARY 28TH I turned eighteen. I didn't expect anything. We didn't really celebrate birthdays at my house—a kiss
and a shirt, maybe, or my mother might make *Wiener Schnitzel*
for dinner—and that was ok with me. Mostly I'd just want to get
through. We'd all put a brave face on it—my father would tell his
joke about the old guy wanting to die in the Holy Land ("To die,
OK, but to live here?") and my mother would smile and shake her
head—the three of us marching steadily on toward the Obsttorte,
straining not to hurry, to say the right things, like people on a tour
of a house they hate.

That night, long after we were done, my dad knocked on my
door and asked if I could talk. I thought he'd gone to bed; my
mother had been asleep for hours. I moved some stuff over and he
sat at my desk and asked if I was still thinking about traveling the
next summer—that he thought it was a good idea, for a young man,
travel. I said I didn't know and he nodded and looked around my
room and said, "I know that it is not always . . . ," and stopped, like
he'd forgotten what he wanted to say.

He reached behind his back and handed me a small box
wrapped in blue wrapping paper with gold noisemakers all over it.
I was just glad it didn't say "Season's Greetings." *That* one I'd hidden in my closet where it lay ticking like the guy's heart in the Poe
story, waiting to bury me. I'd taken it out the night before after
locking my door, terrified they'd hear the bolt sliding home in their
sleep. What would they say if they found it there, hidden like a
bookmark in the first volume of the *Encyclopaedia Britannica*? How
perfect that would be. The bastards had taken their first life, and
now the son who'd taken their second was hiding their treasures in
his closet. It was almost poetic.

It was a watch.

"Thanks," I said. "Really, it's—"

"It is no-sink," he said. Twenty-five years in this country, I thought.

"Thanks," I said.

"It is from both of us—your mother, too."

I didn't say anything.

"So, OK." He patted my leg, then got up to go.

"Thanks," I said again, and he nodded and left.

THE NEXT DAY, Karen returned from Pittsburgh and Christmas break was pretty much wrapped. A day later Frank was released from house arrest straight into school. He still wasn't teaching Sunday school, he said. He had a right. He was gonna come to California with us, he said.

ONE THING I'M SURE, you can't tell about love, or the lack of it, except from the outside, from the way two people look at each other, from the things they do. It's like the way you can tell about a house, about the people in it, whether they're happy, from the way it looks from the street: A small pot of marigolds, a couple of chairs in the shade, tells you pretty much everything you need to know.

I could tell what they had. I could tell by the way he'd wrapped her up in that big coat of his that day in the rain, like he was a magician who could make them both disappear, by the way she'd walk next to him, or look at him when he talked to other people, that look saying, "This man is mine and I like how he is—how he moves, how he laughs—and he knows it and it's the two of us from here on, for everything." It was easy, unforced—walking down the hall, she'd touch his elbow with a finger and he'd turn like a ship; she'd sigh and he'd look up. Sometimes at lunch, or in the library, you'd catch them looking at each other, a kind of calm in their eyes like after a smile, or before it, and know they were talking.

She loved him—what more is there to say? There were times I'd look at them and feel something in my chest and throat, an ache that made it harder to breathe, but I was OK with it. I can say that now. I was OK with it. I didn't know it then, but I loved them both. Who's to say which one of them more?

It was the pot of flowers, the chairs in the shade. I knew they'd get married someday, have kids, that they'd have their shit just like everybody else but that she'd be looking at him the same way when he was eighty and I was OK with it. Some people can't deal with love, can't admit that the thing they wanted once, the thing they'd finally managed to convince themselves doesn't exist, is real and true and right in front of them. So they sneer at it, make it small. I wasn't one of them. I could see it for what it was. What I couldn't see was how deep that kind of love could run, how reckless it could be.

Maybe it had something to do with them being eighteen. At thirty you see options—or invent them. At eighteen it's all or nothing.

THE SUNDAY BEFORE, walking home from Ray's, I'd felt a tickling in my throat like there was something there I couldn't swallow. By dinner I was throwing up in the upstairs toilet. For five days, that whole week, I was down and out, feverish, hacking—too sick to wonder why nobody had called or come by to see how I was doing. My mother brought me soup, took it away, checked the thermometer, left. I was older now. All I could think about was the Cardinal Hayes meet coming up at the Armory. February 2nd was supposed to be our first real test.

Karen called but I never got her messages—not one. Sweating through my sheets, I'd hear the phone ringing downstairs, my mother answering.

I asked her about it later. How could you not tell me she called? I said. It's not right, I said.

She was making out the bills on the kitchen table. "I have other things to think about."

"I'd tell you," I said.

She wrote a return address on an envelope, flipped it over. "Anything else?"

"No, that's it."

She moistened the flap with a yellow sponge, sealed it, tore open another with her thumb. I was glad I couldn't remember a time when she'd loved me.

After a while I went back upstairs.

That week I had the same dream twice. I was flying around a tilting indoor track in the near-dark, leading the pack, when I felt confusion rising in me like nausea. It was completely silent. A huge, empty hall. I had to keep going. I had to. Even though there was nobody there—no timers, no tape, not a soul who would see or know—I couldn't stop. I raced on—curve, straight, curve. Like there was someone behind me. Like it mattered.

I wrenched awake both times and just lay there breathing through my mouth, understanding where I was now, listening to my heart.

WHEN NEITHER OF US showed up at school that Monday morning, she waited through first period, then went to the attendance office. Mrs. Santoro looked in the ledger. I was out with the flu, she said. She turned the page. Nothing about Ray. No surprise there.

At lunch she asked Frank, who hadn't heard anything. He tried to make her feel better. "You know Ray," he said.

She nodded.

"He's probably plannin' something. I mean, look out there. If I had somewhere else to be, I wouldn't be here either."

When he hadn't called by dinner, she tried to call me. I was sick, my mother told her. Sleeping. When she called Frank, he told her to call Ray. Don't worry about his old man, he said. Ray'll understand it's 'cause you were worried. So she called. There was no one home.

Tuesday was the same—no Ray, no answer. She called me from the guidance office. I still slept, like Snow White after the apple.

She walked through her day, bell to bell, gym to lunch, trying to come up with a story to explain it all. In English she missed an entire conversation and couldn't answer when Mrs. Schrot called on her. She had to apologize. She was distracted, she said. This was her senior year, Schrot said. What could possibly be more important? She didn't know, she said.

That evening she couldn't work, imagining cars split around trees, fights—seeing Ray broken on the steering wheel, staring face-up in the ring. She thought about talking to her parents but didn't. Not yet. They were cool, but next summer was still tricky. He'd disappeared? Fights? What was this about?

She made it to Wednesday afternoon. It had snowed the night before, looked like it might again. A sky like steel—the smears of smoke from the houses going straight up. It was cold enough to snow. There'd been no answer. She'd thought about borrowing the car to come see me, had called from school. I was sleeping, my mother said. Perhaps she'd like to call back some other time.

The bus stopped, the driver pulled the door release. Crows, a quick yell, a hard gust of cold. Someone toward the back had a radio, was flipping through stations: "In the news . . . the Dow Jones . . . President Nixon said . . . and then the familiar three-steps-up, three-steps-down opening of "Son of a Preacher Man" and she was off the bus, the doors closing behind her on that sweet, smoky voice: *the only boy . . .*" It was something she could do. It wasn't far. Maybe there was something wrong with the phone.

She had to ask directions once, stopping in at a gas station, glad for the warmth, then walked across the bridge with the river running high and cold and turned at the church. Four o'clock and almost dark. She knew the area. She'd just never been to his house.

She found it easily enough. It looked resentful somehow—forgotten. She'd always felt that he was ashamed of it, now she knew why: the caved-out railing, the stained shingles, the pile of rain-warped boards and chicken wire in the yard . . . there was a light in an upstairs window, another, smaller one, toward the back. A car was parked in the driveway. It had started snowing.

She didn't hesitate when he opened the door, though it was obvious he was drunk. He stood there looking at her throat, his hands on either side of the door frame like he was trying to push down the house from inside. His mouth was slightly open. Was Ray in? she said. He swayed like the house had moved. She said it again. Was he home? Could she talk to him, please?

His eyes climbed up to her face, slowly, and something like a smile closed his mouth. Who wants to know? he said. You?

Ray hadn't been to school all week, she said. She'd been worried. Some of his friends were worried.

His eyes, as if pulled by gravity, had dropped back to her throat, then went further. She'd been worried, she said, pulling her coat tighter around her, feeling the anger and something else growing inside of her. His eyes began their slow climb back. Well, isn't that nice, he said, when they'd reached her chin.

"Please," she said, "I . . . ," but he'd already pushed himself away from the frame and was walking into a small, half-bare living room. She could see a couch, a coffee table with bottles on it. A dog was lying against the wall on some kind of blanket.

"I'll just see if he's in," she heard him say. He walked back and disappeared.

When she walked into the room the dog raised its head, then lay down again. She didn't notice the puppies. She was thinking about the upstairs light, the porch, the door. The man—it had to be his father—came back with an open beer and sank down on the sofa. He'd been in the kitchen, she realized.

She tried again. "Can I talk to him, please?"

"What can I get you?"

"I'm fine," she said.

He smiled, took a pull of his beer.

"Thank you anyway," she said.

"A beer?"

"Really."

He scratched his crotch like a man strumming a guitar. "Somethin' harder?"

"No."

"Whatever you want."

"I just came to see if he's OK."

"What's your name?" he said, and then: "He'll be right down."

She told him. "He knows I'm here?"

"That's a pretty name," he said. "Sure."

"How does he know I'm here?"

He took another pull, looked at the dog, then around the room like he'd never noticed it before, then back. "You don't have to be scared," he said.

She hadn't been. "You know, I really think I should go," she said.

"I told you, he'll be right down."

"Really."

"Really," he repeated. His eyes started to close and he caught himself. "What can I get you?"

She hadn't thought he could move that fast, didn't quite believe that he had. He was between her and the door, still holding the bottle. He'd bumped into the table as he jumped up and the dog had growled from its place by the wall. He laughed. "Can you believe that—my fucking dog."

She could feel her heart pounding against her coat. A voice far back in her head was telling her she was in trouble, but she only half-believed it. This wasn't happening. She looked around for something to grab.

"You don't want to go," he said. He smiled, and the sadness of that smile told her how bad it was.

"I just know he'd like to see you happy," he said.

"Karen?" she heard him say, and her knees almost buckled. She didn't turn around.

"Well, if it isn't my son."

"Get the fuck away from the door," Ray said.

"What did I tell you, huh?"

Nothing moved.

Ray stepped in front of her, tight, his body brushing her coat. "Get away from the door," he said. He was holding a round, thick piece of wood as long as his arm. She didn't know when she'd picked up the screwdriver.

"Well, aren't you a pretty pair," he said. "Sure." He moved to the side. "Enough?"

"More."

"Like that?"

"More."

"Far as she goes."

"I'm not asleep now," Ray said.

He smiled. He was pushing his lips around in a circle with his finger, unaware, his eyes heavy like a child dropping off to sleep. When he smiled, the finger pushed the smile into a sneer, an idiot's grin, a quick baring of teeth like he was snarling or showing them his gums, then a smile again.

"I'm not asleep now, am I?" Ray said.

The head wobbled and he caught himself. "You little fucker," he said, smiling.

They walked toward the door, turning slowly like plants to the sun, then backed up the rest of the way. She felt behind her for the doorknob. She didn't realize she was sweating till the cold air hit her back.

"It was nice meeting you," he called. He was walking toward the kitchen, steadying himself along the back of the couch. "You two have fun."

AND SO, pedaling away in empty air, we fell. We weren't the first—it happens all the time.

I can see them hurrying away from that house, her coat around *him* this time, holding him up. Like the couple in that painting, *The Storm*, except with no scarves or gauze or bullshit. She's the one leading and it's winter and this is another kind of storm altogether. It's over, he's saying. He's not going back. It's done.

Except they're eighteen and it's dark and it's not. It's twenty degrees out. I can see them hurrying down the hill to the store, Ray hugging himself in the cramped little aisle with the chips and the toilet paper while she gets the key and goes out to the bathroom and takes off her angora sweater and puts on her coat again and comes back and gives it to him and he pulls himself into it. They have to think, they have to go.

They try not to look at the clerk, who's leaning sideways, watching them. Like they've done something wrong. Like either of them has ever done anything wrong.

"This ain't no dressin' room," he calls out.

"Sorry," she says.

"That's right," he says.

◆ ◆ ◆

HE DOESN'T WANT the hospital, Ray says. They might call his old man—who knows where that could go? Anyway, it's not that bad. They're out, that's all that matters. Let the bastard find him.

"OK if we just warm up a little?" she calls to the clerk. "Can I borrow your phone?" and he stares at them a long while, then points and she goes to the phone and buys them time. She'll be out late, studying with a friend, maybe a movie later . . .

They have to go, but where? She tells him everything—that I've been sick, that she hasn't been able to talk to me all week. What about her place?

"I can't come to your house like this," he says, standing there in his soaking sneakers and her yellow angora, coatless, bandaged, swollen.

It might be OK, she says. They're cool, they might understand. She'd explain.

Explain what? he says. And even if she *could* explain, they'd never let her go after that. I love you, he says. We're leaving—soon, summer—all we gotta do is get through and we're gone. I'm not gonna fuck that up.

I'd go anyway, she says. I don't care.

He waits, biting his upper lip till he knows he can say it. I know you would, he says. But you do.

He looks ridiculous squeezed into that yellow sweater, like an action figure that's been thrown around a lot.

Anyway, it's just for a night or two, he says. I just gotta figure it out for a night or two—just till Jon's on his feet.

She'd be the one to think of it. She'd gotten thirty dollars for her birthday—a grandmother and an uncle she never saw. She'd been saving it for a prom dress. She'd never wanted to go. It was just her mother kept telling her it was one of those things you'd remember.

And he'd ask her. Right there in the snacks aisle with the lights hitting off his bandages. Like a suitor in a fairy tale, the cooler buzzing in the background.

Would you've gone with me? he'd say.

Are you asking? she'd say.

I'm askin'.

Yes, she'd say. Anywhere.

I CAN SEE THEM walking those four miles to the El Dorado on Route 22, Ray's head and arms sticking out of the garbage bag, rustling quietly. They'd take the tracks just in case, over the trestle bridge, then up to the long shore of the reservoir, walking carefully because stones and shadows change places in the dark and everything looks like something else. And he'd take off the bag in the parking lot and she'd pay for the room and the red-headed guy would keep looking back at the TV and they'd walk up the outside stairs in the cold and let themselves in and close the door.

And maybe they'd make love even though he couldn't move much because they'd just made it through something and because they'd never had a place that was theirs before. And later that night she'd put her sweater back on and he'd take the thin blanket from the bed and wrap it around himself like a Hollywood Indian, then pull the garbage bag over it in the parking lot and walk her the three miles to Putnam Lake, because he'd insist, then back.

WHEN I OPENED THE DOOR that Friday he was wearing her father's old sweatshirt and a winter hat with flaps like Elmer Fudd's. She'd brought him food in plastic bags from the cafeteria. Mary had asked after him, listened as Karen told her what she could— then went to work.

"Oh, my God," I said, when I saw his face.

"Heard you been sick," he said.

"Ray, what the fuck happened?"

"Don't worry about it. Listen, you think I can crash here for a while?"

I pushed open the door. My mother was walking by, dragging her chains.

"Hiya doin', Mrs. Mosher?" he said, taking off the hat.

She stopped when she saw him. "You're hurt," she said.

"I'm fine," he said. "Looks worse than it is."

She nodded, turned to the stairs. Three steps up, she stopped. I could see her small, clenched back. When she turned, our eyes met for a second and she glanced away.

"Come in the house," she said, looking at Ray.

"Really, I'm fine."

"Please." She paused, then said it again. "Please." I could hear the shaking in her voice, like another person in the room we'd all agreed to ignore.

"Sit," she said, when we got to the bathroom.

And she went to work, a kind of current trembling her lower lip like she was cold, carefully peeling back the bandages, cleaning the cuts, even, at one point, shaving along his cheekbone. "It hurts," she'd say, wincing, and he'd shake his head and she'd take the cotton ball I had ready for her, then tell me where to find the little scissors, not like I should have known but just to tell me. When she pressed the cut on his temple closed with her fingers, I noticed how old her hands had grown. "Good," she said when I put the tape across it. I couldn't remember the last time we'd done anything together.

HE COULD STAY as long as he wanted, I told him after we'd gone up to my room; we'd done it before, it was no big deal.

"Could be for a while," he said.

"Long as it takes," I said, and he nodded quickly and blinked and looked at the carpet. He had that look that people have when they're holding on, chin out like he was feeling a sore tooth. It came out as a whisper. "I'm sorry, man," he said.

It took me a while. "Your dad?" I said.

He looked past me into the living room, shook his head.

"Stay as long as you want," I said.

He waited till he could talk. "I don't want your mom and dad to know, OK?"

He stayed a week. Barely.

HE HAD NO CHOICE, really. He had no clothes, no stuff, no schoolbooks—everything was back at the house. He had to go back.

It had all come out—bits, pieces, like a loosening drain.

It hadn't always been bad, he said—you got used to things. He could take him when he was awake—hold his own, anyway. Thing was, lately he'd started coming after him when he was asleep. Sometimes he'd be sorry after.

He didn't know why. Most nights the booze helped because he'd just drink till he passed out. Most nights. Then there'd be a bad one and it would be like somebody had pressed a button under the couch. Something would set him off—could be anything, anything at all—and he couldn't stop.

Why didn't he go to somebody? I said. Tell somebody?

Where do you go when your old man's a cop? You saw it yourself.

Hit him? Fuck, yes, he'd hit him back—more than once. It didn't make things better, didn't make 'em worse. He'd clocked him in the jaw with a lamp, broken his arm. Nothing changed.

One time, lying on the carpet in his room, crying, he told him he'd tell somebody, the cops, somebody.

"I'm pretty fucked-up, just hanging on 'cause you don't wanna black out. 'I'm gonna fuckin' tell somebody,' I'm mumblin', 'I'm gonna fuckin' tell somebody.' I can see him standin' over me. He's got the drawers of my dresser open and he's pissin' all over my stuff. 'Go ahead, call the cops you little fuck,' he says. 'Oh, wait a sec.'"

He'd get into fights to cover it up, he said, figuring if everybody thought he got into fights, because he did, they wouldn't ask. His old man knew how to hurt you without it showin'—it was his job. Problem was, when he drank, he'd miss—or get carried away.

We were sitting in my room listening to the Stones turned low, which doesn't work. Ray had spread out my sleeping bag in the usual place along the wall, set up the milk crate with a t-shirt over the top to keep his things from falling through the holes.

You got used to stuff, he said. It'd been worse when Gene was around. He'd see it starting—could be baby food on the wall, whatever—and get in the way.

"That was a cool thing to do," I said.

"Yeah, pretty fuckin' heroic. They're gonna have a show about me—any day now."

"Seriously," I said.

"Doesn't count when it's your brother," he said. He couldn't split so long as Gene had been in the house, but ever since he'd gone to live with Suze in Yonkers, things had been different. Cleaner. And now they were both out of the house. He was gonna swing by and pick him up on his way out of town, he said. He had it all worked out. He'd stop at the Red Rooster. He'd have a burger and a shake waiting on the back seat.

I asked about Yonkers.

Suze knew. Enough, anyway. She'd be good with it.

We listened to Jagger doing his bad-boy thing.

"Under my thumb," he said, like he'd never heard the words before, then nodded, blinked, and looked at my poster of Marty

Liquori gliding through the tape. "Motherfucker's gonna be under *my* thumb, this time."

He wanted to know if Frank and I would come to the house with him to get his stuff. We could go when his old man was at work, he said.

"Sure," I said.

"Just to get my shit," he said.

"Sure," I said.

It wasn't a laugh, or even a smile; just a quick outbreath of air, amused, dismissive, disgusted—like when you're looking at your own hand cut open on a can.

"What?"

"I don't know. It's just—"

"What?"

He shook his head, and for a second I could see what he'd looked like as a kid.

"What?" I said.

"He's supposed to be my dad, you know?" he said.

WE ATE DINNER that night, the four of us, like we were a real family on TV—subdued, serious, trying to understand this new crisis. My mother brought out the plates, all business. When Ray tried to say it was good, she waved it away: "It's not important."

"And these boys who attacked you," my father said, his jaw set—"they have been arrested?"

He didn't know them, Ray said. Didn't know their names. Nothing the police could do.

"But why would they do this?" my mother said.

He couldn't say. There was this girl he'd been talking to down in the village, Ray said. Maybe that was it.

"You should eat," my mother said.

"And this happened where?" my father said.

"What?"

"This attack—it happened where?"

"The ice pond," Ray said, "out by Dykeman's."

"Do you go to this place?" my father said, looking at me.

I shook my head.

"You must be careful with these thugs," my father said. "Both of you. People are capable of anything."

"This we know well," my mother said.

"Anything."

"Let him eat, Samuel," my mother said.

My father looked down at his plate, then cut a piece of meat but didn't bring it to his mouth.

"And your father, what does he think of this?"

"He'll be back next week. He's on a job. I talked to him on the phone—I mean, he's worried, but you know, what's he gonna do?"

"Your father's away for a week?" my mother said, confused. "Who is looking after your little brother?"

"Gene's stayin' with my aunt, in Yonkers."

We ate quietly for a while.

"You must be careful, both of you," my father said, sounding almost angry. "I don't want you going to this place anymore—this ice pond."

"Let them eat, Samuel," my mother said.

WE DECIDED on that Thursday—it was as good a time as any. Karen would drop us off with the empty suitcases a block away— just in case, Ray said—and the three of us would pack up his stuff and bring it to the car. She could keep it at her house—nobody would know a thing.

We'd be back for dinner, we told my parents—we were just going out to meet some friends.

My father looked up from his book; he'd been coming home early all week. "You're not going near that place?" he said. My mother appeared in the door to the kitchen, wiping her hands on a dishcloth. "No, nothing like that," Ray said, "just around the corner." We'd put out the garbage when we got back.

We found Karen and Frank parked just around the block.

Ray kissed her through the open window. "Thanks, baby."

"I don't like this."

"Frank, man—you good?" They clasped hands.

"This doesn't make sense, Ray," Karen said.

"It definitely makes sense."

"It's just stuff—"

"*My* stuff."

Nobody said anything else while she drove the few blocks, and then she pulled over and we got the suitcases out of the trunk and

Ray kissed her and we started off, walking side by side into the dark like traveling gunfighters.

A wet snow, a soggy dusting on the tops of the bushes and the leaves. He couldn't wait to get his boots back, Ray said—he'd been sucking up puddles all week.

"Your old man have a gun?" Frank said. He'd started smoking since the Sunday school boycott, grown a dirty beard that made him look tougher.

"He's a fuckin' ex-cop," Ray said.

We could see the house now. There was a small light upstairs. No car.

"You think maybe that's a problem?"

"Wanna go back, go back."

"Not what I'm sayin'."

"He's not gonna shoot nobody. Besides me, anyway."

"I'm just sayin', you know, considering we're bustin' into his house and all."

"We're not bustin' into his house," Ray said, turning into the yard. "We're not even bustin' into *my* house. We're just gettin' my shit and closin' the door behind us." He put down the suitcase and pulled his keys out of his pocket. "There's not a goddamn thing he's got that I—what the fuck?"

We walked around to the back, letting ourselves through the door in the fence hanging off its hinge. It was the same thing there. Ray had stopped talking. "You sure it's the right key?" we kept saying. "Try again." Wilma and the puppies had been barking for some time. It was like walking around a kennel.

We had come around to the front again when Frank noticed the piece of paper halfway down the porch. It was wet so it tore but he peeled the two halves off the boards and brought it back and we made it out by the light from the street. "You want your shit?" it said. "Try the weekend."

Ray balled up the note and threw it down the porch. "Fuck him," he said. The dogs were still going, Wilma's mixed in with the thinner yaps from the pups. "Fuck him—that's my stuff."

"It's OK, man," Frank said.

"No, it's not. It's not fuckin' OK." He looked at me. "Your thing's on Saturday, right? You good for Sunday?"

I nodded.

"How 'bout you, man?"

"Sure," Frank said, and then: "Sure it's worth it?"

"Oh, yeah," Ray said. "It's definitely worth it."

We met Karen walking down the street in the dark to find us. Which didn't surprise anybody. She'd been worried, she said.

It never occurred to him to tap a pane, let himself into his own house. Which makes sense, because it wasn't. And we didn't think of it.

THE THUNDER IN THAT HALL. The fear you felt walking in from the bus and up those greasy stairs through the smell of the hot dogs and the heat rub, every step pulling the shell closer to your ear, the roar growing like a coming wave—it's amazing you could breathe at all. I keyed off of him, watched him going through his ritual—his hands tying the headband around his hair, his lean face calm as water, every movement deliberate, measured, unmoved. Who knows? Maybe he keyed off me as well. Truth is, I'd barely slept.

It had never scared me more. Never meant as much. I was ready. If anything, the flu had done me good, made me rest.

We put down our stuff in the bleachers. Falvo returned with the schedule. The two-mile relay was event seventeen. We had three hours. Relax, he said. Pretend you're taking a nap. You know they're watching you. He grinned. Have some fun, he said. Stretch their heads.

We looked around that sea of bodies, trying to find them, pausing at every patch of red. Everyone looked pretty much the same, but somewhere in that crowd was a medium-sized white boy with John Lennon glasses whose legs and heart and lungs could endure what most people couldn't imagine enduring.

"You all right?" Kennedy said.

I nodded.

He grinned. "Gotta throw up, do it early."

"I'm not gonna throw up."

"There he is. Don't sit up."

He led me to him without pointing—second row, three groups down from the purple sweats. "Got him?"

"Yeah," I said. "Glasses, drinking something."

"That's him."

"Didn't he have some kind of beard last time?"

"Maybe. This is this time."

He stretched his leg out to the wooden railing and I lay down on the bench.

"Hey, Peter, man, you gonna run me a 2:08 today?" I heard him say. The crowd roared at something happening in the pit below, drowning out the answer.

Three hours. The week before, on a calm day on a dry track, I'd run a 220 in 23.6. Without sprinter's blocks, wearing sweats. I had the speed, I told myself. I could inflict it when I chose. I closed my eyes. He didn't look like much.

Minute by minute we filled up the time. Like dropping pennies in a jug. Mr. Kennedy found us, sat down a little ways off, unzipped his jacket. When I looked, he smiled and put his fists up like a boxer and bobbed his head a little and I smiled back. John went over to talk to him, then came back. "My dad says to break a leg—the other guy's. His idea of a joke."

"Might be on to somethin'," I said.

We talked a little, tried to sleep, took a walk down to the basement past the food stalls and down some corridor with locked doors, passing groups of other runners in their sweats, their racing flats in their hands or tied over their shoulders. We tried watching the races for a while but it didn't feel right, like we were running down some kind of battery, so we stopped. Moore had brought a radio. When "Fortunate Son" came on, somebody yelled to turn it up but as soon as we did the guys from Archbishop Molloy a couple of rows over turned up "I Can't Help Myself" so for a while it was like a beer milkshake till Falvo yelled at us to turn it down and the Four Tops took over, Fogerty's voice falling down a well, defiance to pleading, "It ain't me, it ain't me . . ."

It was time, Falvo said.

FORTY-FIVE MINUTES OUT he sent us to the warm-up corridor, a long hallway in the basement where runners in sweats jogged, loosened up, then ran quick wind sprints as best they could down the hard floors, then jogged some more. "A twenty minute warm-up, gentlemen," Falvo said. "I want a fifteen-minute jog after you stretch, then repeat fifty's. I want your heart rate up. I want to see some sweat. When you're done, meet me here."

I didn't look at him when he passed, the sheen of sweat on his face, the glasses under the hood making him look like some kind of studious monk, didn't think about the tight little mincing jog, the arms held high like he was worried he might break—it didn't fool me. I'd seen those choked-off little steps on runners lining up for the Olympic final in the 1,500 meters, knew you could hold it in tight as a fist, then open it when the gun went off, unleashing something overwhelming. He nodded to Kennedy as we passed, just a tip of the chin, then jogged to the end of the hall, turned and accelerated so smoothly you could barely tell he was moving except for the posters on the wall flying past his head like windows on a train.

He came by again, looked right through me like he was hypnotized. No nod, nothing. He didn't know who I was. He'd know, I thought. I'd make him know.

We found Falvo in the bleachers, scribbling on the clipboard.

Their second-best was leading off, he said—Balger would be anchoring. Their idea was to break open a lead, hold it, then have him finish it off. They expected us to do the same, to put me in lead-off, Kennedy at anchor. We weren't going to play, he said. He tapped his forehead with his pencil. We'd mess with them, he said, we'd stretch their heads: We'd give them the lead. He wanted Peter running lead-off, then Moore.

Peter started to protest.

Falvo gently shut him down. "Listen to me—are you listening? You play to your strength. Some runners, mentioning no names, need the competition—it's personal for them. You don't. This guy has nine, maybe ten seconds on you. You're not going to see him. It doesn't matter. I know you. You won't get sucked into something you can't handle. You'll run against the clock."

"Coach is right," Kennedy said.

Falvo put his hand on Peter's shoulder. "My boy, you give me a 2:09 or better and I don't care if we spot them twenty yards, or thirty."

Moore would cut it down, he said, then hand off to me. I'd get us the lead, and Kennedy would tie it off. He grinned, cowlick bobbing, then beckoned us closer like a sorcerer in a fairytale.

"Banzai," he said.

FUNNY WHAT NERVOUSNESS can do. Or fear. The runners, the timers, the coaches milling around the end of the track fall away, the crowd is like a highway at night. It's like you're not really there. You can feel the sweat, the drops of pee escaping your dick, even answer when they talk to you—handing you your number, confirming your name, saying "Gentlemen, you will only be allowed to step out for the handoff in the order that your team is coming in"—but you're not really there. You're sitting down to pull off your sweats because you're too nervous to trust your balance, you're watching your lead-off man walk to the line like a lamb to the slaughter, adjusting his shorts, fiddling with the baton, but you're not really there. You're huddled in a cave with your heart, listening to it boom. The noises from the outside world are coming from somewhere far above you.

And then the gun that starts things instead of finishing them cracks and they're off, seven runners, seven teams, racing flats pounding on the wooden boards and he comes by, already five yards down, concentrating on his pace. He comes around again and you yell even though you know he won't hear you and then he's there again and Kennedy is standing next to you. "Sixty-five quarter," he says, because he knows you know what it means, that Mr. Time Tunnel is right on pace, watching the boards ahead of him, beginning to bear down, and then he's there again. This should've been your race, you think. Their guy came through in 59. You could've taken him. You know that. You could've run him down like a dog. It doesn't matter. He's there again, a lap to go, his face changed now, his legs like weights, twenty yards behind and beginning his push. Moore is standing by the handoff line, shaking it out. You wish him luck and the North Salem guy gets the baton and goes and Moore barely nods, waiting, waiting, waiting, and Peter staggers in and slaps it in his palm and he's off.

Five laps to go till it's you. Four laps. Three. You squat down quickly to double-check your shoes. Breathe, breathe. Kennedy's standing there next to you, cool, watching. "Peter pulled a 2:08.5," he says. "We're in it."

"Their guy ran 1:59," you say.

"I know," he says. "We're in it anyway."

Two to go. Moore's working hard now. You can see Balger off to the side—strong, pale legs, big calves for a runner. Moore comes by, already hurting. In second place, maybe fifteen yards down. Balger looks slowly around the crowd, lenses winking white—like a camera panning by. Use it. Make him see you. Make them all see you.

One to go. You're on the line, Kennedy still there, standing by the outside rail. He looks up at the clock. "Might need a little help on this one, Jon," he calls, starting to pull off his sweats. And he smiles and you know what courage looks like. "Just get me that stick, OK? Kill this one for me."

Their guy walks out, arrogant prick, grabs the baton and he's gone and you wait, wait, not feeling your legs, not feeling anything and then Moore's staggering into the infield and that aluminum tube is in your hand and you switch it to your right and go. You want to burn him down, now, immediately, make him pay for those seconds you had to wait but you can't. You can't.

Somewhere there's a crowd, four thousand people yelling, Falvo with his stopwatch, Kennedy's dad punching the air, but you don't hear them, see them. One down and he's coming back to you. Peter's face flashes by. Balger's out there somewhere, that squat little fuck. He thinks he can take it. That it's his. He doesn't know you, doesn't see you. He'll see you. Two down and the alarms are going off in your chest, your gut. It's fast—too fast. Three laps to go. Your legs feel heavy, the snap isn't there. Save it, save it.

Two laps to go and you don't hear your split. He's strong, leaning into the curves five yards up, maybe six, and then the pain starts to come on and you know he's yours because he's feeling it too now and because you know this fire better than anybody, because the hotter it burns the higher you'll build it, because you'll walk into that furnace and sit on the couch.

You're right on his shoulder. He knows you're there. And then you go, leaving him like a bullet leaves a gun. This is everything. Everything you have. First they ignore you, motherfucker, remembering what Herb Elliott's coach said before the 1,500 in Rome: Don't pass them, bury them. Destroy their spirit. Go, go, go—don't let him back. Pull away. Leave him behind. Kill him. This is yours, by God. And the track is unwinding and there's nobody there, just boards and air, and you pour it on like fuel, more, more, more, and you know you've never felt speed like this at the end of a half mile and suddenly Kennedy's there, his hand reaching back, something like wonder on his face, and you slap the baton in his hand. "There you go," you say, and he's gone.

And so you win. Because he's John Kennedy after all, because he takes that twelve-yard lead and pays it out like rope as Balger comes on in the last lap, letting it slip to ten, to eight, then stops it right there and goes through the tape, parting it with his left hand. Moving it aside like you'd move a girl's hair from her face.

And for a while it matters. It matters even after you hear that Balger was sick that morning, that he insisted on running even though he'd thrown up twice before the race, that the wet skin, the glassy look, weren't what you'd thought. It doesn't matter. So what if it took balls for him to get off his knees in that overused bathroom and rinse out his mouth and run? So what if he ran a 1:57 half mile with the stomach flu and then, still in pain, took his hand off his knee just long enough to shake yours and say "Good run, fellas—see you at States, yeah?" Still. You run the race you run—there's always going to be something.

It's quiet on the bus. By Katonah it's night and the snow is coming down, busy in the taillights, lightening the sky. The reservoirs are like puzzle pieces lifted out of the woods. Falvo has the trophy next to him—a foot-high runner welded to a tombstone, one leg back, one arm up like he's racing for a bus. They've given you a medal—you can feel it under your t-shirt, like a welt between your ribs.

You run the race you run.

THE NEXT MORNING Karen drove us over and let us off and we walked down the street to Ray's. Again. The two of them had been living at the motel; she'd stay till midnight, like Cinderella, then hurry home. He'd worked out a deal, Ray told me—odd jobs for a room that would be empty anyway.

"WELL?" they'd said, when they picked me up that morning. "So?" They hadn't been able to make it. When I told them Karen screamed and Ray grabbed me and swung me around and then they got me in a two-way hug.

"What'd I tell you?" he kept yelling. He punched Frank in the shoulder. "What'd I tell him, right? Never fuckin' listens to me." He pointed at me. "We get back I wanna see the medal. I can't *believe* we fuckin' missed it."

"I just couldn't get the car," Karen said.

"States is Saturday, right? I'll make that if I have to crawl," Ray said.

He looked around, the smile slowly pulling back into his eyes. "Fuck it, let's do this thing," he said.

◆ ◆ ◆

IT WAS DIFFERENT, knowing he'd be there. We took the suitcases, started walking. A dull winter day, the sun just a thin spot in the blanket. Somebody was chopping at the ice, then scraping it up with a shovel.

We turned the corner. Mr. Cappicciano's Pontiac was in the drive.

"Let me do the talking, alright?" Ray said.

"No problem," Frank said. I looked over at him—the scraggly beard, the big neck. I was glad he was there.

"You OK?" I said to Ray.

"Fuck it, what's he gonna do?" He licked his lips. "All I want is my stuff, right?"

The dirty snow, the dull little houses—it was like the world had been rubbed with an old eraser. We followed him up the steps of the porch. It smelled like ashes and wet wood.

Mr. Cappicciano answered the door on the second knock. He had Gene in his arms. He smiled, then raised Gene's wrist and flopped his hand up and down like a puppet waving goodbye.

"Say hello to your brother," he said.

IT WAS LIKE SOMETHING closing—you could hear it, a quiet *click*, the tongue in the latch.

"Come in, come in," he said. "It's cold out there."

"What're you doin'?" Ray said quietly.

"Hi, I'm Ray's dad," Mr. Cappicciano said, extending his hand to Frank.

Frank took it. "Frank Krapinski. Pleased to meet you, sir."

He grinned. "Well, I'm pleased to meet you, too, Frank." He'd let Gene down on the ground. "Here, why don't you put your stuff down," he said. "You boys want somethin' to drink?"

I glanced at Ray, who has a smile on his face like he'd been shot in the stomach.

"Something to drink, son?" Mr. Cappicciano said.

Ray shook his head.

"Coffee? How 'bout you, Jon?"

"It's not gonna work," Ray said quietly.

"Now don't be like that," Mr. Cappicciano said. He smiled. "We're family. This is a whatcha-call-it—a new leaf. Bygones be bygones."

"It's just not," Ray said.

"Start from scratch, water under the bridge. Whaddya say?" He pulled Gene over to him by the hand. "Say, 'Whaddya say, Ray?'"

Gene laughed, the inside of his mouth blue from some kind of candy.

"Go ahead, say, 'Whaddya say, Ray?'"

"Whaddya say, Ray?" Gene yelled.

Mr. Cappicciano tousled his hair. "Way to go." He looked at Ray, who hadn't moved since he'd put down the suitcase, and smiled.

"Whaddya say, Ray?" he said.

I DIDN'T SEE much of Ray after that. I left his things out because it made me feel better to see them, but after a couple of days I rolled up the sleeping bag and put the milk crate back in the closet. When my mother asked, I told her Gene was back at home. He seemed fine, I said. I folded up the t-shirt Ray had over the milk crate, put it back in the drawer.

I spent a lot of time talking to Karen, to Frank. There was nothing to do.

He'd probably be missing some school, he told Karen—there was no way around it. He'd figure this out. He would. Just needed a little time, that's all.

She'd caught up to him in the parking lot. He'd told her everything.

"What am I supposed to do?" he said. "What do you want me to do?"

"We can call somebody," she said. "We can talk to my parents."

"About what? He hasn't done anything."

She stared at him like he was losing his mind. "Jesus, Ray. Baby, how can you say that? He's . . ."

"Lately. What has he done lately? What're you gonna tell 'em, that he used to beat me up?"

"Maybe—sure. Why not?"

"And what do you think's gonna happen? Ask Jon. The cops came, the cops went."

"So what're you saying?"

Ray shook his head, pulled his collar up. He was still strong, still himself. "Look, there's a way out of this. I just need a little time to figure it out is all."

"When will I see you?" she said.

"I don't know," he said. The wind picked up, lifting the snow off the roofs of the cars. He pulled her close and she could feel the warmth of his body through his coat and he held her tight, then said it again into her hair.

I WENT OVER a few times to see if he could come out, grab a game of pool. It wasn't a good time. He had to watch Gene. His old man would be back soon. I'm sorry, man, he'd say.

OK, I'd say.

Behind him I'd see Gene sitting on the couch, his legs sticking straight out into the air.

"So how's the runnin'?"

"Good."

"Yeah?"

"Pretty good."

"I'd give you a beer but since my old man's been suspended—"

"I heard."

"Really?"

"Karen told me."

He nodded. "It's just I never know when he'll be back."

"Everything OK?" I said. "You know."

"Listen, you been back to Jimmy's?" he said quietly, like the porch could hear.

Over his shoulder I could see Gene sitting on the couch holding a plate over his head, laughing. A puppy was standing on the couch, its front legs on his chest.

"Not lately," I said.

"Go."

"I—"

"Because I can't right now. Tell Karen—she'll drive if you need to get somethin'."

"OK," I said.

"I got this thing worked out, man, but I need that fuckin' car."

The hot dog rolled off Gene's plate behind the couch and he screamed. There was a rush of puppies. I laughed—I couldn't help it.

"He made me drop it," Gene was yelling.

"Forget about it," Ray called. "Just let 'em have it an' get yourself another. And use the fork—the water's hot." He shrugged. "Fuckin' Nanny Ray, man. Place is a mess. Lucky he's too little to know the difference."

He looked at me. "OK? About what I said?"

"I will," I said.

THE NEXT AFTERNOON I walked down the tracks to Jimmy's. The East Branch was running strong, pushing under the ice shelves growing out from the bank. Some were snowed over, others gray and thin so you could see the bubbles underneath swelling up and shrinking like something under a microscope. Here and there the water gushed up through quarter-sized holes.

The night before, the snow had woken me up—it was like I could feel it in my sleep—and I'd sat up and pulled the curtain over and watched it coming down, trembling in the light from the street. Something moving against the snowy lawn next door had caught my eye. It was Mr. Perillo, clearing his drive like a sleepwalker, pushing the shovel ahead of him, then walking back. It was snowing hard. The shovel would make a black stripe like a finger across a foggy window, then start to pale. It was three thirty-five.

I'd been dreaming—people I'd known forever, who knew me. I'd never seen them before.

I looked upstream—the weighed-down bushes, slumped over the water, the panes of ice, the current pumping through. There'd been no wind—every twig carried its rickety ridge of snow. I'd always liked going this way. How many times had we walked it? It seemed like hundreds.

I FOUND HIM working on a brown Karmann Ghia, sleek as a frog. He had the radio turned low—some guy laughing.

"Don't get to see one of these every day," he said, wiping his hands. "So let's see the hardware. The medal—let's see the medal."

I didn't have it, I said.

"Thought you'd have it around your neck like Superman or somethin'."

"Superman's got a medal around his neck?"

He took a key off the peg board, looked at the tag, then put it back and took another.

"Haven't seen your friend in a while." He pulled his glasses out of his pocket, flipped them open, wiggled them into place.

"He's got a lot goin' on."

He glanced out the window over his glasses. "Nice out there." He went back to looking through the keys. "How's he been?"

"Busy—you know."

He tossed me a key. "Go ahead, turn it over."

"What's this?"

"Might have to do some shoveling."

I was holding the key. "Wait a minute," I said.

"Go ahead," he said.

✦ ✦ ✦

He'd had some spare time, he said. No big deal. Anyway, he needed the space on the lot.

I sat there in that snow cave feeling the engine thrumming under my feet, then rolled down the window, punching away the flat wall as the glass came down. Snow blew in on my lap. "Jesus, Jimmy," I said.

He took off his glasses, flipped them shut like a pocketknife, then stuck them in his shirt pocket. "So tell him she's ready," he said. He nodded. "He did some good work on this car. You, too."

I started to say something and he waved it away, then blew into his hands and looked away.

"Send me a postcard from somewhere," he said.

"OK," I said.

"Anywhere," he said.

I called Ray that afternoon from the phone booth in front of the hardware store. It was done, I said. I said, "It's done, finished."

There was a moment of silence. "It's done?" he said.

"Done."

"Oh, man," he said. I could hear the dogs yapping in the background. "Oh, man," he said again.

"Yeah."

"OK," he said. "OK."

I was looking at the steamed-over windows at Bob's, the little hill of snow on top of the traffic light. A pickup truck with firewood drove slowly down the salted wheel tracks and turned left at the station. My dad's store was a block down.

"Jimmy says you can pick it up anytime," I said. There was an inch of muddy slush on the metal floor of the booth.

"OK," he said. "That's it."

"I think so."

"He's back, I gotta go," he said.

✦ ✦ ✦

THAT WAS SUNDAY. He came to school the next day and we talked about the car. Nobody else could know, he said. Especially now. Not even Frank.

Karen told me she and Ray had started packing. He'd brought a duffel bag out to Jimmy's, left it in the trunk. He'd duct-taped the key to the exhaust pipe—he didn't want it in the house. That way they could leave anytime, he said, whether the garage was open or not.

Things had been quiet lately, she said. Ray's dad had even said Suze could take Gene for an overnight and bring him back Wednesday evening. They might just get through this, Ray'd told her.

He wanted her to finish school. She said there were bigger things. They'd talked about it a long time but in the end he'd promised that if he had to run, he'd come for her.

What about her parents? I said.

They'd have to understand. Still, it might not come to that. Maybe Gene being back in Brewster might even be a good thing. Whatever else Ray's dad had done, maybe he had his limits. Maybe something had changed.

TUESDAY MORNING I could see the sky clearing out, the cold coming in sharp and thin like somebody had drawn a line with a razor. I was up for my run at five—double sweats, hat, gloves, the whole deal. Walking out into the dark, I could see the clouds being pushed east to the horizon, behind them empty night and stars like glass. An easy three miles.

We'd begun peaking, easing back on our training. States were two days away. I did my loop, part way around Bog Brook Reservoir, then up the long hill, listening to my flats crunching on the frozen snow, then headed back, showered, caught the bus. Ray wasn't in school but Karen had talked to him. He was taking advantage of Gene being in Yonkers and his Dad out of the house for the day and taking another trip out to Jimmy's. A camp stove, books, sleeping bags—they had the car pretty well packed.

A sleepy day. They'd cranked up the heat because of the cold and sitting in class you'd feel your head filling with soft gray lines like an Etch A Sketch and the teacher's voice shrinking to a point and then your head would snap up and clear and immediately start filling up again. I saw the kid from the projects, Larry, in the hall and nodded and he said "'S'up, man," and then, still walking, "How's that cat doin'?" and I said "Alright" but by then he was halfway down the hall.

That afternoon Falvo called the four of us into his office. He'd been debating whether to tell us, he said, decided we should hear it from him. The weekend before, running in a college meet in Easton that he'd somehow talked his way into, Balger had run a 1:52.9 half mile. It was the sixth-fastest high school time ever run in the United States.

I WALKED HOME alone that afternoon. Winter dusk, cold. The sky a deep, deep blue. I hadn't walked down Brewster Hill Road in a long time. I could make out the junker rusting on its grill, barred in by trees, and I remembered Ray lying in the middle of the road, his arms out like Jesus, telling me about this girl he'd just met who could walk out of the woods and tell him to lie down in the road and he'd do it. It didn't seem like a year ago. More than a year ago.

It was OK, Falvo had said to us. Balger had run an amazing time, but he'd have to do it again. The world would do what it did. We'd run our race.

For some reason, it worked. Or maybe it was the walk, the road. It was OK. Saturday would come and we'd do our thing and it would be what it was. I looked at the sky, like blue ink in a bottle when you turn it, so still, so beautiful it seemed like a promise.

THE NEXT DAY Ray came by the house. We had the day off—a teachers' day. It was just after lunch. I was in my room, listening to the radio and reading when I heard the knock. My father opened the door for him. Coming down the stairs, I could see the boots first, then the pants, the coat, the sweatshirt hood. He was wiping his feet self-consciously on the mat, apologizing for the mess. He should dress more warmly, my father was saying—it was quite cold out there.

"And how is your little brother?" my mother asked. "Jon tells us he is back home?"

I hadn't heard her use my name in a long time.

"You still have that auger we borrowed from Jimmy?" he said, when I came down.

"It's like ten degrees out."

"C'mon," he said.

IT WAS HARD in the snow because we couldn't see the ties, but going by the tracks was half a mile shorter so that's how we went, me lugging the auger, Ray the folding chairs and the rods, the two of us pushing through, then up into the woods and out onto that great white circle, flat as a coin.

The wind had mostly died. It was very cold. I can see us cutting out from that shore, a pencil ticking the radius, the two of us squinting against the glare. The trees in the distance looked like scratch marks somebody had made with their thumbnail.

It wasn't like he didn't talk. He did. We both did. How you knew it was cold by the way the snow creaked. About Karen. About the meet on Saturday. I told him about Balger, the amazing time he'd run in Easton. We'd just have to run our race, I said, that's all there was to it, and he agreed. "You're just gonna have to do this thing, man," he said, and wiped his nose with his sleeve.

We threw down our stuff. We were a long way out, a quarter mile, maybe more, and I cleared the snow off the ice with my boot and stood up the auger and bit the blade down. I started to crank it and felt it catch, the steel like a circular stairway crisply hissing, then stopped and moved the blade out of the shallow bowl I'd made, and Ray got down and scooped it clean and I put the blade back. It took us a while. The ice was a foot thick. More. Toward the end Ray took off his gloves so he wouldn't get them wet and scooped out the slush with his hands, then waited kneeling in the snow and blowing on his fingers while I kept on till the slush gave way and the black water came welling up.

We scooped out the last of the ice and slush and threw it in the snow and I looked down even though I knew I wouldn't see anything. It was perfect, clean, a bullet through the heart. I opened the chairs, set them up with our backs to the breeze. The shore was far away. Turning the auger had warmed me up so I rigged our rods, pulling the line through the guides. What about trying spinners? I said. He nodded. He was looking off across the lake like there was something out there, slapping his hands together. Since we didn't have bait, I said, looping the line around itself, pulling the knot tight. He could go first.

It was hard with gloves but he flipped the bail and let the spinner fall into the dark, then turned the handle to stop the line and started jigging it up and down.

"You hungry?" I said. "We should probably eat those sandwiches before they're solid."

He didn't say anything when he felt the strike, just swung it up into the air. He yanked off his glove with his teeth and caught it, its tiny orange fins pressed flat under his square thumb, its tail quivering like it was carrying a current, took the hook out and slipped it back in the hole and began to shake—his face, his shoulders, his arms trembling like he could come apart at the joints—the look on his face less terror than disbelief, whispering "Fuck, oh fuck," like a man being shown something he'd never wanted to see and could never forget. "Ray, Ray, you OK?" I kept shouting. I'd jumped up out of the folding chair. I didn't know what was happening. I was scared shitless. "Ray! Ray, you sick? Ray!"

I just held him—I couldn't think of anything else to do. It was like holding a tree in a high wind. I could feel the gusts and then something broke and the sobs started and I just stood there holding him, petting his hair awkwardly, looking over his shoulder across that buried lake. We were a long way out.

The story came out of him in spurts, in horrible clotted bits, and what he couldn't say, I could picture for myself. I'll always see it—it doesn't matter. His old man starting early the afternoon before, standing in the kitchen with the glass next to him cutting up a chicken with the meat shears. Not talking. The house is empty without Gene. The TV is on in the living room: *The Price Is Right*. He can hear the shears cutting, feeling for the joints, springing open, cutting.

He can tell.

"I'm going out," he calls.

No answer.

"You hear what I said?"

Nothing.

He looks into the kitchen. His old man is standing by the counter, a drink next to him, slicing up a chicken. He can tell it's slipping.

"I'm going out," he says again.

"How long you think it would be before I found out?" He doesn't look up.

"What're you talkin' about?"

He can feel it. In the pauses, in the way he's cutting.

"Small town," he says, slicing off a leg.

The shears are bad. There's nothing to grab—a broom, a rolling pin. By his feet, leaning against the living room wall, is a busted picture frame—he could pull the top piece.

"Think you were just gonna leave?" He's still cutting. There's nothing left to cut. "Just drive away?"

"I don't know what you're talkin' about."

"Not much of a car anymore." He's pressing hard, clipping through bone. "Not much of anything anymore."

"We're leavin'," he says. "I don't give a fuck what you say."

"Just leave me here? That it? You and that little cunt?"

"I don't care what you say."

He grunts, snapping through. Ray reaches down and pulls the top piece off the frame. It comes off easily, two thin nails sticking out of the point. It's not enough.

"We're leavin'," he says again. "You hear what I said?"

"That right?" He picks up the glass with the hand holding the shears, his pinkie extended like a socialite, and takes a long drink, the open jaws by his face. "You're not goin' anywhere," he says quietly. "Not in this world."

HE WALKED OUT, listening for movement behind him, wondering if his old man was drunk enough to shoot him. Karen picked him up by the gas station. It was almost dusk. He didn't know how to tell her about the car, their plans—any of it. He had to think. They went back to the hotel, ate macaroni and cheese and apple crumble sitting on the bed with towels across their laps. She could tell something was wrong. He was sorry—he was just thinking, he said. After midnight she went home. At five he woke up and walked back to his house in the dark.

It was dawn when he let himself in the back, the first light just catching the windows. The house was dark, still. The first thing he saw was Wilma whining and scratching at the kitchen door.

It took him a long time to get it out. He hadn't understood what he was looking at—dark socks with pink circles? They were laid out in a row on the counter, legless. Their new fur matted and greasy. He'd gotten them all. One was still moving somehow. He closed his eyes and hit it with the meat mallet. Then hit it again.

WHERE DO YOU GO? When you're seventeen? When there's nowhere to go?

An unlocked bulldozer, a construction on the access road. We climbed up out of the wind. We'd left our stuff.

He had to go, I said. He had to run.

Where?

Anywhere. Oh, my God, I said.

He didn't even know what he was doing, he said. He'd picked them up one by one and put them in a plastic bag. Their faces, he said. He tried not to look at the bowl, just spilled it into the bag with them and walked out.

Oh, my God, I said. You gotta get out.

He didn't see his old man till he was halfway across the living room. It had been dark when he came in. He was lying on his back between the couch and the coffee table like a man in a coffin. His eyes were open and he was looking up at the ceiling as if he didn't remember where he was. Then something passed through him and he knew and he rolled over on his side, his legs banging against the coffee table and brought his knees to his chest and covered his face and whined. Like some kind of animal.

I told him. "Run, I said—you gotta run, Ray."

"Like some kind of animal," he said.

"You can't go back there," I said.

He'd put them in the dumpster at the A&P, he said. He didn't even know he was carrying them. He just looked down at one point and he had this bloody plastic bag in his hand and he walked over to the dumpster and put them in. He hadn't realized he was walking to my house till he turned down our street.

"You gotta get out," I said.

Their faces. He'd never forget their faces.

"Listen to me," I said.

Ever.

"You gotta run."

"I got nowhere to go," he said. "Don't you understand?"

"He'll fuckin' kill you."

"He'll find me. He'll find all three of us. He's an ex-cop. Where am I gonna go? Tell me where to go?"

"The cops."

"The cops?"

"Tell 'em. How he threatened you, beat the crap out of you. How he—"

"What? Killed a bunch of dogs? They'll say he's fucked up, it ain't against the law. Everything else is my word against his."

"He'll kill you."

He was running his hand over a rip in the seat. "I should've fuckin' left 'em there. I should've left 'em for him—to see what he did."

"He knows what he did."

"Fuckin' make him look at it. Make him look at what he did."

"What're you gonna do?" I said.

A kind of numbness seemed to be coming over him. Like he was talking to himself. "What am I supposed to do? What the fuck am I supposed to do?"

"Ray, what about Gene? Ray."

He laughed. "He's comin' back. Today."

"Oh, my God, Ray, what the fuck are you gonna do?"

He looked over at me squatting against the door and started to say something, then shook his head and smiled—an end-of-things smile, a bottom-of-the-well smile.

The wind blew, rocking us. He wiggled the stick shift, like he was looking for a gear. "I don't know," he said.

He KNEW I WAS RIGHT—that he couldn't go back there. I knew he would anyway. He'd go because he had to. There'd be no one to call. And I couldn't come with him. "I know you," he said, "but I swear to God I'll hurt you if you try."

It took me a while to understand what it was inside of him, what it was that let him get out of that bulldozer and pull his coat tight like he was choking himself and start walking till he came to that unplowed street, to that house squatting there in the shadows; what it was that took him up those steps and under the nails coming through the roof and into those rooms still reeking of shit because things in pain will shit themselves and they had. Fingering the end of the copper pipe in his sleeve, the pepper in his pocket sticking to his hand. I thought it was bravery. It was love.

Suze would be bringing Gene back that evening. The puppies would be gone. He'd have to say something.

They could sleep in the same room. He could block the door. It might be enough.

I think I didn't understand where it was going, or maybe I just didn't want to. I was scared, more scared than I'd ever been.

I went home; I had nowhere else to go. It would be fine, I told myself. It would be fine, it would be fine. Sitting at my desk late that afternoon I saw my father walking up the street. It was just about dusk—I could barely make him out. He reached down and opened the little latch on the gate and let himself in and walked up the walk till he disappeared under the roof beneath my window and I heard the door open. As he had a thousand times before. Ten thousand. Holding on. Because that's what he did.

It is what it is, he'd said to me.

We'd watch the news with dinner. Eight dead, seventeen wounded. In other news . . . and they'd ask me about how things were because they were worried, suddenly, and then my mother would say she's going upstairs and pick up her plate and leave the room.

He thought he might read, my father would say.

I'd walk into the kitchen as my mother walked out. Washing the dishes, I'd hear her over the water—twelve steps, the creak of boards, a door quietly closing.

KAREN ASKED and I lied. About everything. About the car, about Gene, about Ray. About them. He'd made me swear and I had. It was easy. Easier than speaking. And what would I have said?

She believed me. It could have been love. Frank believed me, too. That's what friends are for. Ray was fine, I told them. Working it out. I think there was some part of me believed it. Had to believe it.

She'd seen him yesterday, Karen told me. They'd met at the store. He had Gene with him. His dad was working again, he said.

We were sitting in the parking lot. The wind kept pushing her hair in her face. It was strange how he didn't want her to come to the house even when his dad wasn't around, she said.

They'd spent a few hours together. A warm afternoon, little rivers of snowmelt rushing down the gutters, a taste of ashes and sun in the air. They walked down the hill, then out to the Borden Bridge holding Gene by the hand until he got tired and Ray put him on his shoulders. At the bridge Ray stood on the other side and they'd yell across the traffic and then he'd drop a stick in the water and they'd see it come out, rolling in the current.

She'd let them off a block from the house, and he'd kissed her goodbye. She could tell it was on his mind, this whole thing with his dad. She couldn't wait till they could leave. Three months, she said.

We were sitting on the hood of her dad's car while Frank had a smoke. I watched Champbell and his friends come out of the building and get in his Camaro, the four doors slamming almost at the same time.

Was I nervous? she asked. About States? They were all going to be there.

"I'm always nervous," I said.

She looked at me, a small smile on her face. "You're good, aren't you?"

"You'll be watching this asshole in the Olympics someday," Frank said.

"What's it like being that good?" she said, like she meant it.

"I don't know," I said.

I TRIED TO THINK about it. About how much it meant.

Kennedy had told me. He'd wanted to tell me himself. He'd be skipping the spring season, he said. This was it.

But this was his last year, I said.

He knew that, he said, but he needed to work. His dad had been laid off again. Disability only went so far. They'd talked it over, he said. He'd be taking a year off before college. No big deal.

He could see the look on my face.

"Hey, c'mon," he said.

I nodded.

He looked down at the ground, then back. "Listen, I want to tell you so you know I'm OK with it. Coach wants you running anchor tomorrow. So do I."

I started to say something.

"It's OK," he said. "Really. I'll try to keep us in it. If I can do that, you can take him. I believe that. No, fuck believe—I *know* that."

◆ ◆ ◆

THAT EVENING was a blur of nervousness—I don't even know what I did. A light jog, a little TV. I tried to read but couldn't. Everything seemed to tire me out. Walking up the stairs tired me out. It was always like that the day before.

After dinner I packed my stuff, listened to records. Tried not to think. I set the alarm for seven. There was a special activities bus going in to school the next morning. I'd meet the team by the doors at eight-thirty. We'd go to White Plains from there.

THERE WAS LIGHT around the curtains. Winter light.

I dressed, ate a hard-boiled egg and a piece of toast standing in the kitchen, my toes curling up from the floor, sipping a cup of tea. Not thinking. The house was quiet. I put the plate and the cup in the sink, sat down on the kitchen chair and pulled on my socks and training flats, then checked my bag and let myself out the door just as the clock in the hall started to chime, off-tune as always, three minutes late.

They'd find me there, Karen had said. Ray had another ride— he'd meet us. Something about having to arrange for his brother.

The bus was on time. I watched it make the turn, almost running up on the sidewalk, then start up the hill, a black cloud of exhaust rising up into the cold. It was warm inside. A handful of kids, some familiar, going to whatever went on on Saturday mornings. I hadn't even known there *was* a Saturday bus.

Most of them were already there, jogging in place in front of the big glass doors—the pole vaulters with their poles, everybody nervous. I got out of the bus, still half-asleep, did a few lazy jumping jacks. Kennedy was talking to Moore and Falvo by the wall.

They'd meet me there.

Kennedy was walking over.

They'd meet me there.

"Ready to do this thing?"

He'd meet us there. He had another ride.

I nodded.

"You OK, man?"

Ray had another ride. His brother.

"Hey—you OK?"

I could see Frank looking over at me.

Something about having to arrange for his brother.

I started to walk. The morning bus was making its loop around the parking lot.

"Jon?"

"I think I have to go," I said. That's what I told him: "I think I have to go."

I caught the bus at the road and the guy let me in. I didn't know Frank had watched me cross the lot, then started to run after me. I forgot something at home, I said. Could he give me a ride back?

I just had to check. Everything was fine.

"Hop in, kid."

I told him where I was going. I wasn't worried. I just had to check.

He couldn't change his route, he said.

I sat in the front, my leg muscles starting to shake. I left my bag behind, I thought. I left my bag.

Everything was fine. I'd find them on their way out. I could catch a ride with whoever was taking Ray. If I missed him, I could get my dad to drive me. Or even the Perillos. Everything was fine.

We went down Tonetta, then left on Griffin.

"Here," I said. "Stop." I took off my jacket, checked my flats.

"You sure?"

"Stop."

"I can get you closer."

"Please," I said. "Please."

And he pulled over and opened the doors and I started to run.

I've NEVER RUN like that. Never. I knew how far it was, knew the hill up from Kobacker's, the cut behind the church. My last mile. Halfway there I could feel my breath screaming in my lungs, the lactic acid building in my calves, my hamstrings. I slipped turning into somebody's yard, smashed into a low white fence and was up—I hadn't even felt the snow.

It was the only time he'd be sure we'd be gone.

I've never run like that. I never will again. It's all I have in my defense.

The last quarter mile was red with pain. I ran like I'd been shot, the second bullet right behind my skull. I turned up the street. I could see the house now—the rail, the porch. The door was open.

I didn't know what I was looking at. The couch was on its back, the coffee table smashed flat to the ground. Ray and Mr. Cappicciano were on the ground. They seemed to be wrestling but nobody was moving. Mr. Cappicciano was behind him, his legs around his waist. He was holding Ray's hands behind his back with his left hand. Ray's face was in his right. He was moving his jaws for him. "That's right, chew," he was saying. "Chew."

Ray twisted loose when I came in the door, a great gush of blood coming out of his mouth and something I didn't know was the metal end of a lightbulb. He hit his father with his left, awkwardly, tried to scrabble away, to turn, then hit him again, harder, and Mr. Cappicciano, still on his knees, had the leg of the coffee table in his hands and had swung it, following through like a baseball player and Ray was making a noise like I've never heard before, his lower jaw stuck across his face like two halves of a photograph that aren't lined up.

It was to stop that noise that I did it. It was to stop the thing that had brought that noise into the world—a scream of such outrage and pain and helplessness—that I did it, and I grabbed one of the irons from the stand by the fireplace and brought it down. I could hear the bones crack like sticks in a towel but something in my head was screaming at me that he could still turn, still smile, that he could swallow me whole with that disappointed face, and I walked up to him as he was trying to crawl away on his elbows and I waited and then I hit him across the spine to make him stop and then I hit him in the back of the head and it opened up like it was nothing at all. Like it was nothing at all.

What the movies don't tell you is that people can die either quickly or slowly. It depends. Sometimes they take their time. Sometimes they lie on their side with a palm-sized section of their head caved in like a piece of hairy bark and this look on their face like they knew you once and they're trying to remember your name and then it changes and it's like they're looking into a small mirror and then you realize they're not seeing whatever it was they were seeing because they're dead.

And that should be that. Except it's not, really, ever again.

GENE WAS LOCKED in the back room. Wilma was dead. It was Ray who crawled to me as I sank to my knees, his jaw stuck to the side, his mouth a well of blood. He was losing consciousness. He took the iron out of my hand, put his hands on the grip, gripped it again. His movements were stuttering, like a machine breaking down. He lay down on the carpet on his side, his hands between his knees like a child and closed his eyes.

It was only then I heard Gene crying from the back room, then the rising wail of the siren coming up the hill. Frank had guessed where to send it.

Every step you take, a million doors open in front of you like poppies; your next step closes them, and another million bloom. You get on a train, you pick up a lamp, you speak, you don't. What decides why one thing gets picked to be the way it will be? Accident? Fate? Some weakness in ourselves? Forget your harps, your tin-foil angels—the only heaven worth having would be the heaven of answers.

I didn't see Ray for a long time. For a while, I heard, they weren't sure he'd make it, but the surgeons got the glass out of his mouth and stomach and sewed him up, then pumped him full of antibiotics and went to work on his jaw. People said he was different after, like something had gone quiet. I didn't see it.

When he came out from under, they were already there, two cops and a guy in a suit, standing around his bed like he was Dorothy.

"Can you hear what I'm saying, son?" the guy in the suit said. His voice turned away. "Can he hear what I'm saying?"

Somebody said something he couldn't make out. "Little out of it," somebody said.

"Ray, there's been a murder, Ray," the guy in the suit said. "You understand what I'm saying?"

Ray blinked.

"Now I know you're in a lot of pain, but I have to ask this officer here to read you your rights."

One of the cops appeared behind him.

"Ray this is Officer Mayo—you've met him before."

Remember me—your ole pal Hunk? Couldn't forget my face, could ya?

"How you doin', Ray?"

He blinked.

It was just like on TV.

He didn't want a lawyer. He didn't want anything.

"Can you tell us what happened, Ray? Can you write it down? Can he write?"

The cop held a pad in front of him, put a pen between his fingers and closed his hand on it.

"Gene?" he wrote.

"He's fine, Ray. Your brother's fine."

"Go ahead," somebody said.

"Ray—can you hear me? Who killed your father, Ray?"

"Me," he wrote.

"You're saying you killed your father?"

He blinked.

"I want you to think, Ray. I know this is hard."

You just had a bad dream, honey.

"Ray?"

What happened to Glinda?

"I need you to think, Ray—this is very important."

He was still holding the pencil. He underlined the "me."

She'd just been there. A second ago. Maybe if he slept, maybe he'd find her.

"You sure?"

He struggled up again.

"Give him the pad."

"Think, Ray. Your dad."

He still had the pencil. "Fuck him," he wrote.

HE WAS ASLEEP so he didn't hear them talking in the hall.

"What do you think?"

"Does it matter?"

"What do you mean, of course—"

"Not about what I think, about whether it matters."

"You think they're covering for each other?"

"What do I think? I think an hour ago I found something in a dumpster behind the A&P I don't really want to think about—that's what I think. I think somebody should have shot him a long time ago."

"Doesn't exactly solve the problem, does it?"

"Doesn't it?"

IN THE SPRING OF 1970 Brewster was still a small town, which meant the D.A. knew the judge who knew the cops who knew each other. You could be creative. Cobble something. Make it come out. Turn a blind eye.

I'd told them everything—I couldn't *stop* talking—kneeling there in his blood with my sweat gone cold, babbling like a sleepwalker about how I didn't know, hadn't said, hadn't meant, hadn't thought . . . about Ray, about puppies. I was sorry, I said, and started to cry. I was sorry, I was sorry.

They put a blanket over me, the radios crackling like something in a fire.

✦ ✦ ✦

I told them everything. It didn't matter at all.

They weren't stupid. Or cruel. It was a big fucking mess and they cleaned it up. Made the best of a bad situation. Played the hand. Cut their losses.

Your heart went out to the kid—it really did. Still, he'd taken a fire iron to his old man's head. Bashed it in like a melon. An abusive bastard, sure—extenuating as long as your arm—but still. He coulda left, coulda run away from home, started again. Wasn't the first kid born with a prick for a father. Or the last, probably.

The brother? No sign of anything—didn't look like he'd touched him. Couldn't say what might've been. Wouldn't say much about his love for animals. Still . . . he'd taken an iron to the old man's head. Plus the kid was no saint, even before. So what if he came from a fucked-up home—who didn't?

The other one? Clean record, good kid. Lost a brother when he was four. Just got accepted to Columbia. The confession? Protecting his friend. He's a good kid, they're all good kids—that girl, the Krapinski kid.

Tell me about her.

Was in bad shape for a while. Parents are movin' back to Hartford. Getting her out of town. The Krapinski kid's big in the church—he'll be fine.

So what do we do?

What do you *want* to do?

I don't think there's anything to be gained. Would you agree with that assessment, counselor?

He's a good kid. Impressionable. He's protecting his friend. No way I believe he swung that thing.

Heard he's a track star.

That's right.

All right, let's cut him out of this mess, hope he runs in the right direction. The other one's prints are all over everything, there's no remorse—not that I blame him, still.

What are you proposing?

A little discipline, a change of direction. I'm not convinced he's a bad kid at heart. Service did me a world of good, don't see why it wouldn't him.

And so it's resolved. Doesn't matter what the track star says— he can talk all he wants now. They'll save him for himself. They'll send you down to war.

A SIMPLE OFFICE—nothing fancy. He's not wearing a robe. He doesn't look mean. It's March 4—two months to the day before Kent State, when we start killing our own.

They talk for a while. He's like a father—kind, strong face, hair going white.

"Son, it's not like we don't have sympathy," he says, "but it's time to turn it around. Do something for your country for a change."

IT WAS A LONG WINTER that year. Everything locked shut, the river half iced over. The Beatles broke up. "Let It Be" was on the radio that spring. "*Let it be, let it be*"—you couldn't get away from it. I'd walk—I was allowed to walk—for hours sometimes, didn't matter where. I could go back to school when I was ready, they said. I'd had a terrible shock. My parents tried to talk to me, drove me to the shrink, let me alone—whatever I wanted. Even my mother. I'd never seen them so shaken up. I'd been too young when Aaron died.

So this man—his father—he had beaten him, my father said. But of course—that was why he looked like that. All that time. That was why he had stayed with us. Why he did what he did. He was driven to it.

I hadn't known, I said.

"And the baby," my mother said, "my God, what will happen now to the baby?"

My father was looking into his cup of tea, shaking his head. "But this is not possible—any of this." He picked up the teaspoon, started to say something, then lay it facedown across the saucer. "And this man, his father—you knew him?"

I went up to my room, took the volume of the *Encyclopaedia Britannica* out of my closet, came back down and opened it. "He gave this to me," I said, and lay the cloth on the table.

My father just stared at it like he was trying to understand what he was seeing. "These I remember," he said.

"He said it was a gift."

"These I remember very well."

"*Mein Gott*—those boys," my mother whispered, "this was their father?"

"*Aber nicht verstehe*," my father said, confused. "You say this was a gift?"

I nodded.

"But why would he do this?" my mother said.

"To humiliate you?" my father said. "To hurt you? I don't—"

"I don't know," I said.

"But why? Why would someone—"

"I don't know," I said. How could I explain that I hadn't known what to do? That I'd been weak. That I'd taken his gift the way you'd shake a hand that's suddenly offered—instinctively, trapped by politeness—but not for that reason alone. No, I'd taken it because he'd approved of me. Needed me. And because, for years, ignoring who he was, in some miserable, manipulated way, I'd needed him.

"But why would—"

"I killed him," I said.

Maybe I did it to hurt them. To slap them awake. They just stared at me.

"*Was?*" my father whispered.

I said it again.

"*Du? Ich nicht—*"

"He would have killed them both."

My father blinked twice, then reached up and adjusted his glasses with his right hand, wincing the way people do. He opened his mouth but nothing came out.

"There was nobody else," I said. "I had to."

It wasn't until he put his hand over mine, his eyes blinking, confused behind his thick lenses that I realized my face was wet.

"They don't believe me," I said.

I could see his thoughts, racing to catch up.

"You have to help me," I said. "Please."

"I—"

"The police. They think it was him. Please. You have to tell them."

He stared at me and I could see the understanding come into his face and then he reached under his glasses with his thumb and wiped under his eye and readjusted the frame on his face and smiled, a smile of such sadness and pity and resolve that I knew it was over. "This you cannot ask of me," he said. "You're our son."

I hadn't been able to look at my mother till then, too afraid of what I'd see. Her murderer son. Of course. She'd known all along.

She was looking right at me, looking at my hair, my nose, even my eyes as if seeing something inside herself she'd never noticed before.

"It's over," she said. She picked up a cup, turned it, then set it neatly back in its saucer. "There's nothing to be done."

KAREN WAS GONE, away in Hartford, recovering. She'd had a kind of fit when she heard, they said—had to be forcibly kept from jumping in the car. They thought it best—everybody did. Distance and time. Distance and time were the answer. A clean break. They kept saying that, she said, sobbing on the phone. A clean break, a clean break. Like your heart was a bone.

It was two in the morning—a little later. She'd snuck downstairs to use the phone. "Oh, my God, Jon," she said, "oh, my God. I have to see him," she said, "I have to talk to him." She was crying so much I couldn't make out half her words.

"I did it," I said.

There was nothing but quiet.

"I did it," I said again. "It was me."

It was like she was whispering it at the end of a long tunnel. "Oh, my God," she said again. "You have to—"

"I have."

"You need to—"

"I have. Everybody."

"I can't—"

"Ray would've done it. He couldn't. So I did it."

I could hear her crying, then a tiny voice like somebody breaking in on the line, then quiet.

"Thank you," she said.

She'd be finishing school in Hartford, she told me. It didn't matter. None of it. "Tell him I love him," she said.

"He knows that," I said.

"Tell him anyway."

"OK."

"Promise me."

"I promise," I said.

IT WAS A MONTH before they let me. Early March. He looked smaller in the bed, like people do. There were still tubes coming out of him from the second operation on his throat. The wires had come out of his jaw. He couldn't talk too much, they said.

We just looked at each other. The nurse did something with a bag and left. There was no one listening. They didn't care. Their minds were made up.

"Hey," he said, his whisper like a stocking pulled over bark.

"You lied," I said.

"How's she doin'?" he said. "They won't talk to me."

"She's OK," I said. "You know."

He nodded.

"Stayin' up in Hartford for a while."

I could tell by his face.

"Hey, it's not the moon," I said.

He nodded.

"She says to say she loves you."

He nodded quickly and I could see him working hard to hold it back.

"How you been?" he said.

It was my turn to nod.

"You missed your race," he said.

It took me a while. "I'm sorry," I said.

"For what?"

"For everything."

He shook his head.

"You gotta tell 'em," I said. "They're not gonna believe me."

He didn't say anything.

"You gotta tell 'em, Ray," I said. "Please. For me. You gotta tell 'em I did it."

He looked around the room and for a second he was like when I'd met him. That "too late" look.

"Hey, Jon," he said, and that may have been the other time he used my name.

"What?" I said.

He touched his throat like he was loosening a collar.

"Fuck you," he said.

IT HAD BEEN a long time comin'. Like the song said. It would be a long time gone.

Everything worked out perfectly. I went back to school at some point because it didn't make sense not to. People would nod, their voices would change. They'd walk up and touch me in the hall like I was a saint—my arm, my shoulder, my face, that needy, solemn look in their eyes. Like I was a goddamn saint. I talked to Falvo, told him about the deal they'd made. He shook his head. He'd written letters. Others had written letters. He didn't expect they'd do much good.

I told him the truth and he sat there in his teacher's chair and just looked at me and I could hear the clock making a buzzing sound on the wall. "It's OK," he said at last.

"It's not OK," I said. "You don't understand."

"I think I do," he said, "we're all in this, one way or another."

"You don't understand," I said.

"I *do* understand," he said gently. "They needed a lightning rod—they found one."

"But he didn't do it," I said.

"I know that."

"I fuckin' did it."

"I know—it's not the point."

"What *is* the point?"

He didn't answer. I wiped my face on my sleeve.

"I hear the brother's OK," he said after a while.

"Gene's down in Yonkers," I said.

"And the girl's in Hartford."

"Karen," I said. "Yeah."

He nodded. "You hear about Mary?" he said. He smiled. "Who would have guessed—her of all people. She took five sick days in a row—the cafeteria almost stopped without her."

Somebody knocked on the door.

"I'm busy," he called. "Seems she gave the police some kind of note for him—wouldn't take no for an answer. I hear he's living with her now."

Somebody knocked on the door again, more timidly.

He got up and went to the door—I couldn't see who it was. "Not now," he said. "Later."

He came back, sat down. "Anyway, congratulations," he said. He'd heard about Columbia. He'd gotten a call from their track coach—seemed very excited.

I nodded.

"You'll be OK," he said suddenly. "You can't see it now, but life goes on." He looked down at his left hand like a woman looking at her manicure, thinking about how her marriage has died. "That's the thing—it goes on. With or without you."

FOR A WHILE I thought it might be "with." I went back to school. The teachers let me through, passed me for nothing. I hung out with Frank a bit, though we didn't talk much. He'd cleaned up, gone back to church. For his parents' sake, he said. It'd been hard for them—he didn't want to add to it. He was his old self again. Only the smoking had stuck.

I don't know why I didn't tell him. I just didn't, and the longer I didn't, the easier it got. Maybe it was because I wasn't sure what he'd say.

"What was it like?" he said once, almost wincing, like he didn't want to ask but felt he had to—a choirboy forcing himself to look at dirty pictures. "I mean when you got there. I mean if—"

"Not good," I said.

He nodded. "Never thought he could do something like that—did you?"

"Not like he had a choice," I said.

He gave a little shrug, looked away.

"What're you sayin'?" I said.

"Nothin'. I don't know. I mean, don't get sore an' all—I know you were there an' everything so it's hard for you to see but, I don't know, you think it's right for somebody to kill their own father and not be punished? I mean seriously—if he wasn't our friend and all, would you think it was right?"

I couldn't say anything.

"I'm just thinkin'," he said.

"He didn't have a choice," I said.

"Yeah, no, I know, but—"

"I gotta go," I said.

"Yeah, sure, I'm sorry. I probably shouldn't've brought it up."

"It's fine. I just gotta go."

"It's just that, you know, in the Bible it says thou shalt not kill and—"

"But they do, Frank."

"Yeah, I know, but—"

"I gotta go," I said.

* * *

I SAW RAY a few times. He was bagging groceries thirty hours a week at the A&P. He had a little tag on his shirt with his name on it. He'd cut his hair. "Just hair," he said when I came by. He smiled. "Like a bag for that, sir?" The smile hadn't changed, really.

He'd had a letter from Karen, he said. Her parents weren't completely against her seeing him before he left.

"When's that?" I said.

"My date with Uncle Sam? August fifteenth, buddy."

I hung around while he bagged some woman's crap. "Thank you for shopping at A&P, ma'am," he said.

Jimmy had offered him a job but the suits had wanted more structure, he said. Early to bed, early to rise—that kind of thing.

"Name tags," I said.

He shrugged. "How *you* doin'?" he said.

"I'm OK," I said.

He'd almost forgotten to tell me—Karen had got into some college in Boston. Wesley.

"Wellesley," I said.

"That's it."

A short woman with short hair walked up and arranged the bags into a neater pile and kept walking. "Employees aren't allowed visitors—you know that," she said over her shoulder.

"Sorry," Ray said.

"I better go," I said.

"I called it, you know—said this was gonna be a big year."

"Yeah. You did." I could play along.

"I mean, Karen's got into some great college, you woulda won States . . ."

"Frank's stopped playin' with himself," I said.

"Think?"

"Maybe."

He slipped one bag inside another, snapped them out. "And me? Me, I'm gettin' the fuck outta Brewster."

I could see his boss coming back around.

"Good average," I said.

"Fuckin' Ted Williams," he said.

AND SPRING BECAME a summer. Just not the one we'd planned.

Life went on, Falvo had said—with or without you. And Karen came down with her father in June and he left them alone at Bob's for an hour and then she got back in the car with him and left. And Ray, shorn like a sheep and structured up the wazoo, handed in his name tag and kissed his brother goodbye, then hugged as much of Mary as he could and left for Fort Dix. And in September I took the train to the city, then the No. 1 local uptown in the heat and sat in a room on the tenth floor of an ugly dormitory called Carman Hall and tried to breathe.

With me, I thought. Please. Let it be with me.

I HAVE A MEMORY from that spring. For a few weeks, not that long after it happened, I started showing up to practice. Like I was walking in my sleep. Or running, I guess. I hadn't trained. It didn't matter.

It must have been May, a cold drizzle coming down. Falvo had put me in the mile. I'd had to convince him. He wasn't sure. He wanted to bring me back more slowly. I wanted to run. I wanted to hurt in a way I understood.

I don't remember if I won that race. I don't. I remember coming into the third lap, just before the pain came on, and looking up and seeing him standing there on that little hill above the track, smoking. He'd taken off from work. He didn't have much time.

We passed the start and the gun went off for the last lap and I glanced up through the rain as we hit the backstretch. He was still there—tall, thin, his face hidden in the hood of his sweatshirt. Watching me do about the only thing I could.

I WAS ALONE when I heard he'd died, and I hung up the phone and walked back in the room and sat down on my bed. It was just after ten in the morning, March 16th, 1971. It was my father who told me. They'd come to the house, he said. He'd named me as his next of kin.

I don't think I thought about much—or maybe everything, which comes out to the same thing. I'd had a letter, maybe two weeks before. He'd been on the boat for a while by then. He was with the 458th, he said.

I caught the bus for Boston out of Port Authority. If I didn't go now I never would. It was hot, he'd said. The food sucked. He didn't think about the eighteen months. He and Karen had talked about it before he left, he said. They could do it if they didn't think about it. If they thought about it they'd go crazy. I'd told him to take care of himself. To duck.

Six hours to Boston.

He wished he'd brought some things, he'd written. Funny how you missed some shit when you didn't have it. Otherwise it wasn't bad.

If there was one thing he knew how to do it was duck, he said.

He'd been fishing off the boat with a hand line and hooks he'd found in one of the villages, he wrote. He'd cut a kind of spinner from the top of a can. "They got some fucked-up fish in the Mekong," he said.

WELLESLEY wasn't in the city, so I took a cab. It wasn't far.

Bright sun. Warm for March. I knew the name of the dorm from her letters. She wasn't there. I should try the library, somebody said, pointed.

There were strips of snow still under the trees, melting in from the edges. I was still a long way off when she saw me. She was coming over a wide field half in shadow, the pines behind her, and when she saw me she stopped and just stood there awkwardly like a child, the book bag hanging down from her arm, then fell to her knees and buried her face in her hands.

It was the saddest thing I've ever seen.

I CALLED HIM from Main Street after the funeral. "I couldn't go, Frank," I said.

"I know," he said.

"I could see it," I said.

The line was quiet for a while. "Why didn't you tell me it was you?" he said.

"How long've you known?" I said.

"Seems like everybody knew except me."

"Maybe I didn't know what you'd say," I said.

"Guess not."

For a second I thought he'd hung up.

"Where are you?" he said.

WE MET at the end of Garden Street and just stood there looking out over the town past the steeple and the car lots to that ugly little patch shaved out of the woods—a pair of wooden saints tipping back and forth in the gusts that came in cold from the woods, then sickly warm, like breath. He was still wearing the suit, tight across the chest, thick neck crammed into the collar. And he asked me again and I said because I knew what he'd say, that's why, and he nodded, then looked out and said, like it was written in the air somewhere, that it didn't matter, that none of it mattered, that we'd all have to answer for the things we'd done in the fullness of time.

With the leaves down, the town looked see-through, like a scalp through thinning hair. You could see the East Branch running behind the five-and-dime, the pasture walls stitching up the hills. And I told him he could go fuck himself in the fullness of time but he didn't swing at me like I thought he would, just stood there with that pierogi-fed face, then turned half around from the wind without moving his feet like Ray used to and lit a cigarette. Somebody was walking down Main Street, stepping around the ice like he was making his way through an invisible crowd, and I remember making a bet with myself that if he hadn't said anything by the time they reached the movie theater, I'd say something—I didn't know what. Something.

But whoever it was turned into the hardware store and Frank didn't move for what seemed like a long time, then took the cigarette out of his mouth, picked something off his tongue with his thumb and ring finger, and left. I was sorry for it. We'd been friends.

IT TOOK ME FOUR DAYS to sell off everything in my dorm room: the cheap stereo, the hot plate, my records, everything. Cash only. The next day I took the local to Port Authority where I bought a bus ticket to L.A.

I left that night, April 21st. The last thing I remember of New York was watching the hookers working the traffic stalled on the ramp to the Lincoln Tunnel, leaning in through the driver's-side windows.

People talk on buses. I didn't. I went straight through, sleeping in the depots on benches during rest stops. I didn't think I'd seen anything at all—later I remembered pieces of things like something blown back by the wind. A time before dawn somewhere in Arkansas or Oklahoma. The trees had gotten shorter overnight and the sky had spread out and I sat there looking at it for a long time. Other things. The way the shadows of the clouds rushed across the valleys. The Indian woman in the red sari I saw squatting behind a shed in the desert who I thought was begging until I realized she was eating her lunch.

It's a big country. We went through the middle like something pulled by gravity, stepping down the interstates, Harrisburg to Memphis, Memphis to Amarillo. I couldn't draw a full breath the first day. It got easier. I spent hours just watching all that space going by—clouds, a chimney of rain coming down on a mesa fifty miles away. In Flagstaff it was freezing cold and I got a lot of change and put it in a phone, then hung up and listened to it coming back like a slot machine. I didn't call them until I'd been in Bakersfield a week, and they told me how worried they'd been but when I said I wanted to be on my own, they let me. I don't know if it was hard for them. Maybe.

By THE FOURTH NIGHT on a bus you can't think even if you want to. You just go, listening to the gears shifting on the grades in your sleep, watching the mountains and the fence posts lose their shadows then grow them back after lunch, watching the hawks scoring circles around the sun.

Coming into California I was down to eighty dollars. I'd split it into four parts, twenty in each front pocket of my jeans, twenty in each sock. We left Needles at ten, Barstow at two in the morning. It wasn't until well after dawn with the Central Valley crops going by like spokes on a wheel that somebody stood up to get something from the racks and began to yell.

They'd probably gotten on the bus in Barstow, the highway patrol said. Happened all the time: Two guys get on late at night, wait till you're asleep, then pass a few bags to the back and shove them out the window. Their friends pick up what they've tossed, then get them at the next stop.

A cop named Gonzales saved me from just disappearing. He didn't have to.

"Where you comin' from?" he said. We were sitting by his metal desk.

"New York," I said.

He whistled. "Address?"

I didn't say anything.

"You're eighteen—just make something up," he said.

Somebody said something to him in Spanish. "*Lo que diga, hombre,*" he said.

He had a shed out back of his house, he said. Just till I got on my feet.

I nodded because I couldn't do anything else.

"Hey," he said. "You're gonna be OK. We get 'em all the time out here. I know. It's not easy bein' a runaway."

He was wrong. It's not so hard.

I THOUGHT ABOUT THEM now and then over the years, heard some things. That Karen was married, living in Europe. That Kennedy had gone to Nam and come back again. That he was driving a cab in the city. He wrote me once. He seemed happy.

Ray had been fishing off the back of the boat, I heard, had taken his helmet off because of the heat. They'd returned fire, shooting blindly into the green. Putnam Lake had a new war memorial to go with the others.

I THOUGHT ABOUT HIM over the years. Wondered, sometimes, if it could have all played differently. If we'd lost, maybe, before we started.

It didn't surprise me when I heard they'd had themselves named as Gene's guardians, had brought him into their home, made him their son. It made sense. They'd put him in Aaron's room. Everything was there, after all: the toys, the desk, the punching bag dinosaur my mother had patched and reinflated. Like they'd been waiting for him.

I can see him walking up those stairs, bringing both feet together before stepping to the next. Holding my mother's hand. He's three and a half years old, young enough to have a running start before he hits the age my brother was. He stands there in the doorway staring at the colors, the pillows, the sunlight streaming in on the rug—and looks up at my mother, who's finally crying.

THEY MOVED to San Diego soon after the adoption—a place near the beach. At first it was strange to see them walk out into that dry yard with the bougainvillea going up the wall, to see my father reading in the same leather chair with a eucalyptus tree over his shoulder. Basil Street. I was on my feet by then. I'd drive down from the Central Valley, mess around with Gene, the two of us climbing over this yellow cube thing they had by the fence. He remembered me a little. And his brother. Carrying him on his shoulders. And throwing sticks under a bridge. Not much. A girl.

They had a blue kiddie pool on the grass, and in winter I'd carry big pots of hot water from the laundry room to warm it up. In the summers we'd eat outside around the wrought-iron table and when it was time to go my mother would give me a little kiss, my father would touch my back. They were glad to hear I was fine. Now and then I'd catch my mother looking at me like she was thinking about her life, like she was about to say something, but she never did. I didn't expect it. Sometimes it's better not to go back—just settle accounts as they are, call it even.

I REMEMBER one time. An evening in June.

Gene was in his early twenties, pounding nails when the surf wasn't up. A good guy, easy to like. He was still living at home then and I'd watch him with my parents, joking with them. The year before, he'd built them a deck. "So, Ma, you gonna come to the North Shore with me?" he'd say, rattling the plates down on the table for dinner. He'd wink at me. "I'm thinkin' for that right break at Waimea, that ten-six gun would be perfect for you."

"Dad reading?" I'd ask.

"You know Dad," he'd say.

And I'd wonder what Ray would think of it all. If he could see us there.

WHEN HE WAS SIXTEEN I told him. Figured he should know who killed his father. He already knew. I told him the bare bones, left it at that. What was he like? he said. His brother. I thought about it for a while. I loved him, I said.

IT WAS ALMOST DUSK when I turned off the freeway and I drove down Leucadia and up to the cliffs and rolled down the window and watched the sun flatten, pull into itself, go out. A big break was kicking mist into the air, softening the light. You could taste the salt, the kelp.

I recognized him by his walk. He separated off from the others, his board under his arm, the wet suit pulled down to his waist, and I watched him push his wet hair back but it wasn't Ray. He saw me when he was some distance away and stopped, the grin spreading over his face and for a second I could see him trying to stand up on his rashy little legs, pulling himself up on the cabinet, his brother saying "Hey, little guy, you want a beer stein?" The wind blowing against the house. Brewster.

He walked flat-footed over the gravel to the car but I couldn't do the elaborate handshake thing and he laughed and said, "Alright, bro, don't hurt yourself—you hungry?"

He'd cut down the back way, he said, meet me at the house.

And I watched him walk away. Not like his brother. Different.

"Where'd you go, man?" I whispered to myself.

I could still see him, the black hair falling in his face, the way he moved, throwing himself at the world—losing ground but still dangerous, like St. Sebastian with a switchblade. We'd lost—him, me, Karen. Maybe we'd been meant to lose. Maybe, I thought, but he'd never believe it. He'd be sprawled out next to me, taking up space, and he'd smile that too-late smile and call the world's bluff. So what if we'd lost? Fuck it. We'd run it anyway. We'd run it like it mattered.

ACKNOWLEDGMENTS

SOME DEBTS we can be grateful for, and I am, to Paul Graham, Geoff Chin, Paul Neilan, Roger Miller, and Jill Talbot for their conversation, their suggestions, their friendship; to Colum McCann and Brian Hall for their faith and support; to Jill Bialosky and the good folks at Norton, who ran with this book so beautifully; and, far from least, to Bill Clegg, who sees to the core of the story, who just gets it.

My other debts—the life-long kind—are to my family, Leslie, Zack, and Maya, who have lived this gypsy life with me and filled it with so much joy and laughter. Here's to us, guys. Without your love, I'd have nothing to say.

BREWSTER

Mark Slouka

AN INTERVIEW WITH MARK SLOUKA

A common theme in your writing is the question of what it means to be human and how to maintain one's humanity in the modern world. Did that theme come into play in Brewster?

Absolutely, sure. Because the fight to retain your humanity, to do the right thing, is even more desperate when you're young, maybe because you have fewer options, or think you do, because you haven't learned to rationalize your failures, because the forces aligned against you—teachers, cops, so-called "friends," even parents, at times—can feel overwhelming.

Brewster is a real place. Is it anything like the fictional Brewster you've created?

I'm looking out at Brewster as I write: snow flurries, the last crusts of ice on the hills, day laborers huddled on the corner, waiting for work. I've known this place, off and on, for fifty years. Our daughter went to Brewster High. Brewster's changed some; the 5&10 is Levine's Auto Parts now, the A&P is gone, but it's still rough around the edges. Most people drive by—though I like the reservoirs, the woods, the history I've made here. The funny thing is that the Brewster I imagined has taken over the actual place; I see Jon and Ray and Karen everywhere now, walking in the rain, cutting into the woods by the reservoir, throwing stuff into the West Branch. . . . I walk up to Garden Street and I see Jon and Frank looking over the town to the cemetery on the hill.

There are many authority figures in your new novel—parents, teachers, cops—but they are all flawed in some way. It often seems like the teenagers have a stronger moral compass. Is that indicative of the general feeling during the '60s?

There are some strong adults in *Brewster*—Falvo, Jimmy, Mary—but it's true, the moral center is with the kids, probably because

I instinctively side with them. And, yeah, I guess you could say that reflects the "never trust anyone over thirty" spirit of the '60s. But I think it's more complicated than that, and I tried to express that in the novel. For one thing, you can find as many hypocrites and sell-outs in high school as you can in a retirement home; honor and decency aren't age-specific. For another, it's easier to be idealistic at eighteen, before the world's had a chance to work on you. Which is why if you're still holding on to some version of your ideals when you're forty, or fifty, if you haven't given in to the temptation to throw them under the train in the name of "the real world," you're somebody I want to know.

It is interesting that you have two characters, Jon's mother and Ray's father, who suffer from posttraumatic stress disorder in a time when this disorder was just beginning to gain recognition. Why did you feel it was important to have your characters struggle in this way?

Because the hits we take in this life make us who we are. What makes people human to me is their pain and how they deal with it; I've always been moved by the fact that some survive with grace, grow more decent, more compassionate, while others break, or become brutal themselves. My mother, a loving woman when I was young, eventually broke under her burdens; my father, who had his share, carried his into an old age of hard-earned wisdom, humor, love. Go figure.

The loss of childhood innocence is a popular theme in coming-of-age novels. Although Jon and Ray don't have much childhood innocence left in them, do you think Brewster *could be considered a coming-of-age novel?*

I'd like to think it's bigger than that, if only because "coming of age" implies a process with a destination—adulthood—that I'm not sure I believe in. I mean, sure, we grow older, perhaps even wiser, but why is it that the phrase "you're an adult now" always sounds like "come inside, you have school tomorrow"?

The main character, Jon, runs track. Why is this significant, and did you rely on your personal experiences to write the running scenes?

In the '60s and '70s—maybe even today, for all I know—track attracted the rebels, the nonconformists, the outcasts. Jon, like Ray, is a kind of antihero (a classically American character that's gone out of fashion in America), a loner. What else could he do but run track? And yeah, I used my own experience, my memories of those I ran with. At our meets, we had no crowds, no band, no cheerleaders. Maybe a couple of girlfriends huddled in the wind, a few parents, skipping work. And we liked it that way.

Although he often gets in trouble, and society doesn't think he will amount to much, do you think that Ray is a good role model? Why?
He's got a big heart, he's fundamentally honest, he's enduring an impossible situation (foolishly, but he's young) with amazing courage, and he's unswervingly loyal to those he loves. What qualities could make a better role model? As to the fact that society doesn't think he'll amount to much, I'd take it as a compliment considering some of the bastards society has anointed.

Women seem to respond to your work, which seems surprising given that you tend to write from a guy's perspective. Do you think that women read your work because they want to know what men (even troubled, held-in characters like Jon) think?
Maybe. I hope so. I mean, men can be so damn constipated; try going to Bob's Diner and having a real conversation with a bunch of guys and the reaction's going to be, "What're we, a bunch of chicks?" I'd like to find the idiot who first sold us the notion that talking (about anything we might actually be thinking or feeling) is somehow unmanly, that admitting you're hurting, for example, is the same as admitting you're weak. It's a neat trick, if you think about it, because the exact opposite is true: Puff out your chest and pretend you can handle anything on God's green earth, and I know for a fact that you can't and that you'll probably cave when the heat comes down. So, yes, maybe women read me because no matter how locked up they are, how scared of it they are, my guys try to talk, to think, to figure out what the hell's going on in their hearts.

The late David Foster Wallace once wrote something about foreseeing an end to the Age of Irony in the novel; he certainly seemed to yearn for it. Do you think novels like Brewster *might be leading the way?*
I don't know that the Age of Irony has to end, but I wouldn't mind it ceding a bit of territory. I mean, the ironic, clever,

hipper-than-thou voice has ruled the roost for so long now that anything else is considered sentimental slop. It's not—or not necessarily—so. Irony has produced gorgeous, searing books, but it can also become an affectation, a pose; you can almost see the fingers making the invisible quotation marks in the air: "So Sean, is it LOVE?" Which isn't clever, it's cowardice. By the same token, of course, the lack of irony can signal naïveté, but it can also mean that the writer's willing to grapple with the things that move us, trouble us.

Bottom line? I get tired of party chatter; at some point I want to get to the heart of it. Which is why the books I love and remember, the books I hope to write, are the ones that touch something, that aim for the sweet spot of precision and soul.

DISCUSSION QUESTIONS

1. The novel is named for the town it is set in, and it has a tremendously vivid sense of place. Describe the town of Brewster. In what ways is the setting important to this novel?

2. The author portrays a close friendship between two teenage boys in *Brewster*, a relationship less often portrayed than one between girls. Did you think that Jon and Ray's friendship was an unlikely one? What made the two boys close? Did their relationship seem the same as ones you know between teen girls?

3. The narrator of *Brewster* is an adult Jon Mosher telling the story of his past. Why do you think the author made this choice? How would the novel be different if it were narrated by sixteen-year-old Jon Mosher in the present?

4. Jon's affair with Tina feels like a hiatus, a brief escape from his real life and troubles, and she never reappears in the story. What might Jon have learned from his relationship with Tina that he brings to the rest of his experiences in the novel?

5. *Brewster* is set in 1968, a year after the summer of love and at the peak of the Vietnam War, but in small-town Brewster those events feel very far away. Describe the ways in which the novel evokes

the late 1960s and brings that period to life. How has American culture changed in the fifty years since then in terms of racism, notions of acceptable behavior, and how teens get around and communicate?

6. Discuss the character of Karen Dorsey. What draws Ray and Jon to her, and her to them? What do you think made Karen choose Ray over Jon? If you were Karen, whom would you prefer?

7. Who's your favorite adult character in *Brewster*? Falvo? Jimmy? Mr. Mosher? Someone else? Why?

8. *Brewster* can be characterized as a coming-of-age story. Describe the ways in which Jon, Ray, and Karen grow over the course of the novel. What do they each learn about themselves, the nature of love, and the wider world?

9. Describe how the novel treats first love. Did it feel real to you or remind you of the first time you fell in love?

10. Jon's parents and Ray's father all have dark pasts, and both families are abusive, though the abuse takes different forms. Are there parallels to be drawn between Jon and Ray's families? Jon and Ray each find some acceptance with the other's family. Discuss how this happened and why it makes sense.

11. What does running come to mean to Jon? Does it mean something different at the beginning of the novel than it does at the end?

12. In the final chapter, Jon says, "I thought about him over the years. Wondered, sometimes, if it could have all played differently. If we'd lost, maybe, before we started" (279). Discuss the ending of the novel. Do you think that Jon, Ray, and Karen were doomed from the start? In what ways will the characters escape Brewster, and in what ways will it never truly leave them? Do you feel that your own hometown has left an imprint on you?